A LIFETIME
OF NIGHTTIME

D.L. CALVIN

1

Leopold Kaczynski opened the door of his doublewide to let Guinness out for his nightly constitutional of sniffing and peeing. The September moon hung heavy and bright in the autumn sky, making Guinness' eyes shine like two red rubies. Guinness wagged his tail and watched his friend flick his lighter, igniting another cigarette.

Leo stood silent on the back deck, aware that Guinness did not have long to live. Irish Setters rarely lived past fifteen and Guinness was three years overdue. *What do those educated assholes know about dogs, anyway?* Leo thought, taking a deep drag as Guinness lifted his leg and took a whiz on the Lincoln rose bush.

Guinness would probably out live him. Leo's doctor in a most unceremonious manner had informed him of his impending death. The little son of a bitch actually bent over him as he lay in his hospital bed, weak from the countless tests, and in a loud whisper offered his congratulations, announcing to all in the four-bed ward that Leo had lung cancer in both wind bags. Then the doctor asked in an angry voice if Leo genuinely thought doctors were liars when they told their patients to quit smoking? If that was not enough, he added further insult when he asked him if he had a will.

Leo had thought about the will and had taken care of all the details up to and including his cremation. Now all he would do was to sit and wait for death, knowing it would come soon enough.

Staring off into the darkness, he happened to notice Guinness staring at something in the woods behind the mobile home. Inquisitive? Yes. Out of the ordinary? Yes. *Probably a whitetail deer,* Leo thought. Then came a woof followed by a deep-throated growl. Even in the moonlight, Leo could see that Guinness' hackles were raised, his tail between his legs, his ears raised and lying back on his head.

"Who's there?" Leo called out, turning his body to see what Guinness had found.

Leo flicked the cigarette butt, not watching or even caring where it landed. His only concern at this moment was the same concern as his friend.

"Who is it?" Leo asked, walking towards the ramp.

Guinness began to snarl, bearing his old yellow canine teeth, towards the invisible intruder. A deep slow rumbling growl gave warning that he was about to attack something or someone.

Leo stepped off the ramp walking cautiously towards the woods, his eyes squinting at Guinness's silhouette staring into the darkness.

"What is it boy, a deer?" Leo asked in a soft reassuring voice.

Guinness turned his head, nuzzled Leo's cheek, and licked it, just as they both heard the sound coming out of the darkness. It was the sound of dry twigs cracking beneath the weight of something heavy.

Leo stood up and peered into the blackness, straining his eyes as he looked for the deer. Guinness pulled away from his friend and charged into the night, barking at shadows. Leo called out to Guinness, but no longer heard his dog's distinctive voice. Leo walked into the woods. He feared for his dog's safety and wished he had brought his flashlight. He whistled and clapped his hand, calling out to his pet.

What he heard in reply was the sound of someone cocking a shotgun. "Who is it?" Leo called out. His question was answered by a sea of orange flame, followed by an explosion that sent hot copper bee bees into Leo's gut, tearing open his belly and slamming his ponderous frame to the soft cool ground. In the distance, he heard his best friend yelp as Guinness ran deeper into the woods. Again Leo heard the snapping of twigs as the noise got louder and his killer got closer. His life was slowly fading away but he tried desperately to hold in what was left of his belly.

He gasped for air when he heard another snap of a twig next to his head and felt something hard against the top of his head. He turned and looked up squinting, his eyes trying to peer into the darkness, wanting to know the identity of his killer. All he saw was the long dark barrel of the twelve-gauge pointing at his face and then in the desperate voice of a dying man asked aloud the simple question, "Why"?

Once again, the silent woods exploded into a sea of orange flame then the orange flame and smell of cordite dissipated into the night, floating away into an ethereal darkness, the bliss of silence returning to the dark woods.

2

Toby Roth was on the down stroke when his cell phone began chiming Beethoven's Fifth.

"Fuck!" Roth yelled.

"Oh, lover, keep it coming, I'm close," Shaquille gasped between clenched teeth, throwing her legs around his back.

Roth ignored the phone and kept fucking the young caramel colored, green-eyed beauty that lay beneath him, urging the soldier on, telling him how good he felt inside her. He ignored Shaquille's cries as he continued pounding her into the mattress and felt a massive eruption beginning to form deep down in his loins. He could feel it welling up as it traveled up his manhood and ready to explode deep inside her. Like Vesuvius ready to pop, his ecstasy triggered a massive orgasm in the young prostitute that he had become particularly fond of over the last few months. He was right behind her and let go an instant later.

"Hmm…" Shaquille purred, snuggling up to him, kissing his throat and running her fingers through his chest hair. "That was really nice, Toby," she whispered in his ear and kissed his cheek.

Shaquille was the only person alive other than his mother whom he allowed to call him Toby, to his face that is.

Roth smiled, and kissed her gently. "Glad you liked it," he said, rolling over and grabbing his phone. A quick check at his last call and Detective Toby Roth of the "Zanesville City" Sheriff's Homicide

Department knew it was time to go to work. He took a quick shower to remove all traces of the romantic interlude with Shaquille, and a shave was in order to check for telltale love bites, which might otherwise tell everyone he was not a choirboy.

Was this the tenth or the eleventh time, that he had been called out to investigate a murder? *Has to be the eleventh,* he thought as he turned on the red-over-white-get-the-fuck-out-of-my-way lights, and sped off to the farthest corner of the county. *Z Ville* as some of the locals called it, or Y City, another commonly used name.

The city was centrally located off a major highway between Columbus and Wheeling, making the city the perfect town for the drug and marijuana delivery drivers. All they had to do was get off at any one of the four exit ramps and go to a prearranged stop, drop the goods and shoot and scoot down the highway to the next drop, and they commonly did.

The proud little city was once the state capitol until a flood washed everything away. Now the fair city had been reduced to being famous for a bridge built in the shape of the letter "Y," hence the name Y City. It was also famous for its clay pots that were ferried the hundred miles down the Muskingum River to the mighty Ohio River, to be eventually sold in cities all over the world.

Another thing that really bothered Roth were all the damn churches. There were so many for a town so small. The downtown area virtually had a church on every corner. Edifices that once stood proud and foreboding now were seldom used on Sunday as the Zanesville faithful moved away, faded away, or just died away, or perhaps they just became disenfranchised with religion. The Christian children could not pray in school any longer, unless of course the kid went to a private school. *What about the Ten Commandments being torn off some courthouse somewhere and replaced with patching cement...? Thomas Jefferson would turn in his grave,* he thought.

Roth reasoned that the people who went to church figured what the fuck, and started buying drugs and alcohol in lieu of tithing to something as passé as religion that nowadays seemed to take a stand against nothing. Denny's and the Bob Evans Restaurant had more *parishioners* on a Sunday morning than all the downtown churches combined. That was a sign of the times…

That was not to say all the people in Z Ville were bad people, only about half of them— the others were just simple-minded hypocrites. He stepped on the cruiser's accelerator in anticipation of seeing a dead body a few seconds sooner. "Hmm… Now the town is nothing but a cesspool of humanity," he mused, giving the siren another blast as he sped into the darkness of the Ohio countryside.

3

Tim Hill headed Ohio's anti-drug task force for the state's Attorney General's Office of Criminal Investigation. He stood beside his car, sipping a cup of black coffee as he waited for Deputy Sheriff Roth to arrive at the murder scene.

Personally, he thought Roth a first-class asshole, but professionally Roth was considered to be a first-rate homicide detective with a well-deserved reputation that some in the field of police science would envy, although his methods of solving murders could sometimes be considered dubious. His marching orders? Nail the criminal first, worry about how you did it, second.

Roth once got a murder confession by having some beautiful caramel-colored hooker pose as a psychic. He had taken the murder suspect along with the pretend psychic to the actual murder site. With a few facts given to her by Roth the make-believe psychic along with some good old-fashioned bullshit, she coerced a murder confession from the guy. She spooked the poor guy so badly that the suspect told Roth where to find the body of his wife without any further shape shifting.

Hill blew gently across his coffee, taking another slow deliberate sip while gazing into the darkness of the woods and waiting, thinking what he would tell Roth about the victim. Namely, that this man lying at his feet with no face, in fact, the guy that had no head, was just an innocent victim of circumstance.

Roth would say something glib in rebuttal, something like, "No, he wasn't. The asshole pissed somebody off!"

Then Roth would take some of his coffee, pour it into his empty coffee cup, and ask a rhetorical question, like, "I wonder why this man was assassinated?" He would take a sip from his borrowed coffee mug and ask another rhetorical question, "I wonder why the killer shot him at point blank range, removing the man's face, skull, and brains? It's as if the killer was trying to make the man's identity difficult."

Then Roth would kneel down, still holding his coffee cup, pull out his high intensity pen light flashlight, and proceed to point to the victim's mid section with his index finger, moving it up and down, side to side, and in graphic detail explain how the murder was committed. Then, in the minutest of details, explain what probably happened. He would explain why the victim's intestines and stomach were blown to bits, lying all round the body. Then the son of a bitch would look away, take another sip of coffee, and say with practiced perfunctory that, "This probably was the first shot."

With the skill of a surgeon, Roth would then reach into the wound with his finger or perhaps his ink pen and examine the number BBs, then proceed to tell what kind of BB shot the killer used. The little stuff used for small game, or the heavier shot used for ducks and geese? Why Roth needed to know what kind of BB shot the killer used, he did not profess to know, only that Roth would notice that type of detail.

Then would come the big question, "Who found the body?" Alternatively, "Why is the head of the states narcotics task force unit standing over a dead body, in the early morning hours, in the middle of the woods?"

That question was easy to answer. Because the head of the state's narcotic unit is a dedicated asshole committed to doing his job.

Roth pulled his car off the country road and pulled up behind an unmarked state vehicle. Reaching across the seat, he grabbed his coat, being sure to turn the engine off to conserve much needed gas to help the county with its budget problem. He got out of his car. The early morning air was brisk and damp, forcing Roth to put on his jacket to ward off the autumn chill.

Hill looked back at the silhouette walking up the drive.

"Over here, Roth," Hill yelled.

"Who is it?"

"Tim Hill of the Attorney General's Office," Hill replied, watching the detective approach minus his coffee cup.

"Hello Tim, how the hell are you?" Roth asked, extending his hand.

"Fine as wine," Hill replied, taking Roth's hand.

"So what do we have here?" Roth asked, pulling a little high intensity flashlight out of his jacket pocket.

"According to retrieved mail, we have…correction…we used to have a Mr. Leo Kaczynski," Hill replied, taking a sip of coffee.

"What…someone shot the poor bastard because…he was Polish?" Roth asked tersely, shrugging his shoulders and pressing the on switch of his small flashlight. "Goddamn! This poor bastard wasn't murdered. The fucker was executed!"

Hill greatly admired the detective as he watched him work.

"I suppose it would be best to wait until sun up and have a forensic team examine the area," Roth said, walking back to where Hill was standing.

"Have you gone into the house?" Roth asked.

"No— thought it best to wait for you," Hill replied, turning his back to Roth and walking towards the doublewide, Roth falling in step behind.

The first thing Roth noticed when he stepped into the doublewide was how clean everything was. Nothing was out of place. He walked past the kitchen area and proceeded down the hallway, stopping at the first door on his right.

Pointing, Roth called out to Hill, "Laundry room," then moved on to the next open door. "Bathroom," and with that announcement Hill watched as Roth entered the room. Next came the sound of the toilet seat being raised, followed closely by the sound of Roth peeing.

Hill looked at the pictures on the wall and on the end tables observing by the hairstyles of the women and the clothes the men wore in the pictures that they had been taken thirty, maybe forty years ago.

A safety award hung on the wall from some coal company in West Virginia that had Leo's name on it dated July, 1969. *The date would fit the pictures,* Hill thought, unzipping his fly and walking to the bathroom.

Roth searched through the victim's closets and drawers, looking for anything that may help identify the killer. Nothing was out of the ordinary in the entire house that could offer any evidence; he would have forensics run a finger print sweep, which might turn up something. Roth sat down on the bed, sweeping the master bedroom with his eyes, when suddenly he looked down on the soft white carpet and spied a long red hair. Leaning forward, he picked up the hair and examined it.

Just then, Hill walked in to the bedroom and watched Roth pulling gently on something. "What did you find?"

"Do you know if our victim had a dog? Say, a red dog with long hair?" Roth asked, looking up at Hill. "Otherwise, this guy had a red headed girlfriend."

Either the murder victim's love life had something to do with the crime or he owned a red dog. Right now, Roth had only a piece of red hair. However, hair provided DNA.

As Roth approached the laundry room, he decided to look. He opened the cabinets and drawers and found nothing. Then he saw a bag of dog food. Reading the bag's label, it was for older dogs, fortified with minerals and vitamins. Therefore, Leo was a dog lover. Okay, then where's the dog? Maybe the dog knew the killer and sounded no alarm. On the other hand, maybe the dog, like its owner, was dead.

Roth walked back out into the kitchen area, and opened the refrigerator door. The refrigerator was well supplied, indicating Leo had gone shopping. Shutting the refrigerator door, he walked over to the dishwasher and opened it. One plate, one cup, one fork, Leo had eaten alone sometime earlier.

Roth looked around for Hill. He was nowhere to be found. He walked back outside and found Hill talking on his cell. *Funny,* he thought, I *had not heard it ring. Hill must have called someone.*

Back inside Roth looked at the clock on the TV converter box and realized he was hungry. *I wonder what else is in Leo's refrigerator that might be good to nibble on,* he thought, stepping back to the kitchen and opening the refrigerator door for a closer inspection of his dead host's fresh food supply.

4

The eleven-year veteran of the Zanesville Sheriff's Department, James Bean disconnected himself from his wife and rolled out of bed and headed to the bathroom. He turned on the shower, deciding to wash down before shaving. Rubbing the soap on his small pigeon chest, he concluded that he did not like early morning calls, especially from a numb-nut like Hill. *What a crybaby! One would think that a task force commander of the state's anti- drug force would be a man of character, a man of substance, fearless.* "Hill's just another bureaucratic pussy," Bean said aloud. *A sniveling piece of worm shit. The asshole calls and orders me to meet him on some back road off state Route 313 in an hour. Fuck him, I don't need him anymore and I know what the son of a bitch is doing. Yesterday morning Leo had informed him as I handed over three hundred dollars for his magnum that Hill was going into business for himself!*

Bean was late as he slowed his pickup and turned off the state route onto some lonely gravel road that Hill had insisted was the correct turnoff. He dimmed the truck lights and took his foot off the gas pedal, allowing the truck to creep slowly down the lonely farm road, his new truck tires crunching the gravel and announcing to Hill that he was approaching.

Bean picked up his newly purchased .357 Magnum that had been lying securely under his hip, and continued to creep along the deserted road as the amber colored running lights cast eerie shadows on the white birch trees that lined both sides of the road.

He had traveled about a mile down the road when he saw the sanctimonious hypocrite sitting on the hood of his car his arms resting on his chest, waiting for him.

He stopped his truck directly in front of Hill's car and glanced at the dash clock, 5:30 a.m. He had to be at work at six and was about twenty minutes from town, and he had to change into his uniform. He had to make this quick.

Hill slid off the hood of his car and walked towards the big Ford, coughing up a wad of slimy mucus, spitting it to the side. Hill was about three feet from the truck window when Bean hit the power switch lowering the window. The cool autumn air causing him to shiver.

"What's so fucking important that you wake me up in the middle of the night to meet you out here?" Bean asked, his voice betraying his aggravation.

"I killed Leo, emptied my shotgun into his ugly face and blew his guts all over the ground," Hill said, spitting on the ground and sounding proud of his deed.

"No shit!"

"No shit!" Hill echoed back.

"You know of course what this means don't you?" Bean asked.

"Yes, I do, it means more money for us," Hill responded, looking down at his cowboy boot as it scraped the gravel back and forth.

"No, Hill, it means more money for me!" Bean replied, cocking the .357 and squeezing the trigger twice, sending seventeen inches of flame into the Ohio darkness, and removing Mr. Tim Hill of the Attorney General's Office from the land of the living.

Bean rolled up the truck window, straining his eyes into the night and looking for any sign of life. He pressed slowly down on the truck accelerator pedal and pulled away; leaving one of the state's finest lying dead on a deserted gravel road.

5

A tall, dark-haired stranger walked into the *Imperial Bar* and stood a moment. Pam was quick to notice the stranger's deep-blue eyes as he walked past her, heading to the last open booth in the back next to the rear exit.

By his actions, Pam thought he was looking for someone. *Perhaps a woman friend, the kind you rent by the hour or by the job,* she thought.

Pam waited until he took his seat then walked over to him.

"What'll you have?" she asked, looking into the stranger's deep-blue eyes.

"Beer please," the stranger replied, folding his hands and laying them on the table.

"OK, what kind of beer, love?" she asked, knowing by his demeanor he was a top-shelf gentleman. She could tell after a lifetime of pleasing men that he was uncomfortable being in a bar, especially a bar like this. She had a sixth sense about men and reasoned he was probably married. She glanced down at his left hand, confirming her suspicion. She noticed what any sharp bar maid would pick up–that he was either newly divorced or cheating on his wife and looking for a little action–otherwise no decent man in this town would come to a lizard lounge like this.

"A Bud Lite will do nicely," the stranger replied, looking up at her and smiling.

Pam was quick to notice that the smile was warm and genuine, his pale skin hinting that he probably worked in an office. She had noticed the stranger's walk as he stepped by her, a deliberateness of determination, indicating that this guy usually got what he wanted. She was not too sure about him, but he obviously had a serious urge, and her instincts told her that he was unhappy and needed serviced. She assumed a newbie like him would want someone sweet, cuddly and young. She considered the new girl, Heather, then remembered that Heather was already with some well off couple.

Pam found this stranger intriguing, almost alluring, as there was a sinister way about him, yet innocent. Slowly, the up in years, longhaired, retired prostitute bent over the table exposing more of her breasts than the law should allow. She placed the napkin and beer in front of him and stepped back.

"So," she asked," "are you new to town or just new to the *Imperial Bar?*"

"New to the *Imperial Bar,*" he replied, taking a sip of beer.

Pam smiled, wishing she were thirty years younger. "So do you have a name?" Pam asked.

"Yes, ma' am, I do," he replied, taking another sip of beer, but wishing the menopausal old hag would leave him alone.

"It's Roy," he said, looking up and seeing her crooked teeth, yellow from years of nicotine and neglect.

"Well, Roy, if you're here searching for drugs you're out of luck. We serve alcohol and sex, but no drugs. The owner would shoot anyone dealing, carrying or using drugs on his premises, and if you read the paper or watch local news, he means what he says. That's why we're not harassed by the police."

"So, no drugs, but alcohol and sex are served here? Is that what you're saying to me?"

"That's right, Roy, did I pique your interest?" Pam asked. Her smile widening, revealing more yellow and black teeth.

Roy turned away from her and grabbed his beer for moral support, choosing instead not to look at her. He put his beer back down on the wet napkin, raised his head, and looked at the cracked and peeling paint on the ceiling. Not looking at her for fear of losing his nerve, he asked simply, "How much will it cost me?"

"Depends on what you're looking for, sweetie," Pam replied, thinking this guy was a cherry. He would undoubtedly freak out if she told him what a strange piece was going for these days.

"Well, I'm looking for a woman who stands about five-six and weighs about one twenty-five. She likes wearing expensive wigs, sometimes blonde, other times a red head or she will forego the wigs and just be herself, a brunette."

"Oh, you're not a virgin after all. You have some experience with dodgy ladies," Pam said, rethinking her original evaluation of Roy.

Roy chuckled, "That would describe my wife all right…a dodgy lady."

6

Roth sat in his cubical, eyes blurry from fatigue. He looked at his watch and by his calculation he had been on duty for eighteen hours. Not a personal record, but when he was younger he could endure the hours. He had more stamina and of course, more hair. His walk was quicker and his wit, keener. Now he tired easily, and his brain, although still sharp, was just a tad slower. He decided to go home and feed his cat, take a shower, and hit the sheets. With luck, tomorrow would bring him closer to Leo's killer. Hill's killer was not his problem; the Attorney General would undoubtedly send her own homicide detective to investigate.

Roth shaved and showered, turned out the reading lamp, and pulled the sheet up onto his naked chest. Slowly, he placed his hands under his head and stared into the darkness. His instincts were telling him the deaths of Leo Kaczynski and Tim Hill were connected somehow...

* * *

It was a few minutes after 9:00 a.m. Roth looked up from his desk to find a tall, large man standing in his office doorway.

"Yeah, may I help you?" Roth asked.

"Yes, sir, I'm looking for a detective Roth," the stranger said, stepping slowly into the office.

"You found him!" Roth said.

"I'm Joshua Ledbetter of the Ohio Attorney General's Office Criminal Investigation Unit. I've been assigned by the AG to find the murderer of Tim Hill."

"Ok, I guess!" Roth said, standing up and extending his hand to this young giant and motioning him to take a seat.

Roth filled him in on all the details he could think of concerning the murder of Mr. Kaczynski and Tim Hill, putting forth his theory of the murders being linked.

Ledbetter was polite and allowed Roth to finish, then asked him the simplest and most thought-provoking question that he had heard all day.

"How can the murder of a simple retired Polish miner and the head of the state's drug task force be related?"

Roth had to admit it was a long shot for now, but only for now.

7

Heather pulled her car into the old barn, a piece of crap that should have been torn down years ago. She noticed that the holy man was not home. *The self-righteous, hypocritical bastard was probably out fucking one of his congregational flock,* she thought, twisting the well-worn doorknob and pushing against the backdoor that was warped from countless years of neglect. She placed her handbag and car keys on the avocado green, Formica kitchen counter top, worn paper thin from decades of scrubbing with harsh cleansers. She glanced around and tried to place this house, wondering why it felt familiar.

She looked at the lime colored door and instinctively knew it led to the basement. She twisted the cellar door's pearl white doorknob, looked down into the black abyss, and flipped on the light switch.

She started to descend the familiar steps that ended at a dirt floor. At the bottom of the stairs, Heather turned to her immediate left and walked back towards the wall. A quick right, and she was in an obscure alcove that stopped in front of another door. Heather stood perfectly still, trying to remember why she was there, standing in front of a door that had been hung when Abraham Lincoln was president. Then came the memories rushing into her mind. A sardonic smile crossed her face as she opened the door and pulled the string that lit the single light bulb in the middle of a a coal bin that was now used as a closet. This was her secret place, where she transformed into another woman. It was the place where she made all her wishes come true, and the one place where a cheating husband could not find her.

Heather looked into the old, round mirror that she had found buried under years of by-gone headlines. The single bulb cast dark shadows around the room, making self-examination of her face difficult. Grabbing a jar of cold cream, she began applying it to her face. When she had finished cleansing her skin, she removed her wig. This night she had selected the red wig, as Doctor Mike and his wife Doctor Paula enjoyed making love to a red head.

She stripped off her clothing, reached for the lemon-scented baby wipes, and wiped the last vestiges of Mike's semen from between her legs. She dressed in her jeans, and pulled her Steelers sweatshirt down over her well-massaged and very sore nipples. She slipped on her sandals, trying to keep the bottoms of her feet as clean as possible. Her panties and bra, she merely rolled into a ball and tossed into the corner. She would wash them later.

Finished with her makeover, she pulled the light string, walked out of her secret place, and headed back up the stairs. The house phone began to ring, exciting her. She ran up the stairs, which caused the rickety staircase to sway. She was hoping it was another client. Grabbing the kitchen phone on the fourth ring, she gasped, "Hello…," still unsure what she was doing in this place.

"Hello, Robin, where have you been, honey?" The syrupy, deep voice brought it all back to her.

"Oh, it's you… what do you want, as if I didn't know?"

The suddenness of Robin's attack startled him momentarily. Quickly, Roy realized that his wife had not taken her medicine, nor had she eaten the dinner he had prepared earlier.

"Ok, Robin, calm down honey, I'll be home soon," he replied keeping his temper in check, realizing his wife of seven years was mentally ill and had taken to prostitution, trying to fill a void in her life that he obviously could not.

Robin began supplementing the family income by prostituting herself for two hundred measly dollars a fuck but sometimes as much as five hundred. He had to admit it was hard on his ego, especially when she was hell bent on destroying him. Nobody asked anymore where Robin was. They were glad that she was not there as her verbal attacks on the women of his church, especially the state senator's wife and the young intern were most degrading. To Robin, he was a hypocrite who fucked other women. This was true. However, what she failed to understand was that she had pushed him into the arms of other women by cutting him off, moving him into the spare bedroom, saying only she could not stand him anymore.

As a result, he had found a few very giving and loving female parishioners who would spread their legs at any hour of the day, giving him access to satisfy his needs. Somehow Robin found out about these little rendezvous. Now he was sleeping with his bedroom door locked.

The situation came to a head one evening after dinner a few weeks earlier. She had prepared a great supper, and they chatted and laughed, even told some off colored jokes. He helped her clean the table and offered to wash the dishes if she dried. Robin declined, telling him to sit down while she washed the dishes.

He sat down at the kitchen table and opened the newspaper. She was talking about going back to school when the room turned silent. She had picked up an old framing hammer he had placed on the kitchen counter. Fortunately, for him, she came at him from the front, the open newspaper blocking her view causing her to miscalculate the distance.

Having his fill of her anger, he called the squad and had her committed for psychiatric evaluation.

Ten days later Robin was diagnosed with the psychological disorder MPD or DID. What that was and how the doctors identified it; he did not pretend to know, only that they did.

When he went to collect Robin from the hospital, the doctor called him into an empty hospital room and sat him down, explaining the ins and outs of Dissociative Identity Disorder (DID). The only thing he remembered about the conversation was that DID was a fascinating, frustrating and often dangerous psychological malfunction, especially for a woman like Robin.

When he pressed the doctor for specifics, the doctor merely held up his hand and replied, "Sir, what you once cherished will be no more. Everything the two of you held sacred will be destroyed, and your love for your wife tested to the max. At first, you will start noticing little personality changes. Also, you will begin to notice things like forgetfulness, followed by outbursts of vulgarity. She will use it at the most inopportune times, and then will curse you for no reason at all. Her attitude about things will change. I suspect the first thing will be that she will renounce you. If Robin was faithful, she will become unfaithful, perhaps becoming a thrill seeker, maybe sexually promiscuous, although that is extreme. Therefore, I will write her several prescriptions, and you make sure she does not drink any alcohol as these drugs are powerful. I must also warn you—and you have already seen for yourself—that Robin is very capable of killing. So be sure that she takes her meds. If she rebels, and in all likelihood, she will, pull the capsules apart and mix the contents in with her food, same with the tablets. I repeat: no alcohol."

The doctor was emphatic about the alcohol. However, there was no need to worry because there were no spirits of any kind in the house.

8

Lucy?" Roth yelled out from his office, paging his new right hand, Officer Lucy Bell. Bell was on light duty because she was pregnant. Otherwise, she would be in her police cruiser chasing speeders, or driving the back roads of the county looking for anything out of the ordinary.

"What do you want, Roth?" Bell yelled back as he waddled into his office.

"I want you to help me catch a killer—" Roth said, standing up and grabbing a chair. Gently, he pushed it to her.

"OK, I can do that. What do you want me to do?" she said, taking the chair and sitting down.

Roth smiled and handed her a must-do list.

Lucy looked at the list and noticed the numbers down the side of the page.

"When do you need all this? And if you tell me yesterday Roth, I am going to get up from this chair and kick your ass.

Roth noticed she was not smiling.

"Lucy, it would be unrealistic of me to expect anything *yesterday*. So let us start with the murder victim. Find out who this Leo Kaczynski was, where he came from, check his financial data— was he ever arrested for anything, that kind of stuff. Lucy, I am convinced Hill's murder and Kaczynski's are related somehow. The state's homicide investigator thinks I am wrong, and he may be right. However, I have this feeling in my gut that tells me to investigate. So Lucy, start with Leo."

Lucy stood up and smiled. "Ok, Roth, let's catch a murderer," she said, pushing her chair back to him.

Roth chuckled and watched her waddle out of the office. He was about to walk up to the diner on Sixth Street for some ham and eggs when his phone rang.

"Hello?" Roth said to the nameless person.

"Ah, yeah, could you please tell me who this is?" the voice asked.

"This is Homicide Detective Roth of the Zanesville Sheriff's Department, and who's this?" Roth asked, recognizing the voice as Ledbetter's.

"Hello, Roth, this is Ledbetter. I have Hill's cell phone, and I'm calling the last few numbers he dialed, trying to find out who he talked to."

"Tell you what, Josh, check to see who he was talking to around 3:00 a.m. I might be wrong about the time, but he was talking to someone. I gave it no mind at the time, thinking he was calling his wife. Now I am not so sure.

"Josh, I just had another idea," Roth said, scratching his scalp.

"What is it?" the young state investigator asked, realizing he was out classed by experience, and that he had better listen.

"Could you please tell me how Hill's car was parked?" Roth asked.

"Don't understand the question. Why would that make any difference?" Josh replied, his voice sounding troubled.

"Ok, if he was parked in the middle of the road, then he was probably set up, in other words—ambushed. If he was parked along the side of the road in the berm, say with his window down, it stands to reason, he knew his killer, or could have." Roth stopped talking, waiting for Joshua to answer.

"Hmm…Roth, that's good, truthfully, that's damn good. Actually, you have given me an idea that needs to be explored I'll get back to you, OK?"

Roth smirked, shaking his head at the silent phone and wondered what he had stirred up in the young investigator's mind.

* * *

Joshua slipped Hill's cell phone into his pocket and looked up at the clear blue morning sky. Except for the crunching of gravel under his feet and the cawing of crows, it was quiet. *Too damn silent*, Joshua thought. He walked over to Hill's cruiser—the lab boys had found nothing of significance and cleared it for active duty.

Hill had backed his car into a small grassy area just in front of two large oil storage containers as if he was lying in wait. The positioning of the cruiser signified a deliberate act by Hill as if the spot chosen had been agreed upon in advance.

Joshua took Hill's cell phone back out of his pocket and opened it again, looking for the call that, according to Roth, Hill had made. There wasn't one. Of course, Hill could have deleted the number, but why? He would have Hill's phone records subpoenaed.

Joshua slipped the cell back into his pocket and opened the cruiser's door, took a seat behind the wheel and reached for a smoke and lighter. He looked out over the dash and saw nothing, but trees and cows. He was perplexed, and the big question was why? Why was the chief of the state's drug task force killed on a lonely farm road in the wee hours of the morning? Why had he been here? What brought him to this place to be assassinated? Another thing that bothered him, what was Hill doing at a murder scene in the early-morning hours just prior to his own murder? Who reported the murder to Hill? Maybe, just maybe, Roth was correct—the murders were related somehow.

Joshua opened the car door when his mind's eye hit upon something so basic that he and the crime lab forgot about it. The DVD—every state police car had a dash camera. He could feel his pulse quicken as he got out of the car and opened the trunk, praying all the while that Hill had followed procedure and installed a disc in the recorder. If he had, it would prove a breakthrough.

One glance and Joshua felt giddy. Hill followed protocol. Now to view the disc and hope something useful showed up on it.

9

"Mmm…oh yeah, lover, that feels so good—harder sweetheart, I'm close…" April hissed between clenched teeth to the Corporate Vice President of the Power Company. Jack and his wife were always good to her, often taking her to dinner or to the movie. When Joyce, his wife of twenty years, wanted to fly to New York to go shopping, she would call and ask her to come along. Jack had once even told her she was the daughter they never had except this *daughter* gave benefits.

April was the consummate pro when it came to making her clients feel they were the best lover she ever had. Her first lover had been the next-door neighbor. She was only sixteen when she lost her hymen to him. When he had satisfied his lust, he opened his wallet and tossed fifty dollars onto her bed, trying to justify his actions. The dirt bag was her uncle. From then on, April vowed that anybody who wanted her body would have to pay for it, and she would set the price, depending. Her reasoning was simple—why not make the money for doing something she liked when she was young and beautiful?

Slowly over the months and years, April paid her dues learning the oldest profession in the world. To set herself apart from the others, she set up a web page calling herself the "Love Doctor." She made it clear on her web pages that she was not a cheap whore who roamed the streets in search of quick money to buy drugs. She also made it clear that she only did threesomes. It did not matter to her who the other partners were, two men, two women, or husband and wife. As long as they paid her fee of five hundred dollars, she was happy. Within six months of her web page debut, she was making a thousand dollars a day.

She learned as she went along, to loath streetwalkers. Nor could she abide the "B" girls who stood in front of the bars soliciting because to her? They were the type of women who gave her profession a bad name.

She separated herself from the others by the type of clients she serviced. They were the rich, powerful and influential. She catered to their individual needs as well as perversions. To protect herself, she began keeping a work diary documenting in detail what her clients liked, and how much they paid her. She figured that having a little security could not hurt just in case one of the judges or lawyers got pissed off at her and tried to pull something.

She catered to the doctors and their wives, followed closely by prominent businessmen of the city who would hire her services, as an escort for out of town investors. For that service, she would receive a cool thousand a pop, and if the client invested in the person's company, there was another thousand. The city was growing faster than the city services could provide. The influx of new capital began creating a city divided by those that have and those that have not. April was becoming wealthier with each passing month.

April had another great gift—the ability to listen to her clients, especially those that helped her with finances. She began paying taxes and investing in local real estate and setting up an IRA that would let her retire in comfort.

She had it all, the looks, the smarts, and the clientele. At twenty-five, April Kaczynski was on her way to the life she had dreamed that night her uncle Leopold took her virginity.

10

Lucy had just come out of the women's room for the ump-teenth time. Fatigue, lack of sleep, and worry were taking their toll on her and she still had another three months to go before she could unload this baby, which meant two months before she could take maternity leave. Until then, she would suffer and endure the teasing.

Her husband, Larry, was away in Iraq or was it Afghanistan, and it was anyone's guess when he would come home. He had joined the Air Force Reserve to serve and earn. Now he was earning and serving more than he wanted to as a fighter pilot in a godforsaken desert. Larry was a science teacher at the local high school and because of his extended duty, there was a real question if he would be able to get his job back when he came home.

"Hello...Lucy?" a male voice said, surprising her.

"Morning, Bean," Lucy replied, flashing a smile.

"When you due?" Bean asked, inserting three coins into the vending machine and punching E7.

"Three months, I hope," Lucy replied, inserting her coins into the coin slot and punching D2.

Bean retrieved his corn chips and Lucy's candy bar from the vending tray.

"So what does Toby have you doing?" Bean asked, opening his chips.

"Toby, who's Toby?" Lucy asked.

"Roth…I'm talking about Detective Roth. His first name is Toby," Bean said, filling his big mouth with corn chips.

Lucy said nothing more to Bean about Roth's first name. "He's got me investigating a homicide victim," Lucy replied.

"Oh…that must be the state guy who was murdered sometime this morning," Bean said, falling in step with Lucy as she trudged up the stairs to Roth's office.

"Roth has me doing a background check on Mr. Leo Kaczynski. He was also murdered last night, and Roth somehow feels the murders of the state guy, Hill, and Kaczynski are related," Lucy replied, stopping at the top of the stairs catching her breath.

"Oh…" Bean replied, stalling while trying to come up with a plausible explanation why Roth would reason that way.

"Yeah, right now I'm doing Kaczynski's financial records. Then I'll start doing the background checks, employment verification, stuff like that," Lucy said, walking past Roth's office and into her own makeshift space that used to be a kitchenette used by the homicide squad, but now used by Roth for anything he desired.

"Makes sense to me!" Bean said, wadding his chip bag up into a small ball and lobbing it into the waste paper basket for two points.

Lucy smiled at Bean's achievement and took her seat. Bean remained at the door waiting to be invited in. When Lucy averted her eyes to the computer screen instead, Bean took the hint and walked away, once again passing Toby's office while pondering the idea of killing Sir Toby.

Roth happened to look up from reading the Coroner's report on Kaczynski and saw Bean pass by his office. Roth's skeptical side wondered why a deadbeat deputy like Bean would be on his floor.

Bean had interviewed for a detective's shield; it was the only time he had shown any ambition to move up on the food chain. When Roth had asked him why he wanted to be a detective, he replied with a straight face and serious demeanor, "Because it would be fun, and the money's good." Bean-o boy did not get the shield and never applied for anything since. Roth got back to the original question, *why was Bean-o boy on his floor?*

Roth reached across his desk pulled the house intercom phone to him. Holding the receiver to his ear, he punched in the number 12 and waited.

"Deputy Sheriff Bell…how may I help you, sir or ma'am?"

"Yes, Lucy, can you tell me what Deputy Bean was doing on this floor?"

"Sir, he just walked me up the steps, making sure I was OK," Lucy replied. "Why do you ask, Roth?" Lucy said her voice dead pan.

"Lucy, Bean is a dead beat. He has no ambition unless there is money in it for him then he turns into a kiss ass. Best advice, Lucy, be polite to him, be professional, but keep him at arm's length. There's something dark and repugnant about him," Roth said.

"You know, Roth, now that you mention it, Bean did seem really curious when I mentioned Hill and Mr. Kaczynski and how you thought the murders might be related."

"Thank you, Lucy," Roth said, hanging up and returning his attention back to the grizzly details of the Coroner's report which listed the cause of death as shotgun blasts to the abdomen and skull, resulting in a two-page list of body parts either destroyed or missing. *Ok, Doc, tell me something I did not already know,* Roth mumbled to himself.

Just to the left on the bottom of the first page the doctor had made a small grouping of nine little dots. Beside the dots were two 00s with the notation (double-ott buckshot).

Roth laid the doc's report to the right side of his desk and picked up the field teams physical evidence report from the crime scene. He was looking for two spent shotgun shells. "Nothing…" he said aloud. *Not one mention of any shotgun shells spent or otherwise. The killer must have picked them up and taken them with him,* he reasoned. *But why, would the killer do that unless the killer was a hit man, which seemed highly improbable. Another possibility could be that the spent shells could be traced and that was doubtful as double-ott buckshot is almost considered a fair trade item in this county.* Even Roth had a box of twelve gauge double ott shotgun shells in the trunk of his cruiser. All authorized law enforcement personnel carried six-shot pump action, twelve-gauge shotguns in their cruisers. That was common knowledge.

Roth felt his bladder pressing against his backbone and needed to relieve himself. He looked at his watch, almost lunchtime. He had been sitting at his desk for a solid four hours without a break. What the hell he thought. *I need to get out of here and get laid...*

"Lucy—" Roth yelled.

"Yes—" Lucy's small, sickly voice responded, pissing Roth off to no end.

"I'm going to lunch then out to the Kaczynski crime scene."

"Have fun," Lucy replied, never looking up from her computer screen.

11

Roth felt his phone vibrating against his thigh. He had forgotten that he had switched it to vibrate yesterday. Letting go of the steering wheel, he reached his right hand into his pants pocket. A quick check of the caller ID and his concern about finding sex was solved. It was sweet, dumb-as-a-stump, cute-as-a-button Cathy Dixon, or as the men called her, Ditzy Dixon. She was built for one thing, and that was giving pleasure to a sex-starved homicide detective who was old enough to be her father.

"Hello, Dixie, how're you doing', sweetheart?" Roth asked, pulling his cruiser into his driveway.

"Roth I've been promoted to the city beat," Dixie said.

"Sounds wonderful to me, Dixie," Roth said, closing the car door.

"It's a big promotion, Roth. in fact; it's the biggest break I have ever had, and I want to be the best reporter this city has ever seen," Dixie responded, her voice sounding serious and confident.

"So, sweetheart, why are you calling me with this great news?

"I want to discuss the murders of the state trooper and the other guy?"

"Ok, Dixie, come over to my house, and we'll have lunch. I will give you a few gory details and some background information. However, that is all I will give you for now. I will give you more information when things develop and when the case is solved. I will give you the exclusive. Will that help the new cub reporter?" Roth asked.

"What are we having for lunch?" Dixie asked.

"Toasted cheese sandwiches with tomato soup, saltine crackers and a dill pickle, topped off with a diet soda," Roth replied.

"Do you still live on Brookhaven?" Dixie asked.

"Yep, you'll see my car in the driveway."

"Ok, give me fifteen minutes," Dixie, said.

Roth flipped his phone shut and walked into his house, glanced at the kitchen clock and said aloud to no one, in particular, fifteen minutes would just about do it. He pulled out the cast-iron skillet and soup pan from underneath the counter.

The part-time astrologist, part-time obituary writer and now city reporter looked ravishing as she came through the kitchen door. Her emerald-green eyes looked clear and bright, accented by her red hair and freckles.

Roth felt his face flush as he stared at her.

"For Christ sakes, Roth will you please leave me some clothes you old letch?" Dixie said, giving him a kiss.

"Sorry honey, but you look so damn hot," Roth replied, enfolding her in his arms and pulling her even closer, smelling her perfume as he kissed her lips again.

"Wow, that was some kiss, detective," Dixie squealed, delighted that she had such an effect on the normally sedate and somber Roth.

"Sweetheart, you come into a bachelor's house, looking like a beauty queen, and you don't want to be kissed?" Roth said, gently nibbling her ear, still holding her close.

"You're right, I wanted to be kissed," Dixie moaned, offering her lips to him.

Roth kissed her slowly letting his hands fall to the small of her back, gently pressing her body into his. Dixie broke off the embrace, and stepped back looking up at him.

Roth looked into her eyes that minutes ago appeared clear and bright and now were smoldering with lust. He noticed that her cheeks were a rosy pink. She did not want lunch now. She made that obvious when she grabbed her purse, then his hand, and led him through the dining room, made the hard right turn, and headed down the hall towards his bedroom.

The sex was intense, and she lost count of the number of her orgasms. Drenched in sweat, she rolled off Roth's chest and snuggled. Her fingers stroked his soft, silver-gray chest hair, her breath still coming in small gasps as she tried to regain her composure. Roth kissed her and cradled her in his arms as beads of sweat rolled off his face. The hum of the ceiling fan was the only sound, as it made a cool, gentle breeze over their naked bodies, causing Dixie's flesh to break out in goose bumps.

Roth turned, pulled Dixie closer to him, and placed a gentle kiss on her lips.

"Thank you, sweetheart, I needed that—" Roth whispered in her ear.

"You hurt me, Roth," she said, sliding her body around and placing both hands on his chest and placing her chin on them.

"How's that?" Roth asked, softly stroking her cheek with his finger.

"You drove so hard and deep into me; it was like you were angry or something, you completely ignored my scream, and you held me so tight I could hardly breathe."

"Sorry, sweetheart, I guess I was hornier than even I thought," Roth responded, feeling his cock stirring back to life.

"Don't apologize sweetie, I want you to call me the next time you get horny like that. That was awesome; I lost count of how many times I came." She giggled, turning her cheek, and placing her ear to his chest listening to his heartbeat.

"Honey, when you climbed on top of me you asked me what month I was born. Why did you do that?" Roth asked.

"Oh, that—well as you know, I wrote the weekly astrology forecast for the newspaper. One night I am balling my then boyfriend, Scott, and he asks me to put a condom on his *Willie*. Now Scott was a Gemini, and Gemini people are known for their versatility, intellect, and communication skills. So why not develop a marketing scheme for packaging condoms using the zodiac signs and since each sign has its different characteristics all I did was write those characteristics up and hawked them to a generic condom manufacturer I knew in Cincinnati. His business tripled and every month I get a fat check and a dozen condoms," Dixie said, turning her head so it rested in the crook of Roth's shoulder.

"So when I told you that I was an Aries, and you began reciting that stuff; you were reading it off the condom package."

"That's right. I was," Dixie, replied picking up the foil wrap and holding it, so she could read the writing and began reciting.

"The Aries Male is action oriented. His Zodiac symbol is the Ram so it is only fitting that this condom is made from the finest lambskin, reinforced with ribs to support the get it up and go attitude Aries males possess. Aries condoms are also perfect for those opportunistic quickies…"

"And you get paid for writing that mumbo-jumbo?" Roth said, seriously.

"Very well indeed," Dixie replied.

12

Joshua sat in his recliner, a beer in one hand, his cock in the other. He was watching his favorite porno movie, the one showing his wife and the young, single mother-to-be that he had found holding up a sign that simply read, "Will do anything for food."

He took a sip of his beer, feeling the golden elixir as it traveled down the back of his throat. and fell into his growling stomach. As he began to relax, he could feel the day's fatigue slowly creeping into his body, and the movie he took so much pride in only made him want Miss Amanda even more. It had been five months since his wife had left him for another woman. Now she was supposedly living in Florida with some young woman that she had met on line. Go figure...

Amanda's note was simple but direct. It simply said—

Dear Joshua,

Thank you for everything sweetheart, I will love you always. Please do not try to find me for I have found my true soul mate, and it is not a man. I found her on the Internet.

Love,

Amanda

She had him by the short hairs, and he knew it. He could not divorce her because the lawyer needed an address, and he did not have one. Amanda's parents were so ashamed they disowned her, having nothing to do with their daughter from that point on, calling her an abomination of God's law.

Joshua was eating breakfast when his cell phone rang. He looked at the clock on the microwave 6:10. Only two people would call him this early in the morning; one was in Florida; the other was Victor (The Knife) Caruso, aka the state's medical examiner.

"Hello?" Joshua said, pouring his morning coffee.

"Joshua, this is Doctor Caruso. I know it's early, but you asked me to rush Hill's autopsy. Only found one bullet, the other one must have exited Hill's skull. Hill was shot at point-blank range with a .357 Magnum. Death was instantaneous. However, I did denote something peculiar—"

"What?" Josh asked, his voice raised, his adrenalin beginning to pulse through his veins.

"Hill had blood splatter on his pants, and socks," the doc replied in a voice that was smooth and soft.

"That would be consistent with the wounds?" Joshua replied, sitting down at the kitchen table dunking his buttered toast into his coffee.

"No, Josh, the cross match revealed the blood belonged to someone else. I sent the bullet over to the ballistic lab. Maybe they can come up with something." Doc said.

"Thank you!" Josh replied, hearing The Knife ask, *whose next?* Then silence.

Joshua sat holding his cereal spoon at the ready and staring at the playboy calendar, not even seeing Miss October, his thought's spinning around and around in his head, trying to come up with a plausible theory, as to why Hill was murdered.

It was obvious to him that Hill knew his assailant. Otherwise, he would not have met him or her in such a remote area of the county. He could have been meeting an informant. "Hmm, maybe the Pollock that was murdered was the informant and the same guy who killed him killed Hill?" he muttered.

That would make Roth's theory about the murders being connected totally viable. Another thing: if Hill called Roth about the

Pollock's murder, then why was Hill there in the first place, unless Hill murdered the Pollock? However, why would he do that?

Joshua picked up his cereal bowl and his coffee cup and walked into the family room. Carefully, he positioned his breakfast on the side table, and inserted Hill's video disc into his disc player.

He pushed the play button, and walked back to his cereal bowl and began spooning Cheerios into his empty stomach, followed by coffee laced with butter.

Finishing his Cheerios, he walked to the bedroom and began dressing for work. Dressed minus his shoes, he walked back to the family room, pressed the disc player's stop button and hit play. He was not interested in anything Hill had done earlier that day, only the time from the Pollock's murder scene. The disc was running, clearly evidenced by the dash cam. However, the television screen was dark. Impatient, Josh stopped the disc and hit fast forward this time adding another five minutes. He stopped the disc and pressed the play button. He noticed a sudden flash off in the distance on the far-right side of the screen, another flash, then the screen went black again.

Joshua played the disc again, taking it back another few minutes. Once again, he repeated the process of stop and play. This time the film showed Hill on some back county road, the car's camera clearly showing a dead possum lying in the middle of the road, a few deer stealing corn from a farmer's hopper, a raccoon crossing the road. Hill even slowed for the raccoon, letting it cross the road in safety.

A few minutes later, Hill slowed his car and pulled off the road. Joshua could see a mailbox on the left. He could not make out the numbers, but hopefully the lab people could enhance the image and if the address turned out to be the Pollock's then the muzzle flashes were from Hill's shotgun.

Encouraged by what he had seen, Joshua grabbed his empty coffee cup and went to the kitchen to pour himself another cup of coffee. As he walked back into the room, his eyes went to the screen. He saw something explode across the screen. It looked like a face silhouetted in the muzzle flash he knew to be a .357 Magnum. He sat down, grabbed the remote and once again pressed the play back button. He took a sip of coffee and watched the images running backwards, growing more impatient with each passing second.

Joshua pushed the play button and wished that he hadn't after the muzzle flash; he clearly saw the back of Hill's head exploding outward away from his skull. Joshua swallowed hard, trying to keep his breakfast intact. Despite the grossness of Hill's murder, the disc showed a face in what he believed was a truck window, holding a revolver.

Joshua hit the eject button and grabbed the disc, then reached for his coat and thermos, turned out the lights, and he was gone.

With lights flashing, he headed straight to Columbus. He had to show this disc to Scotty Morten in the photo lab.

13

octor Paula Tidwell sat at her microscope studying the latest experiment when her cell began vibrating in the pocket of her lab coat. Annoyed, she checked the caller ID. It was her husband, Mike.

"Hi, honey," Paula cooed.

"Hey baby," Mike said softly. "I'm feeling the urge honey, how about you?"

"What you up for?" she giggled.

"I'm not in the mood for Bean. Hill got himself killed and the Judge intimidates me, although you seem to like the Judge and his wife. So let's try Heather again, or maybe April if she's available?"

"Ooh, I like Heather, plus she's a little less expensive than April. However, April does like to ride my plastic pony," Paula said, her voice taking on a matter of fact tone.

"Let's try for Heather, and you can teach her to ride your plastic pony. But..." Mike replied.

"What?" Paula asked, noticing the change in her husband's tone.

"I don't know how to get hold of Heather, or April, for that matter."

Paula laughed, "Okay, sweetie. I'll take care of it."

"Bye, honey, time to make my money so you can spend it," Mike said hanging up before Paula could respond.

Paula smiled closing her phone, placing it into her pocket. *If Mike only knew the truth, he'd shit himself,* she thought, turning her attention back to her microscope and the lab exercise of the moment.

Paula was not an ugly woman. On a beauty scale, she would rate somewhere between a strong eight and nine. If she wore her contact lenses, and with her long, blonde hair framing her angular face, and with her high cheekbones, she would qualify as a ten. She considered her best features to be her breasts, which were ample. In private intimate moments with a lover, Paula would often confess that she was built for sex.

In truth, Paula could be described as a sex kitten with a sexual hunger of a lioness. She learned over time to use her sexual prowess to control the powerful and influential men and women of Zanesville. Judges, lawyers, the police, the assistant district attorney, even the wife of a state senator; all were within her reach and as such could, when called upon, do her bidding.

Paula smiled when she thought of her husband's remark, "Got to go make the money so my honey can spend it." Mike was a very giving, affectionate man who was in love with his lifestyle, but in truth Mike had no idea what his wife really was.

Mike was a necessary convenience, somebody to go to plays and movies with and give her respectability—more important, someone to give her the status that goes with the lifestyle of being a doctor's wife.

Paula looked at the wall clock and realized that she had been sitting at her microscope for more than five hours; it was time to go home.

As she walked to her SUV, she pulled out her cell and dialed Heather. There was no answer, so she left Heather a message, just in case she was available for tonight.

She was still in the car park when her cell rang.

"Hello Heather," Paula said her voice soft and sexy.

"Sorry to disappoint you, Paula!" the male voice said.

"What do you want, Bean?" Paula asked. She was not amused.

"I need to talk with you right away," Bean replied, urgency resonating in his voice.

"About what?" She placed her Lincoln Navigator into drive and slowly negotiated the parking lot.

"I need money, and lots of it! Detective Roth has a picture of me killing Hill, a picture made from a disc. Before he gets to me, I want to go to South America, possibly Brazil or maybe Columbia and get lost," Bean said his voice now sounding desperate.

"How did this Roth person get a picture of you killing Hill?" Paula asked, pulling her Navigator into the downtown traffic.

"I forgot all state police cars have dash cameras. Hill's dash cam probably showed my face in the muzzle flash of my revolver," Bean replied his voice calmer.

"Bean, just why did you kill Hill?" Paula asked.

"Paula, Hill was a fuck up and a traitor!" Bean said, his voice becoming defensive.

"Well, I hate to break this to you, Bean, but you killed the head of the state's Bureau of Criminal Investigation. A man with connections to the DEA, FBI, and only God knows what else, because to you, Hill was a fuck up. What did you expect? Now you want me to give you money so you can flee to some place in South America. Tell me, Bean, do you speak Spanish?"

"No, I don't!" Bean replied.

"So you want to disappear to a South American country, a white man, who doesn't speak the language and who, in a crowd of Spanish men, would stick out like Frosty the Fucking Snowman, and you call Hill a fuck up? Amazing!" Paula was outraged and her voice clearly showed her displeasure at Bean's stupidity. Bean was going to have to figure things out on his own.

14

It had been two days since he had sex with Dixie, and Roth could feel the urge returning. He reached for the phone to give her a call that was pre-empted.

"Hello Roth. You have a minute?" Roth looked up to see Ledbetter standing in the doorway. *Christ, almighty,* Roth thought. He was *one big son of a bitch.*

"Mr. Ledbetter, to what do I owe this momentous occasion?" Roth said, standing up and extending his hand.

Joshua walked into the office and shook Roth's hand.

"I came for two reasons, maybe three depending on how you look at it," Joshua said, laughing and pulling up a chair, though not invited to do so.

"Oh!" Roth said, and as an afterthought, motioned to Joshua to take the chair that he had already sat down on.

"First I'm here to apologize," Joshua said, smiling at his mentor.

"Apology accepted, I think!" Roth replied, a grin starting to form on his face.

"Second, I'm a bearer of good news," Joshua opened a large manila envelope that had escaped Roth's attention.

Roth sat back in his chair and held up both his hands. A serious look replacing his grin.

"What's this" Roth asked.

"Do you remember when I disputed your theory about the murders of Hill and your dead Pollock being related?"

"Yeah, okay, so—"

"The other day, after I talked with you on the phone, and we talked over the position of Hill's car? I looked at the situation from your point of view. I came up with some questions and developed a hypotheses, and have concluded two things: First, you are correct the murders are related. Second, I know who killed your Mr. Kaczynski, and I have the face of the man who killed Hill."

Roth pulled his chair up to his desk, the look on his face clearly showing disbelief.

"Ok, Joshua, show me," Roth folded his hands and placed them under his desk, pinning them against the desk drawer to hide his excitement.

Before he began to speak, Joshua got up from his chair and closed Roth's office door, something Roth seldom did.

Roth watched in anticipation as Joshua pulled the contents out of the manila envelope, and held the forms and pictures in his hand, reviewing each item before speaking.

"Ok, here we have the ballistics' report on the bullet that killed Hill, the bullet from a .357 Magnum. Our computer indexing log revealed that the gun that killed Hill was also used in another murder, a murder, by the way, which you solved some three years ago."

"That probably was the Wood murder," Roth said.

"Our records show the gun was supposedly sold by this sheriff's department at a silent auction. A registered owner was none other than a Mr. Leopold Kaczynski. He paid three hundred dollars in cash for the Magnum.

"However, I know for a fact that Hill killed Mr. Kaczynski. He then called you personally from the murder scene that he created."

Roth remained silent listening intently to the young detective.

"Look at this medical examiner's lab report. Please note the blood spatter found on Hill's pants and socks. The blood belonged to

Mr. Kaczynski. I also have visual evidence taken by Hill's dash cam, which captured Kaczynski's address in his car's headlights.

"Speaking of muzzle flashes, here are some still photos of Hill walking up to his murderer's pickup truck. Hill knew his killer. I must warn you these photos are very graphic, but if you look at the last three, you will clearly see the face of the murderer silhouetted in the muzzle flashes. Please note the shooters ring finger, he's wearing a wedding band." Joshua had finished his report. He sat back in his chair interlocking his fingers and resting on them across his chest.

Roth leaned back in his chair, looking at Joshua, but saying nothing. His mind working at warp speed, all traces of his overactive libido gone. His concentration was now clearly focused on three things: Leopold Kaczynski, the reappearance of a murder gun, and a face in a flash.

Holding up his finger to Joshua asking for silence, Roth picked up his desk phone and dialed Extension 12.

Joshua heard the female voice say what sounded like "may I help you?"

"Yes, Officer Bell, would you please bring in the information you have on Kaczynski?" Roth asked.

Joshua looked somewhat perplexed at Roth's actions. He thought Roth would be ecstatic about the news.

Roth looked up at Josh and smiled as he replaced the receiver.

"You're not going to believe this, Joshua, but I think we have just opened up a large can of worms. How big a can is yet to be determined. My gut tells me that if Hill was dirty, then there are other law enforcement officials who are dirty as well. I think, and mind you I am guessing, we may have stumbled upon an active little drug ring in my city. I think Hill was protecting either the drug ring or himself, and I think that Kaczynski figured prominently in the ring."

Roth was about to say something else, but never got the chance. He was interrupted by Officer Bell.

Joshua got up from his chair and offered it to her. Lucy smiled and took his chair. She laid several folders on Roth's cluttered desk, avoiding Roth's empty coffee cups.

"Here's the Kaczynski stuff," Lucy said, handing them over to Roth. "I also thought you might want to take a look at Mr. Kaczynski's financial records. They are very interesting," Lucy said, reaching over and taking the folder handed to her by Roth. "This folder is from Interpol, and it reveals that Kaczynski was a member of the communist party back in Poland, and it appears that he had connections to the Russian underworld," Lucy was feeling the need to pee, when she saw the photograph of the face illuminated by muzzle flash. She looked up at Joshua and said, "May, I?" Joshua nodded and handed Lucy the picture.

"I know this person. In fact, I have seen him recently," Lucy said, handing the picture back to Joshua.

"Are you sure, Lucy?" Roth asked.

"Sure. Do you think any girl would miss those diamonds in a wedding band?" Lucy replied, getting up from her chair and waddling towards the open door.

"Diamonds? What about the diamonds?" Roth asked.

"Damn it, Roth! Look at that wedding band! Use your magnifying glass! You will see three small marquis diamonds set in a band of gold. That ring cost a pile, and it is easy to tell that neither of you are married."

"Whoa, Lucy, where do you think you're going?" Roth asked.

'Well, if it's any of your damn business Roth, I'm going to the restroom. Don't fret, I'll be back," Lucy said, closing the office door behind her.

Roth turned to Joshua, who stood laughing at the two of them.

"Hormones," Roth remarked.

Lucy stood at the vending machine, her eyes darting from the soft and crunchy *Payday* to the gooey caramel and chocolate *Snickers*. Today the choice would be the chocolate and caramel. She pressed E1 and waited for her Snickers bar.

"Hey, Lucy Bell— what's the good word today?"

Lucy turned around. It was Bean.

"I know if this damn machine doesn't give up my Snickers bar; I'm going to fill it full of lead," Lucy replied.

"Here, Lucy, stand back," Bean said, throwing his shoulder into the machine and rocking it backwards, causing Lucy's candy bar to fall into the serving tray below.

Bean bent down and retrieved the candy bar from the serving tray, handing it to her.

"How you doing with the Kaczynski murder investigation?" Bean said, dropping his three quarters into the slot and pressing E7.

"Oh, I'd say Roth has already solved that murder. He has a picture of the man who killed that state investigator as well.

"Wow, you don't say—" Bean said, his smile turning quickly to a grimace.

"The funny thing, Bean, is that I know I have seen that guy's face before. I remember seeing that wedding ring with those three diamonds embedded end to end in a band of gold on somebody's finger, but for the life of me, I can't recall where I've seen him before," Lucy said walking away unwrapping her Snickers bar.

"That's too bad, Lucy," Bean said, retrieving his corn chips. "I'm sure you'll come up with it..."

15

April Kaczynski sat at her kitchen table, a cup of green tea in one hand a cigarette in the other. She was reading the article about the murder of her uncle with a certain smugness of personal satisfaction. He was no good, her uncle. He had a way of tainting or destroying anything that was decent.

April took a long drag off the cigarette and slowly exhaled the smoke through her nose. Her cat, Lover Boy, perched quietly on her lap was not amused by his mistress's ability to blow smoke out of her nose causing him to sneeze.

April normally overly loving and affectionate toward Lover Boy was lost in thought. She knew Uncle Leo had nobody left alive in this country. He killed his wife years ago in West Virginia simply by neglecting her medical needs. He could not be bothered with details, such as buying her insulin. Her mother succumbed last year to kidney disease. Leo's brother, her father, was dead from cancer. Her uncle Leo could not even be bothered to attend his brother's funeral. When she had called him and told him of her father's death, all the son of a bitch could say was, "So why bother me?" Yeah, Leo was some piece of work.

April wondered if she could, as his only surviving relative, put a claim against his estate and get her hands on all his money. She would ask Allen at their next get together. Allen was some sort of judge and would probably help her for a piece.

First, she would call Roth and speak with him about her uncle Leo.

* * *

"Dixie?"

"Yes?" came the soft voice.

"This is Roth. Are you up for some lunch?"

"Depends on what you got," Dixie sassed back.

"I've got a story for you that I want you to print. I even have a picture of a killer. Are you interested or not?" Roth said, a smile creasing his face.

Dixie blurted out, "You bet I am! Your place, thirty minutes."

Roth chuckled and shook his head, trying to remember if he had any condoms. But of course Dixie would have some.

* * *

April was about to step into the shower when her cell phone rang. A quick glance at the caller ID told her she would be busy tonight.

"Hello, Paula," April said.

Paula got right to it, her voice upbeat and confident. "I was wondering if you were up for a *ménage a trois* with Mike and me tonight."

"What would be a good time?" April asked reaching for her appointment book.

"About eight?"

"Shall I bring my *toys?*" April said reaching for a clean towel and setting it over the holder.

"As you wish— I have my own," Paula replied.

"See you at eight!" April said, hanging up and stepping into the shower spray.

Paula placed the kitchen phone back in the cradle and a quick glance at the clock told her she had just over three hours to prepare for April. Mike would be home in two hours. She decided to make a large salad, call out for a large veggie pizza, and with a couple of glasses of red wine, it would make for a very romantic evening. First, she had to take a shower and unwind. Bean had her so angry she could not think straight. The only thing she was certain of was that Bean must go. The problem was how?

16

Roth laid perfectly still, trying to catch his breath. Dixie had been insatiable and had exhausted him so completely that he actually had to push her off. Still, she tried to get back on top for another go. *She was ravenous, wonderfully ravenous;* he thought, wondering if Dixie liked women.

Roth turned on his back to allow Dixie to snuggle up to him. He kissed her lips and gently climbed over her body reaching for a large manila envelope that was lying on the nightstand.

"What's that?" Dixie said, placing her chin on Roth's chest, watching him as he pulled out some official-looking papers and placed them face down on the sheet. Next, he extracted high glossy black-and-white pictures. The first picture she saw caused her stomach to roll. She turned and sat up hard, forcing herself to swallow in an attempt not to vomit.

Only then did Roth see her reaction and quickly dropped the picture onto the floor.

"Sorry, sweetheart, murder is often a very messy affair," he said, placing another picture followed by another onto the floor.

"Here it is, honey," Roth said handing Dixie the photo of Hill's killer.

Dixie folded her legs under her body and looked at the photo.

"Wow, Roth, I should ball you all the time. Is this my story?" she asked, looking down at him.

"Not totally—I need you to help me flush out a killer, and then you'll have your story and everything that comes after it," Roth said, turning his back and reaching for his underwear.

"Why do I feel there's more to it than this?" Dixie asked, getting off the bed and walking bare assed to the bathroom, her modesty a thing of the past when it came to Roth.

Roth smiled and reached out to the chair for his tee shirt, choosing not to answer her.

He was becoming fond of Dixie, although their age difference precluded any meaningful romance. By all accounts, Dixie was a beautiful woman. Another thing, the men had it all wrong. She was not a ditz. That was for damn sure, and the best part of all was that she was fantastic in bed.

He would covet her friendship and help her when he could, for as long as he was able. After her shower, he would explain what he wanted her to do.

He knew that trust was often a cop's worst enemy, especially when it came to self-serving politicians and ambitious reporters. But Dixie was new at her job and an eager beaver. She wanted to excel in hopes of getting a better job at a much larger paper and leaving Z-Town forever. Roth felt sure that Dixie could be trusted. Knowing by being patient and trustworthy, over time Dixie would gain the respect and acclaim to success, of that he felt certain.

He sat in the living room and waited for Dixie to finish in the bathroom. His mind was lost in thought concerning the .357 Magnum Kaczynski purchased from the department. That policy had been suspended years ago. He was not exactly sure when, but he would certainly find out. What it did tell him was that the gun definitely established a link between Hill and Kaczynski, as Hill's killer may be the person who ordered the murders.

Lucy had added another wrinkle to his investigation when she informed him that some strange woman named April had called with information about her uncle Leo and asked for Toby to call her. When Lucy asked why Roth would be interested in her uncle Leo, the woman got miffed and said, "…because Leopold Kaczynski was my uncle."

Being courteous and professional, Lucy asked April for her phone number and address. April simply replied he had her number and knew where she lived. Then came a devious giggle followed by silence then a click.

Roth pursed his lips, still waiting for Dixie. He could hear the shower now and knew it would be about twenty minutes. He pulled out his phone and touched the button for auto-directory. He waited, listening to each ring, finally the distinctive, sultry voice of April answered.

"Hello, handsome— where've you been? I miss you," April said sighing into the phone, causing his well-used pecker to quiver.

"Yes, love, I've missed you too! Are you ok?" Roth asked, feeling his lust starting to return and Dixie just a few steps away.

"I have much to tell you about my uncle Leopold, I mean a whole lot, and was wondering if perhaps we could meet for a late lunch, say *The Olive Garden,* I mean tomorrow being Saturday and all?"

"Let me guess, April, and I am just spit balling here: I suppose you want me to pick up the tab. is that correct?" Roth asked.

"Of course, silly, men like you always pay for dinner, and I supply the dessert."

"The Olive Garden at three," Roth said, flipping his phone closed and wondering what a woman like April really wanted from him.

Getting up from sofa, he pulled off his t- shirt followed by his underwear. He rolled them in a ball, tossed them across the room, and walked into the bathroom.

17

Robin stirred, her drug-filled, diluted mind slow to react to the hand cupping her breast and pinching her nipple. She heard herself moan, enjoying the familiar sensation, knowing it was the prelude to the inevitable coupling with a man she had once loved and now loathed. Nevertheless, such was life. Roy was a weak man who often succumbed to sins of the flesh, and it did not matter to him who the woman was. If he wanted her, he would seduce her, using whatever method would work: blackmail, drugs, alcohol, or simply his charm and good looks.

Robin could feel her body betraying her despite her disgust for him, as he slowly rolled her onto her back, kissing her neck, caressing her thigh, pushing her nightshirt up higher with each caress. She could feel Roy's hot beer breath on her cheek as he slid his body on top of hers, aligning his body with hers for the inevitable surrender to his maleness.

Robin began to moan, encouraging her husband, twisting her body back and forth, thrusting her hips upwards and slowly sliding her left leg out of the way making it easier for Roy to access her body. Then, strangely, it all stopped, and he abandoned the offensive. Curious, she opened her eyes, watched him as he sat up on his knees, and started unbuckling his pants.

The son of a bitch did not have the courtesy to undress. She remained silent, her anger building with each passing second waiting for the dumb ass to get naked.

Roy ultimately managed to pull his pants down his legs, forgetting that he was still wearing shoes. She heard him utter his familiar curse as the sound of spare change hit the wooden floor echoing around the room. Again, Robin heard the distinctive word, "Shit!" It was his favorite cuss word.

What an arrogant shithead, she thought. Watching him as he turned his attention back to her, his manhood now clearly visible and pointing at twelve o'clock. Once again, he repositioned himself in front of her and began leaning forward, aligning himself with her.

Through half-closed eyes, Robin watched as she straightened her left leg out, placing it directly under him. Then, with all the force she could muster, she brought her left knee up, hitting him squarely in the balls. His scream was silent as nothing, but a hiss of hot, foul-smelling air passed over his lips as he crumbled into a mass of anguished pain onto the hardwood floor, unable to move, gasping for air.

I wonder what Mike and Paula are up to, she thought pulling the sheet up to her chin and rolling over, ignoring the moaning man on the floor.

18

Saturday morning came early for Bean as he sat at his kitchen table drinking hot black coffee and chain smoking his wife's cigarettes. He had been up since three, his stomach burning all night, and the smoking and morning coffee did little good.

Paula had told him yesterday what she wanted him to do. Then he was to drop by her house around four this afternoon as she had a plan to help him get out of the country. She wouldn't tell him her plan over the phone, but assured him he would be okay with it. Now all he had to do was follow her instructions then wait it out until this afternoon.

Paula walked through her herb garden wearing only her lacy silk camisole. She listened to the cardinal's singing in the trees behind her house and enjoyed the moment. She was also waiting for April and Mike to finish their shower before making breakfast. Last night had been a tempestuous love feast, and she and Mike had devoured April until she begged them to stop.

She would have preferred Heather to April. However, in this case, it worked out fine. The money was well spent and Mike was satisfied for now, and she could get on with the things she must do.

Stooping to her bare knee, she picked some dill, yew, rosemary, and thyme. She was thinking of Leo Kaczynski and how his murder would affect her business. She could not help wondering why

Hill had killed Leo, unless Leo posed a threat to the operation. Hill's murder had blinded her operation as far as the DEA was concerned. Bean was deserting her, and with him gone she would be losing her local police protection and enforcer.

She decided to have Officer Bean come to her house. Yes, she was sure that was the thing to do. She would feed him, fuck him and kill him. The killing would be the most ingenious and insidious part of her plan. Mike had a golf date at noon; he would be gone the rest of the day. Bean was to stop by at four, giving her more than enough time to prepare for him. *The poor bastard will never see it coming,* she thought, *and the best part is I save a hundred grand.*

Breakfast was a simple affair consisting of bacon and eggs, cantaloupe, toast and coffee. The conversation was random, things like Mike's golf game to Paula's homemade recipe for Italian dressing. Very little of last night's escapades were mentioned, only that they enjoyed each other.

Mike smiled as he stood up from the kitchen table. "I'm going to fetch the paper."

Both girls smiled up at him and watched him as he left the room.

Paula then got down to it. "April, do you know a woman...I believe her name is Heather?" she asked, getting up from the table.

"No, I can't say I do," April replied taking a sip of her coffee. "Why do you ask?"

"Oh, nothing much, except Mike ran into her one afternoon at the mall. She was sitting on a bench in front of the *Victoria's Secret* shop. Mike said she looked alone and needy, besides being beautiful. So he sat down and just started talking to her. Next thing you know, he brought her home and for the rest of the weekend we had sex with her. Now we can't find her, and she doesn't answer her phone or return messages," Paula said, leaning forward and picking up the breakfast dishes and placing them in the sink.

"Do you suppose something bad has happened? I mean, maybe she moved away?" April asked.

"That's just like you, always imagining the worst. However, hell, I mean, who knows?" Paula replied, as she scraped the dishes and placed them in the dishwasher.

April was about to speak when Mike entered the kitchen. "It appears, ladies, that our local sheriff's department has a picture of the man who killed that criminal investigator and Polish fellow." Mike threw the paper down onto the table, the headline in bold, black print clearly visible for both women to see: "**Picture of Cop Killer Do you know him?**"

"All right then… I'll find out about it this afternoon as I have a lunch date with Detective Roth at three," April said, standing up and looking around for her handbag and jacket.

"You do?" Paula asked, her voice sounding surprised.

"Yes…Leo Kaczynski was my uncle," April said, looking through her handbag for her car keys.

Paula stood silent and watched April push her chair back under the table.

"Well, until we meet again then," April said, kissing Mike on the cheek and giving Paula a quick peck on the lips.

Damn it to hell, Paula thought. *She's going after Roth to replace either Hill or Bean.* She returned April's kiss with one of her own.

* * *

Roth looked at his watch. He was ten minutes early and debated about sitting in the car or going inside and waiting. He opted to go inside and got a private table. He would tell the lady at the front door and then duck into the men's room real quick to wash his hands and comb his hair.

Roth wore his best jeans, cowboy boots, a dress shirt and tie, and of course, his blue sports jacket to hide his gun. He looked at his watch for the second time in ten minutes; April was late. He felt silly waiting for the city's number one courtesan in a restaurant like *The Olive Garden*. However, when he saw her again he would forget she was a prostitute and concentrate on not being a total slob.

He was looking at the takeout menu when he heard her. "Oh Toby, sweetie, I'm so sorry about being late, but when I show you what I have I think you'll forgive me," April said, walking over to him and kissing him on the lips.

She was right. She was forgiven. Roth looked into her blue-green eyes and could hardly remember his name.

The young host was enthralled with April's beauty as was everyone else in the restaurant. The host took them to a booth in the back of the restaurant away from the kitchen noise and prying eyes of the other patrons, as Roth requested.

A waiter placed two menus in front of each of them and walked away, leaving the two lovebirds to themselves.

"Ok April, what do you want from me?" Roth asked in a whispered voice.

April smiled, reached out and took his hand in hers, catching him by surprise. "I have lots to tell you, Toby, but first I want to say that you look very tired since last we met," she said, reaching into her oversized handbag and coming up with a tissue and a small envelope that she placed on the table next to her napkin.

She wet the tissue with her tongue, reached across the table, and wiped the remnants of her kiss off Roth's lips, causing him to blush.

"Sorry about that, Toby, but I did not want you to look like a clown when you went back to work," April said returning the tissue to her purse. "Now for the reasons I called you," she said, parlaying another moment of waiting as she picked up the menu and quickly decided on lunch.

Roth mimicked her move.

He was about to speak when a college-age young man approached the table, his eyes immediately falling upon April's cleavage.

When April looked up into his eyes, the boy began blushing, causing April to smile.

"Yes, Ken," April, said reading the young waiters nametag. "I would like the stuffed mushrooms and a glass of Chablis, please."

Roth looked at the boy and gave him a smirk. "I'll have the same...KEN!" Roth said, dismissing him.

"Thank you," Ken replied and walked away.

Roth looked across the table and chuckled at her.

"A sweet and innocent boy," April said, reaching for the envelope.

Roth smiled, wondering what he would have done in the same situation, probably have asked for her phone number as he wasn't a shy boy.

"Toby please listen to me before you ask me any questions?" April said.

Roth leaned back and nodded his head, letting her go on.

"My last name is Kaczynski," she said, looking at his face for some sort of reaction and seeing none, went on. "Leopold Kaczynski was my father's brother, making him my uncle. He was a vile man, devoid of any human emotions except greed, anger, and oh yeah, let's not forget incest and adultery. Back in Poland, he worked on the docks and was some sort of big shot in the communist party. Twice, Leo had been asked to kill Lech Walesa, first in 1978 and then again, in 1983, both times he failed and after that, it was too late. Therefore, he fled first to Russia where he became involved in the Russian underground. You call it the mafia...anyway. He got into some sort of trouble in Russia. Murder, I think. Forced to flee, he came to America in 1988. My father and mother were already in America.

"Dad had opened a butcher shop on Linden, and we enjoyed a nice lifestyle—until Leo came to Zanesville. Before that, he lived in Beckley, West Virginia, working as a coal miner. He lied about his work experience back in Poland and managed to intimidate his way to the top job in the union, making big money. In the meantime, Leo re-established contact with his Russian friends who had also immigrated to America, and they started dealing drugs and according to my mother, white slavery as well, enticing beautiful young Polish girls with the promise of money and good marriages. However, when they arrived in America, they were drugged and raped repeatedly until submissive, then sold to pimps as sex slaves. Have you gotten the picture? That was my uncle Leo."

Roth remained silent as he watched the tears well up in April's eyes. He watched her as she picked up her handbag and fished for the tissue that she had placed there only moments ago, his mind already working on a different angle. The thought kept running through his mind, why had Hill killed April's uncle—?

"April what is in the envelope that you want to show me?" Toby pointed to the envelope.

"Yes Toby this is for you. It was written by Uncle Leo to my mother. You will notice it's written in Polish, and I think it may be the reason my uncle was murdered," April said, as she handed the envelope to him.

Roth took the envelope and was about to speak when Ken returned with two wine glasses and two serving dishes of stuffed mushrooms and a large salad bowl. Roth waited until Ken filled the glasses, prepared the table and walked away.

"April," Roth said, leaning towards her, "you despised your uncle and you're glad the son of a bitch is dead. But why are you doing so much to help me?"

"Roth, can I help it that I'm a greedy woman and want my uncle's money, his properties in town and his country place where he was killed? I think the numbers in that letter you are holding are bank accounts. I do not know what the initials next to the numbers mean. Maybe they are the bank's initials. I do not know. However, I know that I am his surviving relative, and I want what's mine by law. Is that clear enough?" April responded taking a sip of her wine.

"So you figure by helping me, I will help get you your uncle's property and all his money, especially if these numbers turn out to be bank accounts. Hmm," Roth said, taking a sip of wine and staring up to the ceiling.

19

Bean sat behind the wheel of his patrol car and waited for the light to change. Saturday morning shifts were normally easy to work. Friday and Saturday nights were a different story. Fridays were usually reserved for domestic squabbles and simple assaults with Saturday a showcase of more of the same except with the added flavor of bar fights and when the weather was warm, hookers who would walk up and down Main and Seventh Streets looking for temporary employment.

Paula had told him to book a flight to Houston, which he did. Then from there he was to take an international flight to Bogotá and simply disappear. He had his passport and tickets plus a quarter-million dollars in traveler's checks. Furthermore, at Paula's insistence, he had no baggage to check through. She suggested that to blend into the normal busy nature of airport pedestrianism would be better than potentially being noticed, and he could buy his necessities when he got to his destination. He knew she was right.

His real concern was whether Paula was going to come across with the money. Roth was closing in, and he knew his time was short. Lucy Bell's memory could kick in at any moment or maybe someone else would recognize him. The only advantage he had was vacation time. Paula insisted he put in his vacation request for this Monday. He was to leave for Houston this evening. He smiled as the light changed. By Sunday afternoon, he would be in Bogotá.

Paula was ready, dressed simply in tight fitting white shorts that left little for the imagination—a loose-fitting halter top and high heels.

She had prepared an excellent dinner for Bean, much better than a person deserved who was on the way out. However, she thought; every *condemned man deserved a good last meal, and I've certainly condemned Bean.*

Her real concern was the sex. She did not know if she could go through with it. Frankly, Bean was lousy at sex. He talked a bigger game than he could deliver, and his equipment was much smaller than his pretense.

Earlier in the morning, Paula had gone to her bank and bought a pre paid visa gift card. Using the exchange rate, the card was good for one hundred and seventy thousand pesos, which was the truth, and the beauty of it all was it cost her only one hundred U.S. Dollars. Besides, the chances were good that Bean would never spend it anyway, and she could easily afford to lose the hundred.

What she really needed to know was how close April was to her uncle, and if he told April about his business dealings. The probabilities were good that Leo hadn't, but she needed to know for sure. She could ill afford any more surprises to her business operations. She further needed to know why Hill had killed Kaczynski in the first place. More perplexing was why did Bean assassinate Hill? She would find out all about it this afternoon while she was killing Officer Bean.

Bean pulled his truck into Paula's drive area a few minutes early. He had taken the time to shave and shower for the last time at the station. He did not want to go home to see his wife and kids. He kissed them good-bye that morning in the full knowledge; he would never see his family again. He thought briefly about taking them with him, but decided against it. He was running away from everything and everyone and it would be difficult to hide with a wife and two small boys. One thing he did however was leave a quarter million dollars in cash, placed in a white plastic bag stashed in his wife's panties drawer with a good-bye note. To him the split was final.

Bean stood on the front stoop of Paula's house and pressed the doorbell, causing the Westminster chimes to echo throughout the house. His stomach began to growl reminding him that he had not eaten anything since Friday.

20

Saturday mornings were lonely for Joshua, especially since his wife had left him. He had already mowed the lawn, cleaned the house and finished off the laundry, and it was still only eleven. Bored out of his mind, he decided to take a shower, shave, and go to the office to catch up on reports that had to be done. On Thursday morning he asked Scotty in photo lab to play around with the picture of Hill's killer. He wanted Scotty to do away with the killer's ball cap, give the person a crew cut, and magnify the wedding band that Lucy Bell found so unique. Hoping something would come of it.

As he drove to the office, Joshua began thinking about Roth. The old' boy was a real piece of work. Slightly irreverent, definitely argumentative, could not care less about politicians or the press. He was truly a cop's cop, of that there was no doubt. Hell, Roth was even known to bed prostitutes and could care less what anybody thought about it. On second thought, Joshua realized it was a good way to get valuable information, especially if these murders were related to drugs.

Josh walked into his office to a desk piled high with files, old newspapers, half-filled coffee cups and candy wrappers. "My wife was correct. I'm a pig. No doubt about it," he muttered to no one, picking up the office trash can. He began clearing his desk of extraneous matter and examining each item of correspondence. Somewhere in the middle of the junk piles, he picked up a computer printout that had a yellow sticky note attached "Per Your Request."

Josh sat the trashcan down beside the desk and pulled his chair out allowing himself to sit down. His one-man cleaning party would have to wait. He recognized the computer printout as being from the telephone company. It was the phone printout from Hill's cell phone. Quickly, he turned to the last sheet, immediately recognizing Roth's number. He circled the next number in red ink noting the duration, only thirty seconds. Hill knew his killer. He started perusing each page looking for anything that seemed unusual. Josh made a mental note that Hill averaged two calls a day to his wife. He called various law enforcement offices around the state, which in Hill's capacity as head of the state's drug task force could be considered normal. There were several calls to a Doctor Paula Tidwell. *Hill's doctor perhaps,* Joshua thought, continuing to peruse the remaining pages.

Two weeks before his murder, Hill had made five calls to the same number within thirty minutes. Judging by the 212 area code it was to somebody in New York City, DEA probably or maybe the FBI. He would call those numbers on Monday. First, he wanted to call the last number on the page.

Joshua dialed the number; he could hear each ring of the phone. He had counted six rings when he heard the woman's voice.

"Hello," the sweet cheery voice said.

"Yes…this is Joshua Ledbetter with the Ohio State Attorney General Criminal Investigation Unit. Is your husband there?"

"No, James is still at work," the friendly voice replied.

"You know, ma'am, usually when I give people my name and title, they get real quiet on me. I don't seem to scare you?" Joshua said.

She began to chuckle. Her voice had a delightful lilt to it now, causing Josh to smile.

"My husband is a Deputy Sheriff, so why would your name and title scare me? I often take calls from various people in law enforcement, especially from a Mr. Hill. I think he was also from the Attorney General's Office. You know; he was the fella that was murdered out on Route 313. In fact, he called here early that morning before he was killed. Beanie talked to him. Then he went and got himself killed. He used to call here all the time. He and my husband were working together, trying to catch drug smugglers."

Joshua decided to go for broke.

"Ma'am, do you know if Beanie still has his .357 Magnum? A gun he bought from Leo Kaczynski for three hundred dollars?"

"You mean that big silver gun that looks like a cannon?" the woman said, her voice changing from sweet and gentle to angry.

"Yes, ma'am," that's the one!" Joshua replied, his voice sounding enthusiastic.

"Why, that lying' son of a bitch you just wait until he comes home. I am going to kill that little prick. He told me he took the gun off a drug dealer named Leo whatever. Now you tell me he gave three hundred dollars and our sons both need braces for their teeth."

Joshua was about to ask another question, but she hung up on him obviously upset over Beanie lying to her. *I wonder what's going to happen when we arrest your hubby for murder,*" he thought.

He did not need Scotty's help after all, the murderer was a Deputy Sheriff named Beanie, probably a nickname for Bean. Somehow, Joshua could not help, but feel that Roth was correct when he said they had opened a can of worms. Oh, well, he loved to fish, and he was betting Roth did too. He reached for his desk phone. It was time to call Roth.

21

Heather rolled over and looked at the clock, trying to remember where she was. One thing was certain—she was hungry and had to pee. She thought about staying in bed and peeing, but that was too gross even for her.

Humiliated and dejected, Roy was in the den, sitting in his favorite chair, a bag of ice resting on his privates. He had decided to ask Robin for a divorce, something he should have done months ago. Having a wife who doesn't like you is one thing, but having a wife who tries to de-ball you in a moment of intimacy is quite another. He also decided to ignore what the congregation would say or even his own father. "To death 'until you part" did not include being kicked in the balls or going without sex, minister or no minister, and he had taken into account what the doctor had told him. "Your wife has the propensity to kill," and besides Heather no longer the same woman he had married.

His concentration was broken when he heard the flush of the upstairs toilet. He looked at the mantel clock. He would give Robin thirty minutes then ready or not he would climb the stairs and walk in on her and simply ask for a divorce. After the good news, he would go to his room shut and lock the door and write his sermon for Sunday morning. Fittingly, the topic would be a timely talk on divorce.

Heather pulled the shower door open and stepped into the musty smelling shower stall. Reaching out she turned each valve one turn, then the hot valve a half turn more. She waited on the warm spray, she stepped back, adjusting the spray nozzle to her liking. She reached through the shower spray, checking both the water temperature and grabbing the green colored bar of soap and washcloth lying in the dish behind the spray. She sniffed the soap, for some reason, smelt familiar to her. Stepping into the warm spray, she lathered the well-used pink washcloth and began to think of Dr. Mike and his alluring wife, Paula.

Roy placed his coffee cup down on the coffee table. It was time, a prelude to freedom and sanctity. He stood up tossing the ice bag back into his chair. He still felt a deep gnawing pain in his groin, but ignored it shuffling over to the stairway. He looked up at the bathroom door and began feeling the tears forming in his eyes as he took the first step. The pain was agonizing, but he had something to do despite the pain. He took another step holding tightly to the stair railing feeling the nausea begin to burn the back of his throat, which created a bitter metallic taste on his tongue. He swallowed hard and took another step, the sweat beading up on his furrowed brow as he fought to keep both his pain and nausea in check. Just a few more steps and it will be over. He thought.

Roy took another step and thought perhaps a better idea would be go to the emergency room and get help, but no…he had to go through with it. Then again, if he opted for the emergency room, when he returned home, Robin would be gone, and he could write his sermon in peace and deal with other matters later. He took his last step and stood on the top landing in front of the bathroom door. He reached out and grasped the doorknob of the bathroom door. He had arrived at his destination, and although his legs were wobbly and his sweat fell like rain onto the hardwood floor. He paused and wiped his face using his tee shirt as a sweat rag. He realized that Robin had hurt him badly, how bad he didn't yet know, only that his pain had become more excruciating. However, the time to ask for a divorce was now. The only thing he had to do was knock on the door and tell Robin to leave the house, ridding himself of the evil Jezebel.

Roy could hear the shower running and knew if he opened the bathroom door that Robin would pitch a fit. However, in truth he was beyond caring what she thought. All he really cared about was that she would be gone forever, and when he needed female companionship, he could ask the senator's wife or maybe his intern pastor to comfort him.

Heather heard the knock. Knowing who it was she yelled, "Go away asshole—"

Roy opened the bathroom door and stepped inside, and for one of the first times in their marriage he ignored her completely.

"Robin, please step out of the shower. This won't take long," Roy, said his voice deep and threatening.

"Fuck you!" she replied ignoring him.

Roy became livid, "Robin; I'm not going to ask you again, please step out of the shower now. I have something to tell you."

"Just a second, let me rinse off!" Heather said, her voice sounding calm.

Frantically, she looked around the shower stall for anything that could be used as a weapon to defend herself from this strange man who kept calling her Robin.

"Hurry up, will you" the stranger's voice asked, in a tone that seemed somehow familiar to her, and at the same time threatening.

"Ok, my love, I'm almost done, just wringing out my hair," Heather said, twisting the washrag so tightly that her knuckles turned white. Daintily, she placed the damp washrag over both tap handles, and then an idea sprang forth, grabbing the bar of soap with her left hand and the washrag with the other; she placed the bar of soap into the washrag and twisted it making herself a weapon.

Opening the shower door slowly, Heather stepped out of the warm shower stall not knowing what to expect from this crazy man who now stood before her wearing only a wet tee-shirt and a pair of maroon colored underpants. She looked for a bath towel to wrap herself in as the cool air of the large bathroom had enveloped her causing her body to break out in gooseflesh.

Roy averted his eyes as her nakedness actually offended him, especially now that he was going to ask her for a divorce and had already made the emotional break.

"Ok, now what's this all about, and who are you exactly?" She asked, holding her makeshift blackjack in her right hand, and looking around the bathroom for a towel to dry herself. Spying no towel, she turned her body towards this crazy man letting him view her body, hoping the pervert would go away.

Roy looked down his nose at her, his look disapproving and sad. "Robin, there is no easy way to say this, I want a divorce!"

Heather looked up at him her lips pulled back exposing her teeth her face becoming contorted in her anger.

"Who the fuck do you think you are asshole. Coming into my bathroom and calling me by another woman's name. Then asking me for a divorce. I don't even know who the hell you are? Get out of here! Do you hear me, you crazy son-of- a -bitch. Get out of here right now." She yelled walking up to him, pushing him backwards towards the open bathroom door.

Roy stopped standing his ground refusing to be bullied.

"Now, Robin, there is absolutely no need to be angry or hateful towards me. I don't feel that way towards you," Roy said his voice soft and condescending towards her.

"Fuck you!" she screamed, swinging her makeshift blackjack, striking him in the face. Instinctively, he pushed her back causing her to slip and fall to the wet hardwood floor.

"Quit this!" Roy yelled looking down at her naked body splayed out like some grotesque fish flopping on its side trying to right itself so it could swim away.

Heather managed to sit up resting on her knees. Her breath coming in giant gasps as tears of humiliation trickled down her cheeks. Her contempt for this so-called husband of hers clearly changed to hate. His harsh voice and immense size did little to stop her as she reached out and grabbed her weapon and stood up. She would be damned if she was going to back down from this asshole.

Roy stood at the open bathroom door looking at her, watching her as her chest rose and fell. A steady contemptuous glare was staring back at him. He could not believe that this feline creature from Hades had been his wife of many years. He shook his head, turned his back on her, and tried to leave, which infuriated her.

With all her strength, Heather swung her weapon, catching Roy off guard. The blow caught him in the right eye, blinding him, causing him to stagger aimlessly around the bathroom his outstretched arms trying vainly to grab her.

Heather kept backing away from this crazy man, ducking his wild swings and all the while listening to him bellow like a wounded animal.

She darted to his blind side trying to flee the bathroom when he managed to grab her by her hair. Twisting and turning, she screamed trying to break his grip. She saw a nail file on the vanity top and grabbed it with her left hand and began flailing wildly striking him on the side of his neck slashing deep into the right carotid artery. Roy's blood began spurting out, drenching his tee-shirt and the vanity mirror. He looked at the grotesque figure of a man in the mirror, a man bleeding out with only moments to live.

"You crazy fucking bitch, you killed me," Roy gasped falling to his knees then slumped onto his side, the blood flow pooling around his head. He felt his pulse slowing down, reducing the blood spurts to regularly timed pulsating geysers. He watched as Robin ran out of the bathroom screaming, "Oh, my God, what have I done?"

A few moments passed. He heard her bedroom door slam and hoped she was calling for help. Slowly, Roy felt the rapture of death enveloping him and knew it was a race against time. He closed his eyes and began to pray to the higher power asking forgiveness and begging for another chance. He could still hear Robin yelling, "Oh, my God, what have I done?"

Then as he felt, the last burning embers of life begin to fade. Roy knew help would not arrive in time and smiled remembering that Robin did not have a phone in her bedroom. There was an upside to all of this—he wouldn't have to deal with the bitch anymore.

22

Roth opened his eyes momentarily, darting his focus from side to side and trying to remember. He sat up on his elbows and noticed the shadows on the wall, which told him he had overslept. Turning his head, he surveyed the bedroom. He thought it odd he had not noticed how opulent it was before. Then he saw April lying there and realized how beautiful she truly was even in sleep—a real postcard.

Retracting his elbows, he fell back down onto the bed, gently inching his body towards hers his desire clearly showing under the satin sheets.

Gently, he placed his hand on her hip and rolled her onto her back. Rising up on one elbow, Roth looked down upon her face, finding it without flaw, and wondered why she bothered to wear makeup. He kissed her lips then her cheek, slowly aligning his body between her legs. Tenderly, he slid both his hands under her, pinning her to the bed with his body. He had passed through the desire phase the first time they had made love. Now he was in pure animal lust. Despite April's screams, scratching and biting, Roth consumed her, leaving the beautiful prostitute a quivering mass of human flesh begging for more. There was a God…

Roth was physically and emotionally charged as he left April's condominium. He knew April would call him again, and he would take her to dinner, and she would give him dessert. What a setup…

Walking towards his car, he wondered what April's neighbors were thinking about seeing a Sheriff's cruiser sitting in their private parking lot. *To hell with what they think. It's nobody's business;* he thought, reaching into his jacket pocket for the car keys.

Opening the car door, he noticed his phone lying on the front seat. He threw it there not wanting to be disturbed. He started the car and pulled the safety belt across his chest. He clicked it closed, reached down, picked up his phone and checked for missed calls. Joshua had called three times. *It must be important,* he reasoned, dialing Josh's cell phone.

"Hello," the sleepy voice muttered.

"Sorry to wake you, Josh," Roth said, putting his car in gear slowly backing out of the visitor spot.

"Oh, it's you, Roth. I've been trying to get hold of you all afternoon," Josh said, sitting up in his lounge chair and waiting for his brain to engage.

"What've you got, Josh" Roth asked, pulling out into late-afternoon traffic.

"Yeah, well the man who killed Major Hill is a Deputy Sheriff named Bean. Do you know him?" Joshua asked.

"Hello are you there, Roth? Answer me?"

"Yes, Josh, I'm here," Roth replied. "I had to pull off the road! Let me understand what you just told me. Deputy Sheriff Bean murdered Hill. Do I have that right?"

"Yes," Josh replied, wondering where Roth was going with this.

"Ok, we both know Hill murdered Kaczynski," Roth said aloud, allowing Josh to follow along.

"Yes, Roth, we know for sure that Hill murdered the Pollock."

"I think I have it now, Joshua," Roth said, moving his phone to his other ear allowing him to gain access to the inside pocket of his jacket.

"Ok Roth, I'm listening—" Joshua said, lifting the toilet seat.

"April Kaczynski is Leo Kaczynski's niece. This afternoon I met her for lunch, and she handed me an envelope that Leo had given her mother for safekeeping. It is written in Polish, but April thinks the numbers are bank accounts and the initials next to each number are the bank's initials. She also told me that her uncle was an evil pig, that he had murdered someone back in Russia, and oh yeah, he was linked with the Russian Mafia in New York." Roth stopped talking, waiting for Joshua to reply. All Roth could hear was water running in the background, he thought it odd that Joshua would be making coffee this late in the afternoon.

"Ok, Roth, if April is correct, then where did *Uncle Leo* get all his money?" Josh asked flushing the toilet.

"Drugs," Roth replied.

"Bingo! I have two telephone numbers, both in New York City on Hill's phone records. How much do you want to bet that Hill was dealing?" Josh said.

"I'm betting Hill was cutting himself in big time by disposing of poor old Leo he was eliminating the middleman and increasing his retirement fund," Roth said, shaking two breath mints free and removing the taste of April from his mouth.

"Roth, if you're correct, then Bean killed Hill for exactly the same reason."

"Or was he ordered to kill Hill by a person or persons unknown?" Roth replied.

"Either way, Roth we have little to go on. I think you should arrest Bean before he disappears, just to cover your ass," Joshua said, sitting down at his kitchen table, looking up at his playboy calendar and wishing Miss November was with him now. "Tell you what, Josh, I will need an arrest warrant signed by a judge and I seriously doubt on a late Saturday afternoon I will be able to find one. How about you bringing all your evidence here on Monday, then we can walk over together to the Assistant District Attorney's office, show the evidence to her, and let her get the warrant. We can then arrest Bean at work on Monday in front of the other sheriff's deputies."

"Sounds like small-town politics to me, Roth, but it's your city and your call. I'll see you Monday morning around nine…"

23

The flight from Columbus to Bush International was on time; a rarity. Bean had taken the Greyhound Bus to Columbus then a cab to the airport. He left his truck in the police parking lot and walked the block to the bus station.

All Bean had to do now was walk the miles of public space to the very specific location designated concourse "D," Gate 30. First, he had to find a men's room. Something Paula had served was disagreeing with him, and he could only hope he would be in time to dip his head and lean over the toilet without soiling his clothes.

Dinner had been polite conversation and a series of questions concerning Leo and his niece, April. Bean had been quick in denying April's relationship with Leo, saying he never knew April's last name, which was a true statement.

Then somewhere between the steak and the salad, Paula asked Bean why he killed Hill. He was prepared for her question beforehand, knowing he was no longer in her favor. He brought along proof of Hill going freelance on her. Without saying a word, Bean reached into his back pocket and produced photographs of Hill taken only a week before he killed the traitor.

She asked what they were, and he explained how Leo had called him all upset over Hill trying to cut him out of the operation. Hill even threatened to kill Leo if he said anything to anyone. Leo told me that Hill was going to Ashtabula to pick up a hundred thousand dollars worth of cocaine and heroin. Bean told her how he followed Hill taking numerous pictures of Hill at a rest stop along Route 90, just inside the Ohio border.

Paula studied each picture and listened carefully as Bean described the two men in detail—both Russian.

Paula was quick to remark the fair man was rather good looking. The darker man had a sinister look about him, something some women found exciting and dangerous. Bean smiled as he told her that the man was no one to mess with.

The series of photos was revealing. One photo showed Hill talking with two men, the next photo showing a fair-haired fellow extending his hand as if he were saying hello to Hill. The following photo clearly showed the dark man standing behind and to the right of Hill, his right hand resting on something under his blazer. The next pose showed Hill laughing as he produced a thick white envelope from his back pocket. The last photo showed all three men loading packages into Hill's cruiser trunk. The sequence was obvious as to purpose.

Between the apple pie and his second cup of coffee, he informed Paula that Hill had set them up for a major drug bust. He would probably claim he was working undercover and only he and one of his pals, probably someone within the state police or perhaps the Attorney General herself, knew about it. Then he would step in and steal everything. "Hell, Paula, he even offered me a cut, so I killed him—" Bean found it odd when Paula began to cry, but figured she was just grateful for his protection.

* * *

Bean was not sure if he could walk the distance from Terminal "A" to "D" as he was feeling much worse. His stomach cramped, and he was beginning to feel nauseated while sweat began to form on his upper lip. He wondered if he should rebook his flight and get a hotel room until at least the nausea passed. He looked at his watch debating the pros and cons of making such a decision. Time was now an enemy. Just then, he heard the agonizing sound of a shuttle car approaching on his left. Quickly, he walked towards it and held out his hand. *Next stop, Terminal "D," then Bogotá,* he thought.

* * *

The last traces of sunlight filtered into Paula's den, casting long shadows across the white carpet. She sat silently, her only sounds being whimpers of guilt. She was clasping a handful of damp tissues. It was ironic. She had never killed anyone before, but she had thought about it. Now she had killed without really thinking about it.

She had simply broken off two twigs of a yew bush from her flower and herb garden and ground the evergreen leaves to a very fine powder. Holding some back for garnish, she had mixed the powder with rosemary, thyme, olive oil, and vinegar.

Being a toxicologist Paula knew the fatal dose of poison would take about six hours before the effects started to show and by that time, it would be too late, providing Bean's flight from Houston left on time. *Taxus Canadensis,* or Yew bush in street lingo had often been used by early American women to abort an unwanted fetus, oftentimes over dosing, and once the poison had entered the body the user died an agonizingly painful death.

A painful death serves Bean right...if he is guilty. Oh well, too late to think about it now—

Fittingly, Bean would die somewhere over the Caribbean at some god-awful altitude. The medical examiner in Bogotá would rule the cause of death an apparent heart attack and Deputy Sheriff Bean would probably be shipped back home in a tiny box, his cremation destroying the real cause of death. So sad, to avoid scandal, the county fathers would undoubtedly bury Bean with police honors and give his widow a full pension, thus burying another crooked cop and keeping another dirty little secret safely entwined within the Sheriff's Department.

24

Deacon Jeremiah Woods loosened the bell rope and held it in his left hand. In his right, he held his grandfather's pocket watch, given to his grandfather by the school board for fifty years of faithful service. Jeremiah's eyes were on the second hand as it pushed the big hand closer to the twelve. When it reached the top of the hour, he would pull hard on the rope signaling from horizon to horizon that it was 8:00 a.m. and time to come in from the cold and worship God. He would pull the rope for exactly one minute then as he had done since he was a boy, he would coil the rope and return it to the same hook his grandfather had used before him when he rang the bell.

Mrs. Woods, who stood in as organist and church secretary, played the hymn. *Down by the Riverside* softly on her Hammond as the church regulars filed into the chapel. Emily Lutz walked down the aisle towards the choir loft, looking around the church and counting. How many had braved the cold rain to come and rejoice in the Word. When she was not exercising her role as principal at the elementary school, she served as choir director and had been for nearly forty years. She actually knew every song in the hymnal by heart.

Mrs. Olive Maycourt stood in the doorway of the anteroom just to the left of the choir loft. She was becoming concerned as it was almost time for church services to start, and Roy was not here yet. *Very odd,* she thought. *This never happens.*

Olive looked at her watch again, becoming extremely agitated with her pastor. It was her turn to serve communion, and he told her on Friday not to worry, that he would be at church in plenty of time for her to set up the communion table.

Olive's agitation was being felt among the other parishioners as well. Even Alicia, the young intern, sensed something was wrong as she walked down the center aisle, smiling, chatting with the folks and working her way towards the pulpit.

"Where's Roy," someone asked from the back of the sanctuary.

Alicia held up her hand asking the congregation for quiet.

"I don't know what has happened to Roy." I shall give the sermon this morning."

With those words, she took a deep breath then a sip of water and reached down into the deepest recesses of her mind to recall a sermon she had heard as a little girl. The sermon would be about Forgiveness. What the others did not know was that Roy had warned her one afternoon as they lay in bed together that if for any reason, he did not show up for Sunday worship, she was to give the sermon on Forgiveness and after church services, she was to call the police and report his murder. At the time, she thought it folly, now she was not so sure…

Roth sat at the kitchen table reading his favorite cartoon strip when his cell rang. Checking the caller ID it was Sheriff Swanson.

"Hello, Otis," Roth said.

"Morning, Roth, sorry to disturb your reverie, but we have a situation that requires your immediate attention," The sheriff said, his voice sounding both authoritative and angry.

"Yes, sir," Roth replied. "What's up?"

"I just received a call from the American Embassy in Bogotá, wherever the hell that is… Deputy Bean is dead, Roth. There is no reason for him to be in Columbia, so we can only assume he was running. He died on the airplane, of an apparent heart attack. Anyway, I want you to find out why one of my deputies was flying to Bogotá. I think something stinks here. You hear me?"

"Yes, Otis, of course I hear you," Roth replied.

Otis hung up without saying good-bye. Roth shrugged his shoulders and smiled.

"Now what?" he muttered out loud.

25

Dixie couldn't believe her good luck. Last week, she helped Roth flush out a murderer and this morning she was standing outside some preacher's house who was murdered by his deranged wife. The police detective in charge told her the victim had been stabbed and his wife Robin Willingham was a person of interest. That is all the detective would say. She thought the detective in-charge to be a smug and arrogant prick.

Dixie watched as the EMTs wheeled out the body and placed it in the city's ambulance. They would take the body to Good Sam's where Doc Morgan, the county's medical examiner, would examine the corpse and make the determination as to the cause of death.

No one spoke as the small crowd of curiosity seekers watched the firefighter secure the gurney and close the large ambulance door. She became acutely aware of bird's singing and could even hear the lawn gnats buzzing around her head. She was pondering a rather indelicate question: *When does a body become a corpse? She was not exactly sure, but she reasoned that if someone could identify the corpse, then it was a body and if no one knows the name of the body, then it was a corpse. Dixie girl, you are just too smart for your own good. She thought.*

As she turned to leave, she spied a tall young woman wearing the white collar of the clergy. Curious, she walked over to the woman and stopped directly in front of her. Dixie looked up into the most beautiful set of silver blue eyes she had ever seen.

"Hello, my name is Cathy Dixon; I'm a newspaper reporter with the *Times*. I was wondering if you knew the deceased."

"Yes, Ms. Dixon, I knew Reverend Willingham. He was my spiritual advisor and teacher."

"Are you the person that called the police," Dixie asked.

"Yes, from the church, just before the service. Then after church, I rushed over and found the police and the EMTs," the young preacher said, sticking her hand in her pocket and pulling out her car keys a silent signal that she was ready to leave.

"Please pastor what is your name," Dixie asked.

"Alicia Adams," she replied softly with a practiced smile.

"Thank you, Alicia," Dixie replied, writing down the name as she walked back towards the murder scene and looked for anything she could find to fill in more details.

Alicia Adams watched as Cathy walked away, thinking... *if that lady only knew how despicable Roy Willingham was she would thank Robin for killing him. That asshole was a user and abuser of women. He would charm them, then seduce them, then use them for his perverse pleasure. When he was done with them, that's when the blackmail started. Not always for money, sometimes for favors as simple as an introduction to another woman, only so he could charm and seduce her. If our God in heaven embraces a charlatan like Roy Willingham, then he truly is a merciful god. Alicia thought.*

Sunday afternoons in the pressroom were dull unless you had a front-page story to write and Dixie definitely had a front-page story. She figured her story to be at least a column. However, Frank Parson the copy editor would probably chop it to pieces. However, it was still front-page news and even in places where murders were an everyday occurrence, a story like this would make the front page. She read her story again, checking her facts and the all-important punctuation that Frank was such a stickler for. Satisfied her story was accurate, she hit the send button and immediately what she had composed was in the electronic box waiting to be published come Monday.

Dixie hated herself for feeling the way she did—very needy and wanting to be held kind of woman. For some reason she just could not let go of the look she saw on Alicia's face. It was not exactly an evil look, more one of disdain, and those silver blue eyes showed no emotion at all. It was as though she was glad her "spiritual advisor" was dead. Still, Dixie's feminine instincts told her something was wrong, dreadfully wrong. She decided to call Roth, sit on his lap, and have him just hold her close and tell her everything would be all right.

Heather sat in the park watching the river pass by. She had emptied the contents of her purse looking for money and discovered she had a total of twenty-six dollars and some change. Her biggest surprise came upon the discovery she had someone else's purse someone named Robin Willingham.

Carefully she folded the money and stuck it in her jeans along with the coins and the tube of used lipstick. *No, sense it throwing it away,* she thought. The rest of the stuff she gathered into one big pile and scraped it into Robin's purse. Then with a deep sigh, she stood up, walked over to the trash receptacle, dropped the purse into the round crevasse, and left the park.

Roth was well into his twelve-pack when the cell rang. He did not want to answer it, but his sense of duty obligated him.

"Hello," Roth growled, "how might I be of service to you?"

"Roth, are you drunk?" the vaguely familiar voice said.

"Depends on whose asking," came Roth's terse reply.

"It's me, Dixie! I wanted to come over and talk with you about something, but you've shot that idea in the ass!" she said, smiling into her cell phone.

"What time is it?" Roth growled.

"Almost two," Dixie replied.

"Tell you what, Dixie darling', I'll put on a pot of coffee, take a shower, even shave. So come on over and we will chat. I have something to tell you, too!" Roth said in a seductive voice.

"Good, I'll be there in fifteen to twenty. See yah then!"

Dixie rang the doorbell and turned the door handle, letting herself into Roth's apartment. She could hear the shower running and wondered if Roth had even heard the doorbell. She debated on calling out but decided to pour the freshly brewed coffee and wait for Roth to finish.

Roth had heard the doorbell. He was going to invite her into the shower, but decided against it. He walked into the kitchen clad in his underwear and tee shirt and carrying an old purple bath towel that should have been discarded years ago.

"Hello, honey, what do want to talk to me about?" He said nuzzling her neck in greeting.

"This morning I went to a murder scene on the lower north side," Dixie said, handing Roth a cup of coffee. Roth said nothing as he took a seat, discovering too late that the wooden chair was cold against his still wet flesh causing him to shiver. He sat quietly sipping his coffee listening to Dixie talk about the events of the morning. From the gist of Dixie's story, she was more upset about some female clergy named Alicia and her complete and utter hatred for the deceased man. Who supposedly had been her teacher and spiritual advisor than for the murder victim who was killed by his lunatic wife? She continued about some homicide detective who would not answer her questions, even down to the detail where she told him that she thought the detective a smug and conceited asshole.

Roth smiled and shook his head. It was clear that Dixie had a lot to learn about murder investigations.

"Dixie, are you finished?" Roth asked her, taking another sip of coffee.

"Yes, for now. I mean, I guess I was just appalled at her behavior towards her spiritual advisor," she said.

"Dixie all men who wear the collar of faith are not honorable or spiritual. He well could have been an evil man hiding behind his collar to give legitimacy to his evil doings. You say his own wife killed him. Well then, find her, Dixie and ask what her husband was like. Maybe she killed him out of self defense…"

"Roth, no wonder I like you," Dixie said, grabbing his hand and kissing it.

"I have something to tell you and it can go no further than this table," Roth said putting down his coffee cup and placing his bath towel across his lap.

"Ok, what is it?" Dixie said, looking into Roth's eyes.

"The story that I asked you to write last week to flush out Hill's killer did its job. We flushed out a Sheriff's Deputy named Bean. Anyway, I got a call this morning from Otis, who informed me that Bean died en route to Bogotá from heart failure. The body has been cremated and is being returned for proper burial. We cannot, at least at this time, reveal that his death was more than a heart attack, but I suspect Bean was murdered to keep him quiet, perpetrated by someone in the drug smuggling business. With Bean's death, we now have nothing more to go on. The trail has gone cold."

Dixie remained silent pushing herself away from the table. Taking both their coffee cups, she placed them in the sink. Roth sat perfectly still as he watched her, wondering what she was up to. When she reached down, took him by the hand, and smiled.

26

Roth looked at his watch. It was almost 9:00 a.m. The cold west wind had forced him to turn up his collar as he walked the three blocks to the county building. He wanted to talk with Otis about Deputy Bean. He knew Otis would take the news hard as he truly believed all his deputies were infallible. Before he left his office, he had phoned Joshua asking him to come to the sheriff's office before they visited the District Attorney's office on the next floor. In reality, he saw little need to bring the DA's office into this mess now that Bean was dead. However, he wanted to talk with both Joshua and Otis about an idea he had been kicking around in his head. His idea was simple, and he would merely ask Otis to bring in an undercover narcotics officer from Cincinnati or Toledo, somebody not known by the local buyers and users of the county. The other thing that was bothering him was why the drugs were not on the streets yet. He thought it peculiar as if the drugs were being horded. A more realistic possibility was clients with money were using the drugs. The upper crust of the city and county, denying the locals the taste of the truly good stuff. How far up the social ladder this problem went, he did not even pretend to know. The only thing he was sure of was somewhere near the top of that social ladder was a drug dealer—and a murderer.

Otis looked up from his desk and smiled, motioning for Roth to come in and take a seat. Roth smiled, nodding his head in acknowledgment of his boss's invitation. He entered his friend's office and unbuttoned his overcoat. Otis held up one finger, signaling that the call was about over. Slipping off his coat, he nodded, placed the coat on the back of the chair. Wishing he was any place, but here. He seated himself in front of his friend.

Otis hung up the phone and cursed.

"Politicians are whores, Toby, remember that if you ever decide to be one," Otis said, crossing his arms across his massive chest.

"No thanks, Otis, I'm a simple cop with a dirty job, and I'll remain so until I hang up my holster," Roth replied.

"Ok, Toby, what is it? You want to tell me?"

"Deputy Bean was dirty. He was also a murderer. I suspect he was an enforcer for a local drug dealer." Roth said crossing his legs and arms as if doing so would ward off the evil news that he had just told his boss.

Otis sat back in his chair, stunned by Roth's statement. His eyes narrowed to slits; his face turning crimson. Roth noticed Otis had grabbed his biceps so tightly that his knuckles had turned white.

"Of course you can prove this?" Otis said, his voice soft but intimidating.

Roth looked across the desk, and merely nodded his head.

"Let's see the proof," Otis said holding out his hand.

Roth shifted in his chair feeling the need to urinate.

"I'm waiting on Joshua, who's a little late. I suppose morning traffic is the reason," Roth said stalling.

"Who's this Joshua fellow, and why are we waiting on him?" Otis asked leaning forward grabbing his Cleveland Brown's coffee mug.

"His name is Joshua Ledbetter, and he's a criminal investigator with the State Attorney General's Office," Roth replied as he looked down at his watch.

"Ok Toby, and just how is this Joshua fellow involved in your case?" Otis asked, leaning back in his chair and taking a sip of his coffee.

"Before I begin explaining everything I want your promise you'll bring in an outside narcotics officer, and no one in the sheriff's or police department will know," Roth demanded, his voice showing that no compromise was possible.

"It's that serious that we cannot trust our own officers." Otis asked.

"Yes, it's that serious!" Roth replied, looking at his watch and wondering where Ledbetter was.

The meeting lasted an hour, and not once did Roth refer to his notes as he carefully led Otis step by step through his investigation. When he had finished giving his oral report, he sat back in the soft leather chair and waited for Sheriff Otis to comment.

"That's it" Otis asked, looking like a schoolboy who had just been told an exciting bedtime story.

"Yeah…except for this—" Roth said as he handed Otis the envelope that April had given him.

Carefully, Otis opened the envelope, gently pulling out the two pages. He slipped on his glasses, the bi-focal line clearly visible revealing that Otis' eyes were getting old.

"I can't read this!" Otis said, sitting back in his chair examining the second piece of paper. "This one looks interesting. It's either a pay record for blackmail or perhaps numbered accounts and these initials must be the bank's, indicating where the money is deposited." Otis was now convinced that Toby and Joshua had stumbled onto something big.

"It is written in Polish," Roth said.

"Hmm… you know we might have someone here who can read this and just perhaps shed some light on this letter," Otis said, reaching for his desk phone.

Roth watched Otis dial his phone, and then waited for some strange voice to respond to his summons.

"Yes, is Sawicki around? Good, please send him up, I want to ask him something."

"Is he what? Not with me" Otis remarked and hung up the phone. Please tell why Toby, do people assume whenever, I want to speak with them; they're in trouble?"

"Otis, if you're asking me, then I would have to say it's your winning and pleasing personality," Roth replied, a smile forming on his face.

"To hell with you, Toby" Otis said, his laugh, quickly turning into a smoker's cough.

"Otis do they know" Roth asked.

"Know? Probably not, and let's keep it that way," Otis replied, wiping the tears away from his cheeks.

Roth smiled and nodded to his friend that his secret was safe. Otis would announce to the county and city that he was dying when he was good and ready and not before. Otis hated to be pitied, he felt that pity was a weakness of character, and he despised that.

"You wanted to see me, sir?"

It was Sawicki standing straight and tall in the doorway, his buttons straining against his shirt, his massive biceps cut by the hem of his sleeves. Roth had never seen the young deputy before, but found him intimidating.

"Yes, deputy, I seem to remember reading on your profile sheet that you speak Polish?"

"Can you read this, Sawicki?" Roth asked, not looking up from his chair.

"Yes, sir," Sawicki replied.

"Then from this moment on and until further notice you're under orders not to divulge one word, I repeat, not one word, about what you're going to read. Do you understand that deputy?"

"Yes, sheriff, I understand perfectly, sir!"

Otis handed the envelope to his deputy and sat back in his chair, interlocking his fingers across his stomach that once was rock hard in his youth. However, was now big enough that he could rest on a cup and saucer on it.

Sawicki held the letter, perusing it before he started to read.

"Alina

I'm very sorry for all I have done to you and your family. I ask your forgiveness on our sainted mother's grave. I want you to have these numbers, and please keep them in a safe place, and upon my death you will go to your bank and present this letter to your friend, Dorota, she will know what to do. You are not to tell anyone, not even April.

All my money is yours as is all my property. I will be killed some-day by one of my business associates, and I can assure you they will not hesitate to kill you or April to gain access to my money and the names of my clients."

"That's it?" Otis asked.

"Yes sir that's it" Sawicki replied, handing the letter to Roth.

"Hmm… It's actually more than I expected," Roth said, not caring if he was understood or not.

"That will be all, Sawicki!" Otis said, pointing to the door.

"Yes sir."

Otis remained silent until the young deputy closed the door.

"Ok, Toby, what gives?" Otis asked.

The deputy just confirmed that the numbers listed were dollar amounts and not bank account numbers. Then the initials next to the numbers must be his clients. Moreover, this Dorota person holds the key. However, since Alina has been dead for some time, it will be difficult to find this Dorota."

"And if Dorota is dead, then what?" Otis asked.

"We look someplace else!" Roth replied.

27

Joshua opened one eye then the other and then moved them from side to side scanning the bedroom. He could tell by the shadows on the wall that he had overslept again. "*Shit!*" he muttered as he slowly rolled on to his side, trying to engage his brain and legs and finding it difficult. *Too much booze*, he reasoned, pushing himself off the bed and stumbling towards the bathroom.

As Joshua looked at his Gillette shaving cream lathered face, he remembered there were still two maybe three numbers on Hill's phone records that he had to call. The calls to New York were especially intriguing, and then the call to Hill's doctor, that call would be merely a formality just to wrap up loose ends.

After those calls had been made, he would call Roth and apologize for not being there. I hope that if he had good news Roth would forgive him, and if not so be it.

Joshua walked into the headquarters building and pushed the elevators up button. Arriving on the twentieth floor, he proceeded to walk the hall towards his office and noticed that each office he passed was empty. Another thing he noticed was the silence. The phones were all silent, allowing the admin staff to play catch up. He smiled as he did not have to make up a lie as to why he was late for work. However, one thing became abundantly clear to him—the drive time to work seemed shorter, and then a quick check of the wall clock told him why. It was after nine and the morning rush hour traffic had passed. *Wow! Am I smart!* He mused, walking into his office.

Paula lay in bed thinking, her right forearm lying across her eyes to block out the morning light. To her left, Heather was sleeping peacefully, obviously exhausted from last night's sexual cravings. Her conscience was bothering her over Bean's death. She had murdered a man, and knowing that he had died an agonizing painful death made it all the worse. She had tried to justify her actions by using the self-defense thing, him or me, but that didn't seem to work, so now she was learning to live with it.

She was also in need of two key people to help her run her organization. She needed a trusted enforcer, someone to keep people in line and someone who could tell her what the DEA and local cops were doing. Hill had filled that function—until he got greedy. Now all she had for protection and respectability were Riley Swanson who was married to a state senator, and pretty little Rebecca Colt, the Assistant District Attorney, and a few local judges who liked to party with each other's wives, and of course old' Otis.

With Leo gone, she had no go-between to insulate herself from the bad guys in New York, which was not necessarily a bad thing. Leo had told her stories about the Russian Mafia, and how ruthless they were. He had warned her from the very beginning to keep her distance from them, advice she had followed religiously.

Now without Leo, she had no negotiator and buyer to supply her customers. She was virtually deaf, dumb and blind and she knew it. What she needed was a change in direction using a different plan, something simpler and closer to home, and no more Russians, and certainly no more killings unless it couldn't be helped.

Paula turned onto her side and looked across the bed at the alarm clock, almost 9:00 a.m. She smiled, realizing that today was Monday and Monday's were her scheduled day off. As she moved her naked body closer to the edge of the bed, an idea sprouted forth, but first she had to get up and answer the damn phone.

After a quick shower, she would be off, putting her plan into action.

"Hello," Tidwell residence!

"Oh, I'm sorry, ma' am, I was looking for a Doctor Tidwell," the deep male voice asked.

"Yes, which Doctor Tidwell are you looking for?" Paula asked politely.

"Umm...I don't exactly know for sure."

"Maybe we can do it this way?" Paula asked. "Tell me what this call is in reference to and then maybe I can help you."

"Ok, ma'am, this is Joshua Ledbetter and I'm a criminal investigator with the state's Attorney General's office. I'm investigating the murder of one of my colleagues. His name was Hill, a Mr. Timothy Hill. Was he one of your patients?"

Paula felt her chest tighten as the blood drained from her face. She did not respond as she tried to come up with a plausible answer for the investigator, knowing that whatever she answered, it would be followed up.

"Yes, he wasn't exactly a patient, more of a family friend, and anytime he was in the area he would call and stop by for coffee. Tim was more of a golfing buddy and friend to my husband than me," Paula said holding the receiver tightly as she found it difficult to breathe, and feeling her heart beating against her chest as she tried to keep it together.

"So you have no idea why he would call your home at one in the morning the day before he was murdered?" Joshua asked.

"If Tim called here as you suggest, then he did not speak with me!" she said flatly, hoping to convince Joshua enough that he would hang up and go away.

"Ma'am what kind of doctors are you, you and your husband?" Joshua asked, momentarily changing the subject.

"Mike is a Doctor of Holistic Medicine, and I'm a Doctor of Toxicology at Ohio State," Paula replied with pride.

"Impressive," Joshua replied.

Joshua was pushing the proverbial envelope, and he knew it. She was lying of course as Hill did not play golf. However, why lie at all she wasn't a suspect. One thing he had learned over the years as a criminal investigator was that people lied for three reasons. Personal gain, self-protection, or to protect someone they love. Which reason was she lying for? Joshua decided to push her just a little bit more, hoping she wouldn't hang up on him.

"Wow, so you're a toxicologist?" Joshua asked, trying to draw her out of her self-protection mode.

"Yes, sir," she replied flatly.

"What is it exactly that a toxicologist does?" Joshua asked his voice smooth and soft.

"Look, I don't have time to explain all the myriad details of my profession right now, so if that's all I will say goodbye—"

"Hmm…" Joshua muttered as he leaned back in his chair, gripped his seldom-washed coffee mug and took a sip of coffee. His investigator instincts were telling him she was scared. He heard the fear in her voice as she responded to his questions. But, scared of what? What could or would scare a Doctor of Toxicology to the point of lying to a criminal investigator during a routine investigation?

* * *

Joshua decided to wait and talk to Roth…that is if Roth was still talking to him.

He picked up his office phone to call New York. He dialed the nine for an outside line then the two followed by the one then the other two. He hesitated and placed the receiver back into its cradle, deciding to use Tim Hill's cell just in case the number he wanted to call wasn't a good guy number.

Joshua opened Hill's phone and noticed that the battery was dead. He would charge the phone in his car as he drove to ZANES-VILLE. Slipping Hill's cell phone into his jacket pocket, he locked his desk. He looked at his watch; ZANESVILLE was an hour away, putting him there just a little before eleven. He flipped open his phone and dialed Roth as he wanted to inform him that he was on his way.

Mondays sucked for newspaper reporters. Only the sports guys had fun on Monday's. Everyone else just tried to look busy hoping no one would notice how bored they really were. Dixie was no exception and had she waited until this morning to file her story she would have something to do. However, she wrote and filed her story on Sunday, and now she had absolutely no idea what she should do. She sat silently tapping her pencil on her desk staring off into another place. She sipped her green tea and tried to decide if she should follow Roth's advice and look for Robin Willingham. The problem wasn't a small one. Where does someone begin looking for someone that doesn't want to be found? The preacher lady, that's where—

28

Otis pushed his glasses up onto his nose and reached for his phone. He coughed as he dialed, hoping she was home. "Hello, my friend. How are you?"

"As well as can be expected, Paula!" Otis replied.

"Is this a social call or a business call?" Paula asked.

"I would have to classify this as a business call, Paula," Otis replied.

"Ok, how much is it going to cost me?" Paula asked.

"I'll let you be the judge of what this information is worth," Otis said, a small chuckle escaping his lips as he took a sip of coffee.

"Oh, how gallant of you, kind sir," Paula said chuckling.

"Sweetie, please watch that beautiful ass of yours—my chief of homicide, Roth, along with some guy out of the attorney general's office are closing in. He is also bringing in an undercover nark from Cincinnati. I'm advising you to remain inconspicuous, and tell your people to do the same," Otis said, sitting back in his chair and resting his coffee mug on his Buddha belly.

"Will do!" Paula replied, hanging up the phone and making a mental note to mail Otis five hundred dollars.

"Who was that on the phone?"

"Otis," Paula replied, having been so absorbed in phone calls and personal thoughts that she had forgotten about Heather.

"Who's Otis?"

"Just a friend, Heather, who called to say hello."

"I wish I had friends that did that," Heather said, walking into Paula's bathroom as if she owned it.

Dixie didn't need a street map to find Pastor Roy Willingham's church. All one had to do was make a right turn onto Main Street and then follow the morning sun east. At the traffic light, she hung a right then made a left at the next light, then straight up the big hill. She found the Evangelical Church with ease and followed the flower delivery van up the hill. She made the left turn into the church parking lot noting the church faithful had already hung the black sash over the portico and black wreaths adorned all the doors, signifying to all that a man of God had passed over to the other side.

How quaint that people still did that, she thought. She parked her car close to the building as the November wind was cold despite the sun-filled clear blue skies.

She turned off the engine, suddenly becoming aware of the silence that surrounded her. She tried placing her handbag under the front seat then decided better of it and popped the trunk, deciding to throw it in the hold for security, not that these people would steal but still one never knew. With her notebook in hand, she proceeded to enter the church by the side entrance. Quickly, she looked at her note pad and found the name for which she was searching, "Alicia Adams."

"May I help you, miss?"

Dixie turned around startled by a deep voice that sounded like it was coming from on high. She smiled as she looked up seeing a distinguished looking black man. His white hair was long and wavy and glistened in the sunlight.

"Yes, sir, my name is Cathy Dixon, and I'm a reporter with the Times. I'm looking for Alicia Adams," Dixie said, looking into the stranger's eyes and seeing the tranquility of a true believer.

He smiled down at her, nodded his head and walked in front of her. Taking about six long strides, he stopped and lifted his long arm and pointed down the hallway.

Dixie noticed his fingernails were manicured.

"She is down this hall, Miss Dixon, first door on the right."

"Thank you," Dixie said, smiling at her tour guide as she turned and headed down the hall.

Dixie was hoping that Alicia might just help her find Robin. She had overheard one of the detectives telling another yesterday morning that Robin hadn't taken either car. The smug detective, the one she thought such an asshole, had remarked that the murder was shaping up as a crime of passion and since both cars were still here, the wife and her lover may have fled the state. It certainly made sense.

Dixie stopped in front of Alicia's office and knocked on the door.

"Come in, Deacon."

Dixie turned the handle and opened the door only to be greeted by the sweet aroma of marijuana.

"Hello, Alicia, I'm not the deacon. We met yesterday at the murder scene. My name is Cathy Dixon, Dixie to those who know me."

"Yes, Dixie, I remember. I also read your story this morning. So what can I do for the press?" Alicia asked guardedly.

"Phew, it is really smoky in here! Do you have a window to open?" Dixie asked, praying for some relief.

"No, but I do have a window air conditioner I can turn it on if you like," Alicia said, getting up and stepping over to a unit that should have been junked years ago.

The knob turned hard and Alicia set the speed control to high, hoping the unit could clear the smoke before they both froze to death.

"I asked how I may be of service to you. You surely did not come here to pass the time," Alicia said.

"Yes, I'd like clarification to some questions, some for a follow-up story and a couple to satisfy my curiosity."

"Oh, I'm guessing you want to know more about Roy. That's easy— Roy was a blackmailing asshole, liar and fornicator, and if that word is too big for you Dixie darling', he was a fucker and a half. Now you know the inside word, so you can go tell the world," Alicia said throwing her arms out wide.

Dixie looked down at the beautiful preacher lady noting how her tears made her eyes look even brighter.

"Did you love him?" Dixie asked softly.

"Love him? I loathed him!" Alicia said, venom resonating from her voice.

"That would explain it!" Dixie said, placing a chair beside Alicia's desk.

"Explain what?" Alicia replied, looking at Dixie through her tear stained eyes.

"Yesterday when I asked you a question about the deceased, it was strange the way you responded, cold and detached without the slightest sense of remorse. Furthermore, for someone who had just lost her spiritual advisor and teacher, one would think you would've shown a little more emotion. So I suspected right then and there that something was wrong."

"Aren't you the smart one," Alicia remarked coldly.

"Well, if you didn't like me yesterday, you're really going to hate me today— Listen, Alicia, you're not the only woman in the world who has been betrayed by a man. You're supposed to be a leader in the community, so suck it up and lead out—"

"You just don't understand."

"What don't I understand?"

"In the eyes of God, I'm corrupted and allowed Roy to do it to me. I allowed him to use me like a whore, and that's exactly what I was, a whore, and Roy was my pimp, and you know what, Dixie darling, I enjoyed it—"

"Shit! No wonder his wife killed him!" Dixie said.

"You mean Robin?" Dixie asked.

"She was a lamb led to the slaughter. Roy actually drove her insane. He told me one night she tried to kill him with a hammer. I just hope she's safe and warm and being cared for. She did not deserve this," Alicia said, opening her small refrigerator and taking out two diet colas.

"So you have absolutely no idea where Robin is?" Dixie asked, popping the tab on her cola.

"None, however, I do know the police are wrong about Robin having a lover. She was totally anti-man to the max!" Alicia said, taking a sip of her cola.

"Do you think her lover could be another woman?" Dixie asked finally.

"I would think so— I did her and she liked it," Alicia replied.

Dixie was taken a bit off guard by Alicia's remark but quickly regrouped. "I guess that's something. After all, love is where you find it," Dixie said, taking a deep swig of cola.

29

Roth walked quickly back to his office as the sharp cold air caused his lungs to burn. He stopped at the corner of Fourth and Main waiting for the traffic to clear and it was just his luck that a funeral procession clogged up things from the direction of Saint Nicolas Church. He cupped his hands over his nose and mouth, warming the air before he inhaled, trying to stop the burning in his lungs.

The wind was obviously coming up the river, which meant the wind was coming from the south and every time the wind blew from the south, the city got dumped on by rain or snow. As he began climbing the steps towards his office, he heard Lucy Bell yelling he took off, running taking the steps two at a time. At the top, he saw Joshua holding Lucy's head in his lap.

"Easy, sweetheart, I've got you," Joshua said, grabbing Lucy's hand.

Roth grabbed his cell and hit the auto 911 as he rushed to Lucy's side. As he knelt down beside Joshua, he saw that Lucy's water had broken.

"Yes, operator, this is Detective Roth of the Sheriff's Department. I need an ambulance. Officer Bell is having her baby. My address? Ah…third floor of the county jail, and please hurry."

"Nice of you to show up, Joshua," Roth said, taking Lucy's hand.

"Believe it or not, Roth, I was doing my job, and I have some interesting stuff to share with you, that is, after we get Lucy all squared away," Joshua said, smiling down at Lucy and praying the ambulance would arrive soon.

The EMTs were quick and efficient as they picked up Lucy off the floor and placed her on the gurney. Joshua assisted the fireman who placed a blanket over her as Roth knelt down and kissed her forehead.

"Whew, that was a close one, Roth," Joshua said, walking into Roth's office. "Too close!" Roth replied as he followed behind Joshua.

Joshua smiled at Roth as he slid his chair up to his desk.

"Ok, what are you smiling about?" Roth asked, motioning to Joshua to be seated.

"This morning I called the last two numbers Hill dialed. Both calls were interesting. A real eye-opener was the one to a Doctor Tidwell. I was thinking of course that it was Hill's family doctor."

"Makes sense!" Roth interjected. "And…"

"There are two Doctor Tidwell's! One is a voodoo doctor and the other one, a woman, a Doctor of Toxicology."

"A voodoo doctor?" Roth asked, puzzled by Joshua's reference to voodoo.

"Yes, I think she called him a Doctor of Holistic Medicine, something I've never heard of before," Joshua replied.

"Ok, Josh, keep going."

"Right, well, she told me she knew Hill as a friend of her husband. Now get this, she told me Hill was her husband's golfing buddy."

"I'm not following you—" Roth said, sitting back in his chair and interlocking both arms across his chest.

"Hill didn't play golf! So why should she lie to me? When I asked her if Hill was in the habit of calling at 1:00 in the morning, she denied getting the call, saying Hill must have spoken to her husband. Hill's call lasted for five minutes and the call was made the night before he was killed."

"Ok, so what else?" Roth asked.

"I found the next tidbit truly interesting," Joshua said.

"On my drive from Columbus, I plugged Hill's cell phone into my car charger and dialed a number in New York City. What was intriguing was that the message prompt was in Russian and broken English—" Joshua then sat back in his chair and crossed his legs showing his expensive specialty cowboy boots.

Roth leaned forward and placed his forearms on his desk, tapping his fingers as he evaluated Joshua's report. "Russian you say, and a Doctor of Toxicology that lied to you for no apparent reason. Interesting!" Roth said, slapping his desktop with both hands.

"I wonder what this all means?" Joshua asked.

"Yeah— how does this get us any closer to Hill and Deputy Bean's murderer?" Roth thought out loud.

"Wait a minute— I thought Bean died of a heart attack?" Joshua asked.

"Supposedly so, Joshua," Roth replied, picking up a red folder from the corner of his desk.

"I take it you disagree with the medical examiner in…where was it…oh, yeah, Bogotá?" Joshua asked.

Roth looked at Josh and smiled.

"Here, read this. Then we'll discuss it," Roth said, handing Josh the folder.

Josh reached out and took the folder. After a few minutes, Josh said, "This case gets crazier, and crazier; it's like we're going around in circles trying to catch our tails."

"Otis asked me to investigate Deputy Bean and find out why he was on a plane to Bogotá," Roth replied.

"Ok, so why was he on the plane?" Joshua asked.

"Don't know, but I suspect he knew we were onto him," Roth replied.

What intrigued Joshua about the folder's contents were the first hand accounts of the flight crew and especially the transcript of a Doctor Emanuel Gonzales of Turbo, Columbia. According to Gonzales, who was returning home after attending a medical conference in Houston, an airline attendant asked him for help. She led him back to coach where he encountered a young man about twenty-nine to thirty-five. The young man appeared to be in severe gastroenteritis pain. His skin was pale and his pupils dilated. He was also euphoric and began convulsing, and then the young man's heart simply stopped beating. At first, the physician thought the young man may have been reacting to some sort of drug, but he kept screaming that his stomach was on fire so when the man's heart stopped as the attending physician, he listed the cause of death as a heart attack. When the plane landed in Bogotá, he told the medical examiner at the airport that the man had died of an apparent heart attack. In reality, the doctor really didn't know what killed the man. He alluded that it could have been some sort of poison but didn't come right out and say it.

"Christ!" Joshua exclaimed. "What next!"

"I've brought in an undercover narcotics officer from Cincinnati. His name is Sam Rossi. Do you know him?" Roth asked.

"No—" Joshua replied, handing the folder back to Roth.

"Ok, then let's look at what we do know." Roth pushed his chair back from his desk and crossed his legs.

Joshua stood up and walked over to Roth's grease board and picked up two magic markers, green and red. He drew a line down the center of the board. On the right side, he wrote what they knew for sure; on the other side, he placed a red question mark at the top of the grease board.

The brainstorming went for on for two hours, working even through lunch, each man playing the devil's advocate for the other. Emotions ran high as did their tempers. Both men put their egos in check and kept brainstorming until mentally exhausted. When they had completed putting everything in one column or the other, they sat down and took a mental inventory.

"Let's go to lunch!" Roth said.

Joshua looked up at Roth and chuckled, shaking his head.

"Yeah, let's do lunch. By the way, did anyone ever tell you that you're a shit head? Because you are, you know that?" Joshua said.

"Yes they have and, yeah, I know!" Roth said, grabbing his jacket.

30

Rossi, come here please—"

"Sure thing, Lieutenant," Rossi said, taking a cream filled doughnut from its box.

"Oooh…Rossi's in trouble again!" someone yelled from across the squad room.

"Fuck you, Schneider, you ass-kissing pervert," Rossi yelled, giving the entire squad room the Italian salute.

"What you need, Lieutenant?" Rossi asked with her very pronounced Italian accent.

"Some homicide detective named Roth in ZANESVILLE has asked for an undercover narcotics detective to help solve the murder of a deputy sheriff and a criminal investigator from the state's Attorney General's office. So Captain Lacy has nominated you as your partner is still in the hospital and you're not due in court to testify for another ten days.

"Do I have a choice, Lieutenant?" Rossi asked, taking a bite of her breakfast.

"No…no you don't!" the Lieutenant replied, smiling at her.

"Didn't think so!" Rossi said, standing up and taking the info sheet from his hand.

Lieutenant Mick Foley had been a police officer ever since he got out of the air force before Vietnam escalated in earnest in 1965. In all that time, he had never met a police officer like Rossi. Pound for pound, she was as tough as any man as many of Cincinnati's drug pushers and prostitutes had found out the hard way. Rossi held black belts in both Karate and Judo. She had joined the army out of high school and did two hitches, working first in military police then for the Office of Special Investigation (OSI). Foley smiled and shook his head, knowing this was one detective who was the equal to Roth, someone who could out think most senior detectives.

* * *

Paula had taken Otis's advice and decided to revamp her business. She would not deal with the Russians, or anybody else for that matter. She decided to go freelance and use her federal license as a toxicologist to order and produce the various pills to keep her customers happy and well supplied. Using her prerogative as a department head, she had purchased a used pill-making machine off the Internet. The machine was capable of making large batches of little round pills, which could easily be stored in Tic-Tac containers.

She decided to start making the Alphabet drugs, probably the E GHB or GBL and of course, the rich kids' drug Ketamine, or special K as it was referred to on the streets. There were still the die-hard users that liked their Roofies or as toxicologists called it, Rohypnol. The Oxycodone would come later. She figured she could make at least six thousand a week or more when she went into full production. Her only concern being a homicide detective named Roth and that special investigator Joshua. Otis and Bean had told her about Roth, but it was Joshua that had called her, and some small little voice was telling her that she had miscalculated by lying to him.

Another concern was Heather. What to do with her? She couldn't stay at the house indefinitely, even with Mike's voracious sexual appetite as he'd soon tire of her. Besides, she was acting weird. Last night after sex with Mike, she rolled over onto her side obviously surprised that someone else was in bed with her. She rose up and looked down at the naked body and asked who she was. When

Paula responded using Heather's name, Heather asked in a voice that was dead serious, "who's Heather?"

Surprised by the question, Paula got up onto her knees and asked, "If you're not Heather, then who do you think you are?"

"My name is Robin."

"Oh, you say your name is Robin?" Paula asked.

"Yes, Robin Willingham, my husband is a minister."

"You say your last name is Willingham and your husband is a minister?" Paula asked, grabbing Robin by the shoulders and pulling her close.

"Robin, your husband is dead," Paula whispered. "The police say you killed him. Do you remember killing him?" Paula asked.

"He's dead?" Robin replied.

"Yes," Paula replied, gently stroking her hair.

"Then I'm free, I'm totally free of him. The beast is dead and you say the police think I killed him?" Robin said, staring into Paula's eyes.

Paula did not respond as she took Robin into her arms and held her close, feeling Robin's tears as they fell softly onto her shoulder and slowly trickled down her arm.

April did not respond to her cell. Instead, she concentrated on aiming her Corvette through the hairpin turns on a backcountry road that would take her to Newark. She had always thought that driving while talking on the phone was unsafe, unwise and just a bad case of dumb ass but as the road curved to the left she slowed and pulled off the road at the Dillon Dam entrance. Opening her handbag, she fished around until she retrieved her phone. She had missed two calls, one from Roth and the other from Paula. One call was a business call, the other undoubtedly for pleasure.

She dialed Paula's number, pulling out her Blackberry checking the schedule. She was booked solid this week starting late this afternoon with Jerry the County Auditor at 7:00 this evening and finishing the day with Owen, the state senator and his wife at around 10:00.

"Hello, April, nice of you to return my call," Paula said, her voice soft and warm.

"Yes, how may I help you?"

"Do you remember when I asked you about a woman named Heather?"

"Ah…yeah, I remember. Did you find her?"

"Not exactly. She found me and she's staying here with Mike and me, but she cannot stay with us indefinitely," Paula said.

"Ok, so what do want from me?" April asked, concern registering in her voice.

"I want you to take her under your wing and teach her how to be a professional escort," Paula asked.

April began to laugh. "You want me to teach her how to seduce men and women and steal clients away from me? That's what you're asking me to do?"

"I didn't look at it that way, but when you put it in those terms my idea isn't all that good," Paula responded.

"Is Heather a drug addict?" April asked.

"No, she's not," Paula, responded.

"Is she a bar girl or street walker?"

"No, she's more an abused house wife who just had enough, and to support herself she resorted to selling her beautiful body to put food on the table," Paula responded, her voice beginning to crack with emotion.

"I'm not trying to be a downer here, but a hateful woman doesn't make a good call girl. Good call girls are articulate, well read and must learn to give pleasure at will…and without prejudice. I'm afraid Heather, if that's her real name, is full of anger. Hell, Paula, she's apt to cut her clients' dick off. I would suggest you hire her in some capacity, maybe as a personal assistant or something like that. Buy her new clothes and fix her up, so she's even more beautiful," April said, hurrying the conversation along as she had to call Roth then rush home to get ready for her dates. The phone conversation ended with nothing much really resolved but it was a start.

Roth had just returned from lunch when his desk phone rang three times. Roth became annoyed when Lucy didn't pick up on two rings but then remembered she had skipped out to have her baby.

"Hello, Roth here—"

"Wow, how forceful and so authoritative," April said laughingly.

Roth began to chuckle. "Hello, sweetie, how're you doing' today?" he asked.

"By the way, you answered your phone, honey. Obviously, I'm doing' much better than you," April replied her voice soft and warm.

"Listen, I wanted to ask if you remember a friend of your mother's by the name of Dorota. I believe she worked at your mother's bank?"

"My Aunt Dorota, yeah, she was my mother's childhood friend. They came over from Poland together just before the war," April replied.

"Is your aunt still alive and if so where does she live?" Roth asked.

"Yes, Roth, she's still alive and lives in Florida I believe, with her new husband," April said. "Why do you want to know about my aunt?"

"Ok, sweetheart, we've trusted each other this far so I might as well go the distance," Roth said chuckling.

April began to laugh. "You're right, Roth, we have trusted each other for a long time, and it's been fun… Now, what is it?"

"Just this— the letter you gave me speaks of a woman named Dorota. According to your Uncle Leo, she has the money your uncle had accumulated from blackmailing and extorting people here in Z-Town. Those numbers beside the initials are not bank account numbers as we thought but the actual dollar amounts your uncle extorted," Roth, said, remaining silent and waiting for April to respond.

"You still there?" Roth asked.

"Yes, sweetie, I'm still here. I'm trying to figure out what I should do about the money. I don't know if she figured since mom was dead and Leo was dead, the money was hers. I don't know what to do about it," April said, her voice dead serious.

"Let's meet tomorrow, and we will assume you have her phone number and can call her? I want to know, along with the money, if there was a list with names on it. If there is, I want that list. The money, April, well…that will be between you and your aunt, and of course your conscience."

"Ok, sweetie we can do that, but I'm going to be very busy tomorrow. How about calling me when you get the chance and then we can decide on a time and place?" April asked, starting the Corvette's big engine.

"Sounds like a plan," Roth replied, hanging up on her.

Damn that man! How rude to just hang up on me like that. I like to be the one to hang up, April muttered to herself, throwing her cell into her handbag and dropping the shifter into first gear.

31

Trench coat in hand, Roth locked his desk. He was tired and hungry and wished that April could be with him. A little depressed, he looked at his watch to find it was going on 7:00. He wasn't exactly sure but thought he had heard the clickity-clack of a woman's high heels coming up the steps and quickly thought of calling Dixie for a dinner date. That thought was put to rest when something startled him. It looked like a woman and was built like a woman but if this was a woman, it was one he'd never seen the likes of before.

"You Roth?"

Roth was taken aback, saying nothing, merely nodding his head and stepping back leaning against his desk and gazing at it—

"I'm Rossi…from Cincy. You requested an undercover Nark."

Roth shook his head and began to laugh. "I thought Lacy was going to send a man."

"I can do anything a man can do and twice as good!" Rossi said as she walked into the office extending her hand.

Roth took her hand and grimaced, he was not expecting such a powerful grip from a woman half his size.

"Rossi, is it?" Roth asked.

"Yeah," Rossi replied.

"What's your rank, Rossi?" Roth asked, looking down at her.

"Detective Sergeant First Grade. What's yours?" she said, a smirk beginning to appear on her face.

Roth chuckled, "Higher than yours...and call me Roth. No titles used here. You have a place to stay yet?" Roth asked, walking past her and motioning at her to follow.

"No, sir just arrived a few minutes ago." Rossi grabbed the guardrail and headed down the stairs one-step behind Roth.

"Ok, then, have you eaten yet?" Roth asked.

"No, sir!" came Rossi's quick reply.

"Good, I'm hungry and we need to talk about the obvious. Then I'll place you in a hotel that could best be described as a flop house," Roth told her as they walked outside into the cold night air.

"Gee, Roth, you really know how to impress," Rossi said as she pulled up the hood of her fleece lined sweatshirt.

"Hmm," Roth muttered, ignoring her comment.

* * *

Otis was surprised and thankful to see the five crisp one hundred dollar bills that Paula had sent him. He actually despised himself for what he had been doing, but between Edith's medical bills and his own, and with their combined life savings rapidly disappearing, he needed all the money he could get. His cancer was still spreading despite the treatments and the pills that were supposed to ease his pain were not doing the job. He knew his time was drawing near, and then he would be free of this constant pain. However, until that time, he would remain a sheriff and die with his boots on, gun at his side, and a big shiny star pinned to his brown shirt.

Otis knew that Paula was no match for Roth, not in any circumstance, especially once Roth got her in his sights. She would be burnt toast, but until he died, he would continue selling out his deputies, collecting all the money he could.

Rossi had declined Roth's flophouse offer, deciding instead to stay at a more convenient and certainly more comfortable hotel, one located behind the roadhouse café where they had just eaten. She walked into the hotel lobby and noticed the looks of disdain. She didn't mind. She was dressed in her street costume and the taunts, whistles and looks of disgust only confirmed her disguise was working.

Once she was safely in her room, she began undressing, starting with her multi-colored chiffon wig, next came the costume jewelry. First the lip rings, then those god-awful, clip-on nose rings, and the birdcage-sized earrings that adorned her ears, finally the half-carat red ruby navel ring. Next came the knee high spiked boots and last she pulled off the tattered pink and yellow jeans, and debated removing her female security device. The damn thing was such a pain to remove, but it did save her more than once from being raped. She loved the fact that the security device was all-inclusive and she merely placed the device within her vaginal cavity. Because of the dangerous nature of her job, she used the contraption to protect her from any physical damage caused by physical or sexual assault. The device was simple in design, a cylindrical housing with one end open and the other end closed. The closed end was inserted slightly deeper within her vaginal cavity, while the open end had a thin membrane inner surface, which would absorb any dispensed seminal fluid. Pressure sensors were positioned around the cylinder for sensing any contractions in her vaginal cavity, and in turn, these contractions would cause the pressure sensors to activate a needle that was positioned at the closed end of the security device to extend into the rapist's penis. The needle would actually puncture the penis and take a tissue sample of the assailant. A microcomputer, connected to the external and internal sensors, would then be activated, releasing an identification dye containing an irritant to discolor the rapist's organ and cause a severe skin reaction. She could also connect an auditory recorder to the microcomputer, which would be activated upon penis insertion, recording all the sounds occurring during the sexual attack.

She opted to remove it at this time and clean it in the morning. Right now, all she wanted was a shower to remove her makeup and eye shadow and then to lye down and sleep. Tomorrow would be another long day.

32

Roth sat in his lounge chair watching his old RCA TV; his hairy right leg draped over the chair's well-worn arm. In one hand, he held the TV remote, with the other a four-finger high ball. The television simply provided background noise as he tried to shut down his brain and relax for the evening. He hadn't been sleeping well for some time, in part because of Shaquille's murder last evening then the unholy trinity murders of Kaczynski, Hill and Bean occupying all his time with no end in sight.

He missed Shaquille terribly. She wasn't a bad girl actually, though she did do sex for money, but that was only to pay her way through college. She had wanted to be veterinarian and was in the process of applying to several well-known schools, but so much for that. Her clients had been mostly well-heeled sugar daddies that indulged her and made love to her on a steady basis.

That was until Harley Curtis took her life. The exact reason why Harley cut her to ribbons wasn't clear, only that with her dying breath she called him on the phone, crying like a wounded coyote and begging him to help. Fortunately, he was only a block from her apartment when the call came through and he actually heard some of her last screams, as Harley killed her. Roth hadn't bothered knocking, simply twisted Shaquille's apartment doorknob like he had done so many times before and, with gun drawn, rushed into the apartment yelling her name.

Hearing a low guttural growl, Roth proceeded slowly towards the hall taking small stutter steps as he moved into the living area giving him a better view of the hallway with more time to react. He removed the safety on his pistol and held his gun at the ready. Expecting whomever to come directly at him from the hallway that led to Shaquille's bedroom, Roth took two more steps widening the angle from the living room to the hallway. Then out of the dark shadows of the hall way came what could only be described as the biggest, blackest man Roth had ever seen. The animal was covered in blood, its eyes glazed by blood lust snarling his intent to kill again like an animal.

Roth yelled, "Halt!" only once as the crazed man closed the distance lifting his left hand revealing a large butcher knife. Roth fired once placing the bullet just above the man's heart, but still the crazy man kept coming closer and closer, snarling all the way, foaming at the mouth, and forcing Roth to fire repeatedly. The animal fell dead at his feet.

Roth placed his gun back into its holster and called out to Shaquille. Something told him she was dead, but until he saw for himself, he would not accept the worst. Roth stepped over the man's body and walked down the hall to her bedroom, calling out her name as he went. He stopped at the bedroom door and gazed into the darkened bedroom. He saw her lying on her back, her eyes wide open staring at nothing. He flipped on the light switch and immediately wished he hadn't. His eyes fell first upon the blood then her sliced and stabbed body. Shaquille wouldn't be going to Veterinary School any time soon.

Sitting down next to her, he gently lifted her up and placed her head in his lap. He started to cry as he picked up her phone and dialed 911. He had a murder to report.

* * *

When Paula arrived at work next morning, a pleasant surprise awaited. The pill machine ordered six weeks earlier had arrived. The machine was larger than expected, about the size of her dishwasher, and surprisingly light. She secured her purse in her desk drawer and hung up her winter jacket. She plugged in the coffee pot to boil water for tea then took a pair of scissors and opened the box, pulling out an instruction manual. She couldn't believe what she was reading, nor could she get over all the electronic bells and whistles the machine offered. She decided to take the machine home, and if the school property administrator asked to see it, she would simply tell him the machine was at her house waiting to be assembled by her husband.

Paula pulled her Navigator into the garage and quickly closed the auto-door behind her. Not wanting any of her neighbors to see what was going on. She opened the Lincoln's door hatch, pulled the bags of chemicals she would use out of the trunk, and stacked them on Mike's workbench. As she pulled out the pill machine, she thought how shocked her neighbors would be if they knew, what she was about do right under their noses.

Paula figured at the most she would have a week before she had to bring the machine back to the university for inspection and identification. This was necessary to be in compliance with state and federal law as the machine had been purchased with official, traceable funds. Once the machine was properly identified, it would be recorded into the universities property log, and after that, the machine was hers to do with as she pleased. However, until then she had a week to begin making alphabet drugs, and according to the literature provided this machine was capable of making twenty thousand pills an hour. Based on the formula for Rohypnol, she had enough chemicals for five hours of continuous operation. She would then switch over to Ketamine, which should make the college kids happy. Paula figured with the quantity and quality of drugs, she could discount the drugs and sell the Rohypnol for two dollars a pill, the Ketamine for three dollars each, figuring she would gross a cool two hundred thousand dollars.

Roth sat at his desk drinking his morning cup of hot black coffee, still feeling the effects of last night's whiskey. He always maintained his mental processes were better when he was buzzed. However, at this precise moment in time he had absolutely no idea how he was going to keep his idea a secret from acting Sheriff Roland Lavey.

Roth wanted to set up a small task force of his own, away from prying eyes. He and Joshua could then go after the murderer of Deputy Bean, and then Rossi and Deputy Sawicki could go after the drugs. He was betting that both teams would end up at the same place. That was his idea anyway, but knowing Lovey he would sure as hell want in on the investigation and there was no way Roth would let the conniving, lying, backstabbing son of a bitch in on his investigation. So his dilemma was how to direct Sawicki without anyone, especially Lavey, knowing what was going on.

His desk calendar reminded him that he had a meeting with Joshua and Rossi to discuss how they were going to proceed with the investigation. He needed Deputy Sawicki and Rossi to get the Russians to tell them to whom Leo had been selling. Once they had that information, they could begin closing the noose around the murderer of Bean…and those involved with distributing the drugs.

However, the immediate concern was getting Sawicki away from the immediate supervisor. He needed help; in fact, he needed help from someone high up who could keep his mouth shut. Roth smiled as he reached for his desk phone and dialed 611.

"Sheriff's Office," the invisible voice said.

"Hello, you beautiful hunk of woman, you— When are you going to ditch that old man of yours and hook up with me?"

"Hello, Toby!" came the terse reply.

"Damn it, Marsha! How'd you know it was me?" Roth asked feeling defeated.

"Well, two reasons, Toby. You're the only dumb ass who would talk to me like that. Not even Otis himself would dare say anything like that to me, and the second reason—well I'll keep that a secret," Marsha giggled, looking down at the inter-office caller ID LED.

"Marsha, I'm in trouble and I need your help," Roth said.

"Ok, Toby, what's her name and how old is she?" Marsha asked, her voice sounding serious.

"No, no, Maggie, not that kind of trouble. I'm talking about work trouble," Roth replied, his voice soft yet authoritative.

"Roth, I'm only an office manager, I have no authority to help you."

"Listen, since I have no administrative assistant and I really need someone to help me with all the bullshit, I need to officially hire an assistant, plus I know who I want to help me."

"And who would that be?' Marsha asked.

"His name is Sawicki!" Roth answered.

"Sawicki is not an Administrative Assistant Roth—he is a Deputy Sheriff, not a secretary," Marsha replied in a serious voice.

"I know that, and I'm involved with two murders, one a Deputy Sheriff the other a State Criminal Investigator, both killed because of drugs. I need Sawicki, Maggie, because he speaks Polish and Russian. I know the Russians are providing drugs to a distributor here and when I find that person, I'll have my murderer. The problem is I don't want that butt-fucking Lavey and the ass-kissing Carroll Luke involved with my operations," Roth said, unaware that he had raised his voice to Marsha.

"I thought Bean died of a heart attack?" Marsha said, surprised at Roth's news.

"No, Bean was poisoned by some slow-acting stuff that made it appear like a heart attack," Roth said.

"Ok, Toby, I understand now," Marsha said.

Roth could hear Maggie typing something into her computer.

"I can send Luke to that disaster preparedness school in Virginia for ten days, paid for by Home Land Security. As for your butt-fucking buddy Lavey, I can send him to the governor's three-day conference in Columbus, starts this Monday. You can have Sawicki this Tuesday, but that's the earliest," Marsha said, all traces of joviality now gone.

"How long can I have him?" Roth asked.

"Ten days or until someone discovers he's gone, whichever comes first—" Marsha replied, hanging up on Roth as Sheriff Lavey walked into her office.

33

Dixie pulled her car into the Denny's parking lot. She had invited Alicia to breakfast so they could discuss Robin and attempt to figure out where she might be. Both rejected the police theory about Robin having a lover. That idea was just preposterous, conceived by two naïve police detectives who took it upon themselves to make Robin a murderer rather than a person of interest.

Dixie stood by the side of her car waiting for Alicia and slowly reached into her coat pocket. She pulled out her leather gloves and inserted her hands into the warm, soft rabbit fur that lined each glove. She looked up at the dark-gray clouds moving west to east and knew winter would be coming soon…

Dixie stood in line to pay for their breakfast. Alicia stood patiently at her side, her eyes looking upward and staring off into emptiness. Dixie heard Alicia utter, "If Robin has dropped off the radar and is not hiding with friends, and she has no family in the area, no access to money and no car—then she's hiding *in plain sight,* as someone else. That's the only thing it can be. That's what I'd do."

Dixie paid the cashier and walked outside Dixie asked Alicia if she had a key to Robin's house. "Yes, I do!" Alicia replied, wondering why she hadn't thought of it.

"Meet you at Robin's," Dixie said, hurrying to her car.

Fifteen minutes later, Alicia honked her horn as she pulled off the street and maneuvered around to park beside Dixie.

"What kept you?" Dixie asked.

Alicia smiled as she got out of her car and pulled her winter jacket closed with her left hand. Dixie noticed the jacket had no zipper. "I hit both red lights then had to run over to the church to get the spare key then rushed here and got stopped by the same two red lights. You can't win—"

Dixie began to laugh. "Oh, well, at least you're here now," she said, walking up to Alicia, putting her arm around her waist and pulling her body close in a vain attempt to shield her from the wind.

The yellow ribbon which denoted a police crime scene, was lying at their feet, ripped and torn by the wind. They hesitated momentarily looking down at the yellow ribbon then proceeded to climb the back steps to Robin's house. Alicia inserted the house key and turned the knob. She began bouncing her body against the door, making it move an inch at a time until finally the old door gave way, allowing them to enter.

Besides the silence, they were greeted with the smell of mildew and rot. Not unexpected, the house was cold and damp. Dixie opened the refrigerator door and quickly closed it the smell of spoiled milk and rotten chicken were more than a stomach could take.

Alicia moved through the kitchen door into the dining room, looking for anything unusual. Seeing nothing of particular interest, she moved on towards the den. Dixie followed a few feet behind her and noticed a room devoid of warmth. No pictures or paintings graced the walls. The China hutch had a few dishes that matched, but most didn't. She opened the middle drawer of the hutch and found porno movies and various men's magazines. She closed the drawer and opened the next one finding more of the same, except for two DVDs that had no titles. Those she slipped into her coat pocket.

Dixie entered the den and found Alicia standing in the middle of the room and looking down at a hot water bottle that was lying in the recliner. Except for the hot water bottle and an old picture of Moses holding the Ten Commandments hanging on the wall, nothing else in the room seemed out of place. Dixie walked towards the steps that led upstairs.

Alicia began to shiver as she looked back into the den and hall-way. Everything was there that should be there—chairs, tables, even drapes with window shears hung pristinely in the den and dining room, but it was obvious the house was impersonal and no love lived here.

Alicia smiled at Dixie as she offered her gloved hand to her. Neither woman spoke as they climbed the steps side by side, each feeling the damp cold of the house as it began to permeate into their bodies despite their winter coats.

When they reached the top of the stairs, they found another yellow ribbon crisscrossing the door immediately in front of them. They stopped and momentarily glanced at the ribbon that adorned the door. Dixie turned away from the door that hid the murder scene, and slowly continued to walk down the hall towards two open doors.

"This must have been Robin's room?" Alicia said, picking up a small bottle of perfume and pressing down on the plunger, releasing the pungent smell of Shalimar.

Dixie opened the closet door and began examining the labels on Robin's dresses and blouses. They were hand-me-downs, some very chic but out of style. She had only three pairs of shoes, white, black and brown.

Alicia opened the chest of drawers that dated back to another century and began searching for anything that would help them locate Robin.

The search took less than ten minutes and revealed nothing that could help them. However, Dixie had learned—and obvious to any woman—the marriage was loveless. Alicia stopped at the bottom of the steps and started to pray. Dixie ignored her prayer and headed towards the kitchen and the back door to escape the foul smell of the refrigerator. As she opened the door to leave, she spotted a lime green door with a pearl white doorknob attached to it. *A food pantry,* she thought. She twisted the doorknob and pulled open the door, at the same time shutting the back door.

"Alicia, come quick!" Dixie yelled.

"What?" Alicia asked as she walked into the kitchen.

"Look —a basement! How and the hell did we miss this door?" Dixie asked.

"Looks like hell's hole, don't you think?" Alicia remarked staring into the darkness.

"Yes, and it smells," Dixie replied.

Alicia reached across and flipped the old wall switch. "Darn it!"

"What?" Dixie asked.

"I was hoping the bulb was broken," Alicia said taking the first step downward. "Oh, my god…the floor is dirt!" she remarked as she stepped off the rickety basement stairs into the basement.

Dixie ignored Alicia's comment and moved passed her towards the washer and dryer. Pulling a crumbled tissue from her coat pocket, she placed it over her nose and mouth and opened the washing machine's small door. The smell of wet, rotting clothes covered in black mildew caused her stomach to turn. Quickly, she closed the door and stepped back, watching Alicia as she traced the basement's old limestone wall with her hand and then simply disappeared from view.

After a few moments, Dixie called out, "Alicia, are you all right?"

"Yeah—I've found something you should see," Alicia replied.

"Be right there!"

Dixie turned into a hall and saw a light flickering out from what appeared to be an old and probably forgotten root cellar.

Alicia held her cigarette lighter high causing the small orange blue flame to cast eerie shadows on the musty walls of the little room. She stepped forward and found a pull string hanging from a board above. She gently pulled it, sending the room into a soft, dim light. Looking up at the bulb, Alicia saw that it was encrusted with dirt from the ages.

"What do we have here?" Dixie asked walking into the room.

"I'm not really sure, Dixie," Alicia answered.

"Hmm…so what's that over in the corner behind you?" Dixie asked, pointing to what looked like a pile of clothes.

"Alicia reached down and picked up a bra and thought it odd that there were two elliptical holes cut in each cup. She handed the bra to Dixie and picked up two pair of crotch-less panties.

Dixie found two dozen condoms lying on the wooden shelf next to two expensive wigs.

"I think you're correct—Robin is hiding in plain sight and earning her living the old fashion way!"

34

Rossi gave herself a final check in the hotel's bathroom mirror, dressed in her big girl's clothes—a chic little black dress that accentuated a svelte body as well as ample cleavage. She wanted to look respectable for her potential landlord and life's experience had taught her that a soft smile opened up a lot of doors that would otherwise be denied wearing her street costume.

She also wanted to gauge Roth's reaction when she walked into the meeting this afternoon dressed like a lady. Her cop instincts told her that Roth had a plan and she was to figure prominently in its execution. Roth was no fool, a conclusion she reached last evening, but still he seemed like a man on a quest, and that made him vulnerable to error. She would make up the difference.

Joshua sat quietly in his office reading his interim report on Tim Hill. He was very late with the report, and he knew it. He just hoped that when Big Mama read it, she wouldn't rip him a new ass.

Big Mama was actually the Attorney General, and the investigators referred to her with affection as Big Mama, however, not to her face as that would be disrespectful. She was tough but fair, and didn't play favorites except for Smitty, her advisor in homicide cases. Dakota Smith, aka Smitty, was a legend in Ohio law enforcement circles. He held two medals for Valor, plus a Distinguished Service Cross and at least a half dozen Purple Hearts.

Smitty should have been pensioned off to greener pastures years ago. However, he was always able to convince every Governor and Attorney General how important he was to them and the state. Smitty was as wide as he was tall and had these beady little deep-set eyes that were hidden under two bushy eyebrows that resembled caterpillars making it difficult to read his thoughts. He also possessed a set of jowls that actually flapped as he walked, making him look like some grotesque lizard-man.

Josh pressed the almighty send button and took a sip of coffee. He wondered what would happen to him when Smitty read his report.

He looked at his watch, 10:50 a.m. His meeting with Roth was at three. That would allow time to get a haircut, a decent lunch, and maybe a three-mile run in before he left for Zanesville.

Joshua zipped up his winter jacket and started across the parking lot towards his car when he heard his name.

"Ledbetter!"

Joshua knew who it was before he even turned around.

"Yes, Smitty?" Joshua retorted as he stopped and turned just in time to block a roundhouse right. "What the fuck are you doing?"

"Kicking your lying' ass!" Smitty yelled, taking another punch at Joshua's jaw.

Joshua blocked Smith's second punch and returned the punch with one of his own, dropping Smitty with one punch to the nose.

"What the fuck is this about?" Joshua yelled, looking down at the old warrior.

"I read your report asshole. It's a pack of lies!" Smitty said, holding his white hanky to his nose in an attempt to stop the bleeding.

"No, Smitty, it's all true, every word of it, and I have the proof to back it up." Joshua said extending his hand downwards hoping Smitty would take it.

"You have the proof?" Smitty said, taking Joshua's hand and pulling himself up off the cold pavement.

Joshua looked into the warrior's tear stained eyes and nodded his head.

"I want to see this proof," Smitty said, dabbing his nose with his white hanky.

"Right now?" Joshua asked.

"Fucking yeah, right now... If the press gets hold of this, there will be hell to pay. I'll tell you that!" Smitty yelled.

"Ok, let's go back inside," Joshua said, putting his arm around the rotund legend shielding him from the cold wind.

35

Joshua sat quietly in Smith's office waiting for Smitty to return. He had politely excused himself saying he was going to the men's room to clean up, but Joshua doubted it. Smitty had an agenda and Josh knew that straightening out his nose wasn't on the agenda. Gripped tightly in his hands were two folders, one containing the coroner's report of Leo Kaczynski and the other the video of Hill getting killed by Deputy Sheriff Bean; the photo of the muzzle flash of Hill's shotgun as he murdered Mr. Kaczynski.

Joshua was brought to his senses when the door opened and Smith's booming voice called the room to attention.

Joshua complied with the command without reservation, standing straight as a board, his massive shoulders thrown back, his chin neatly tucked into the V-notch of his sternum.

"Please be seated, Joshua," the soft feminine voice said.

Instantly, Joshua recognized the voice and knew that it belonged to the Attorney General.

"Please, Joshua, be seated," she said walking around him and sitting on Smith's desk. "Smitty tells me you have evidence against one of your colleagues. Is this correct?" she asked, her voice soft and motherly.

"Yes, ma'am, I do!" Joshua replied.

"Before you show me this evidence, Joshua, tell me what were you going to do with it?" she asked, looking down at him as if he were a young schoolboy being scolded for playing too rough on the playground.

"Really, ma'am, nothing at all. I figured that since Tim Hill was murdered by a corrupt sheriff's deputy who, by the way, is also dead, then nothing can be gained by dragging Hill's name through the mud. We would be better off leaving Tim a hero in the eyes of his family," Joshua said, looking up and staring into the Attorney General's soft, blue-gray eyes.

Neither she nor Smitty spoke. They just looked at each other, creating an awkward silence in the room. Then Joshua saw a sardonic smile begin to form on the Attorney General's face. Smitty grimaced and nodded his head as if some sort of telepathic dialogue had just occurred.

"Ok, Joshua, you can go."

"So you don't want to see what I have?" Joshua said, shaking Smith's hand and suddenly wishing he hadn't as the old man squeezed his hand so tightly he might as well have crushed an egg in front of Big Mama.

"No, Joshua I don't need to see your evidence," she said. "I know it's in good hands and will be used wisely if the need arises. Oh one thing more, what county was Hill murdered in?" she asked.

"Muskingum," Joshua replied.

"So that would be Otis' county. Tell me, Joshua, what is the name of the homicide detective you're working with?" she asked respectfully.

"Roth, ma'am!" Josh replied looking into her eyes once again and seeing what could only be described as a familiar smile.

"Do you know him, ma'am?" Joshua asked.

"Yes, Joshua we're old friends!" she replied, walking past him towards the office door.

* * *

Dixie had a blush on her cheeks as she walked into Toby's kitchen from the cold. She looked at the kitchen table and smiled at the place settings. *"Toby's going all out to seduce me."* She thought placing handbag on the kitchen counter.

"Toby," she called out wondering why he wasn't there to greet her.

The sudden flushing sound of a toilet answered by the grinding, growling sound of calcified water pipes answered her question as to Toby's whereabouts.

"Hi, Dixie, I'll be right there," he called out.

She could still hear the loud growling sound of the houses water pipes protesting as Toby washed his hands. She looked across the kitchen and saw a pan boiling over with tomato soup, and one of those new fancy sandwich makers. Noticing the blinking red light, she knew the toasted cheese sandwiches were done.

She took the pan off the burner, grabbed two small plates and two bowls from the cupboard, and removed each sandwich, placing them on the plates and cutting them in half diagonally.

"Hello, Dixie," Toby said as he walked up behind her, encircling her in his arms kissing her neck causing her to shiver. She giggled and snuggled against him. He had shaved as she could smell the scent of Old Spice, reminding her of her grandfather.

"Toby, pour the soup! And remind me to show you what I found at the Willingham house yesterday," she said, elbowing him aside and walking towards the kitchen table.

Toby followed dutifully, carrying two hot bowls of soup that burned his fingertips. Gently, he placed the bowls on the table and went back to the old Amana and retrieved two diet colas.

"What were you doing at the Willingham house? I thought that was a closed crime scene," he asked, taking a bite of sandwich.

"Yeah and will continue to be until the police find Reverend Willingham's killer," Dixie replied, looking Toby in the eyes as she took a sip of cola to wash down her cheese sandwich.

"I can only assume you did not disturb the actual crime scene. So go ahead and tell me what you found."

"Remember you told me to find Robin Willingham and get her side of the story?" Dixie asked.

"Yeah, yeah, go on," Roth mumbled to her.

"Yesterday morning I took Alicia, she's the intern minister that Roy Willingham was fucking to breakfast. Anyway, she thought since Robin had no family and hadn't left the city, and then ironically Robin must be hiding in plain sight. So Alicia having a key to the Willingham's house, we simply let ourselves in and went exploring, and boy did I found out a bunch of stuff," she said smiling as if she was proud of breaking the law.

"Ok, Dixie, what did you find out that the police didn't already know?" Roth said, pushing himself away from the table and crossing his legs.

Sensing Toby's agitation, she pushed away her soup and sandwich and turned her body, facing him eye to eye. She even leaned into Toby, something she had learned long ago from an old psychologist boyfriend and if she remembered correctly, it was something about dominance.

"Robin Willingham has taken up prostitution to support herself. She disguises herself by wearing very expensive wigs. Secondly, she was an abused wife, not physically abused but mentally abused, by a husband who cheated on her and exploited her for sexual favors among the rich and powerful of Zanesville."

"Tell me more!" Roth said.

"A walkthrough of the house revealed the house was devoid of love and warmth, sort of a medieval devil's island."

"Besides your personal observations, what proof do you have that this minister exploited his wife for sexual favors among the upper crust of Zanesville?"

"I thought you'd ask me that question—" Dixie replied, pushing herself away from the table and walking over to her handbag and extracting two DVDs.

"Here, look at these. I think you're going to be as shocked as I was," she said, handing him the two DVDs.

"You have aroused my curiosity," Roth said, looking up into her eyes and feeling a tinge of lust.

"Is that all I have aroused?" Dixie said, looking down at his crotch.

"We have time, Dixie," Roth remarked standing up and walking towards the front room. "Pull the blinds," Roth said, half-asking, half-demanding.

She smiled at him and complied with his request, watching him as he bent down and inserted the disc into his DVD player and hit START. Roth stood and backed up exactly three steps and sat down in his favorite chair. Without looking, he grabbed Dixie's hand and pulled her gently down onto his lap and held her close, his eyes staring at the plasma screen waiting for the action to begin.

The blinds did little to filter the bright light of the winter day, but Roth could still make out many of the very important people of the city. Even without sound coming from his television, he could imagine the oohs and the ahs and the grunts and groans of the actors on the screen.

"Now watch this, Toby!" Dixie said.

"There! Right there— Toby, what are those two women doing?" she shouted, pointing at two very naked woman that Roth recognized as Becky Colt, county Assistant District Attorney, and Maggie Hennessey, Attorney General of Ohio. She was wearing a wig and dark glasses, obviously trying to conceal her identity but there was no way she could conceal the half-heart tattoo as he had the other half.

"They're snorting cocaine," Roth replied.

"Now see that tall, blonde girl with the beautiful breasts? That's Alicia, and the woman standing next to her making out with that good looking guy, that's Robin Willingham," Dixie said snuggling back into Roth's embrace.

"The guy Robin is making out with is our state senator," Roth said, "and the woman wearing the dark glasses and tattoo is Maggie Hennessey, his voice rising slightly in righteous indignation. "Dixie, do you have any idea who is videotaping this?"

"Yes, the esteemed Doctor Tidwell!" Dixie replied, with disgust clearly showing in her voice.

"What's on the other disc?" Roth asked, softly kissing the top of Dixie's head.

"That one is really strange, Toby, it shows a tall, beautiful, blonde woman and a tall, dark-haired male enjoying a lust-filled evening with a beautiful, dark-haired woman. I don't know who videodiscd that one," Alicia said. "They probably had the camera on a tripod because the camera isn't jerking up and down.

"Hmm, you say the name is Tidwell?" Roth whispered in her ear as he nibbled her ear lobe.

"No, I said Alicia say's her name is Tidwell, and stop that, you letch!" Dixie said slapping his hand.

"Sweetie, put the other disc in while I make a quick phone call," Roth said, slowly extracting himself from Dixie and giving her a peck on the cheek.

"So what have I missed?" Roth asked as he walked back into the room munching on his left over toasted cheese sandwich.

"Not a lot so far, only the tall blonde and that dark-haired woman are kissing," Dixie replied, scooting over to allow Roth to sit down beside her.

"Dixie, I'm going to confiscate these discs and swear you to secrecy. Somehow, you and Alicia have stumbled onto what I've been searching for, the reason Tim Hill and Deputy Bean were murdered, and now I have it. They knew too much and one of these people is a cold-blooded killer," Roth said, taking her by the hand and leading her towards the bedroom, looking at the wall clock and trying to decide if he had time to enjoy his young protégé.

36

The cold air followed her up the gray stairway, causing Rossi to pull her coat tighter as she braced against the elements. She wasn't positive but thought Roth's office was up one more level. She thought picking up the pace her high heels echoing off the cement steps sounding more like Morse code than a woman's step.

Joshua sat silently in Roth's office, his mind racing through a myriad of thoughts past and present concerning the case. First in his mind was Roth's prophetic words—*I think we have just opened a can of worms.* Now it was ringing true. He also remembered Roth saying ...*dirty cops and politicians are involved and I don't know who I can trust anymore.* It was just Roth and he—until they got some re-enforcements.

He was also curious as to why Smitty had tried to knock his head off over a seemingly innocent comment concerning Tim Hill. Why didn't he just pick up his desk phone and call him about Hill? Or could Smitty and Hill have been working the illegal drug trade together? If so, it would have been a dynamite team. Joshua smiled and dismissed the idea as ludicrous, blaming Roth for his thinking that way. He took a sip of lukewarm coffee and allowed his mind to move on to his impending divorce. He had come to the conclusion that being celibate for a woman who would never return was a waste of time. He was going to start using women like Roth—for his enjoyment and comfort only, no emotional strings.

Suddenly, he heard the sound of clickity-clack on the steps. He couldn't tell if they were coming up or going down, but he did recognize the sound as high heels. He looked at his watch, 2:45, fifteen minutes more before the meeting and Roth wasn't even here. *He'd probably be late for his own meeting,* Joshua thought.

"Excuse me, sir, is this the office of Detective Roth?" the soft female voice asked.

Joshua had been so engrossed in his own concerns that he had already forgotten the echoing sound of a woman's high heels.

Slowly Joshua turned his neck and looked over his shoulder, seeing the woman framed in the doorway.

"Is it?" she asked again, her voice still soft but showing some agitation with him.

"Ah…yes…ma'am it is!" Joshua replied, standing up for this beautiful woman and wondering what he should do next.

"Then you must be, Joshua?" she said, walking towards him and smiling.

"Yes, ma'am," he said.

"My name is Samantha Rossi," she said, extending her hand.

"Hello and how may I be of service to you, Ms. Rossi?" Joshua took her hand and was surprised by the strength of her handshake.

Rossi began to chuckle. "I haven't been called Ms. since I was in high school. Joshua, I'm going to be your partner. Didn't Roth tell you? I'm a narcotics officer from Cincinnati. Roth requested an undercover nark, and I was selected to come here and lend a hand."

"Roth told me that he had requested a narcotics officer, but not someone as beautiful as you—" Joshua replied, feeling his face beginning to turn red.

"A nice thing to say, even if not quite true," Rossi replied.

Joshua regained his composure long enough to walk round Roth's desk and pull out a chair. He was careful to wait until she was seated before he sat down, something he had been taught by his Grandma Ledbetter years ago and he had never forgotten the courtesy.

Quickly, Josh scooted Roth's chair up to the desk and sat down folding his hands, feeling a long overdue, familiar stirring in his loins. He looked across the desk, stared into her eyes and started to smile as he imaged her naked in his bed.

"Samantha, technically you're correct, we are indeed partners. However, our assigned missions will not put us in direct contact with each other. You see, Roth and I are homicide detectives and you are a nark officer. Still, I do see Roth's plan, and if I'm correct there will be one more of us for sure and he or she will undoubtedly be a narcotics officer as well."

"Oh…and what do you think Roth's plan will entail?" she asked, smiling up at this gentle giant whose immense size dwarfed her.

Joshua cleared his throat, impressed with Samantha's matter of fact style and coolness.

"I think he is going to have you two go after the suppliers, the people distributing drugs. Roth is convinced the drugs are being distributed to the rich and powerful in the city and surrounding county. I'll tell you something else, Samantha, we're all alone in this investigation because we are convinced crooked cops are involved as well as politicians, and we already know they will kill to protect their secrets. If they find out what we're up to we will all simply disappear never to be seen or heard from again—that is, if we don't get to them first."

A knock on the office door interrupted their conversation.

"Excuse me—I'm to meet with Detective Roth at three. He called me a little while ago and told me to be here."

"Samantha, meet your partner!" Joshua whispered as he stood up, motioning the deputy into the room.

"I'm Joshua Ledbetter, Criminal Investigator, and this beautiful lady is Samantha Rossi from Cincinnati, and you are…? Joshua asked as he walked towards the deputy, his voice falling off as he extended his hand.

"Deputy Sawicki, sir." The young deputy took Joshua's hand and felt a strength equal to his own.

Sawicki bent down and extended his huge hand to Rossi.

She looked up and smiled, taking his hand in hers and discovering that her hand was too small to grip his.

"Deputy, do you have a first name?" Rossi asked, looking deep into her intended partners hazel eyes and seeing a lion's heart.

"Yes, ma'am, it's Paul!" he said, retracting his hand.

Paul was about to speak but was interrupted by approaching footsteps as the sound of hard rubber heels echoed off the concrete floor.

"It's Roth!" Joshua said in a casual voice.

Paul took a step back and Joshua stepped to the side and stood beside Paul, wondering what was going to happen next. Rossi remained seated, using the woman's prerogative to stand or sit.

Roth walked through the door, his face ruddy red from the winter's chill.

"Hello, Joshua, nice to see you again. Have you two met?" Roth said pointing to Deputy Sawicki as he hung up his overcoat and suddenly realized that a woman was sitting in front of his desk.

"Who's this?" Roth asked looking at Joshua.

"Roth, I would like to introduce Samantha Rossi on loan from the Cincinnati Police Department," Joshua said, smiling down at Samantha.

"No way! I met Rossi last night, even took her to dinner!" Roth bellowed, showing his displeasure.

"Yes, Roth, we did have dinner last night, and you treated me like a slut. I wanted to show you that I'm a woman with a dangerous job. I want to hear your plan and if I like it, I'll stay. But if it's bullshit Roth, I'll go home. Do you understand me?" Rossi said looking at Roth directly in his eyes in a subtle act of defiance, yet still maintaining her soft and lady-like voice.

"Ok, let's sit down— Sawicki, close and lock the door. Joshua, if you would, please inserts this into the DVD Player," Roth said, handing him one of the two DVDs in his possession.

"What you are about to see is a bit shocking and may even serve to make you horny," Roth said, pulling another chair over for Sawicki. "But that's the nature of our work as police officers…"

As the DVD player began to play, Sawicki killed the lights then took a seat.

The room remained silent as they watched the Zanesville lords and ladies frolicking, fucking and snorting their way to euphoric bliss.

No one noticed Roth as he crept away from the others and turned on the light switch, cascading the room into fluorescent white light, temporarily blinding them.

Joshua took his cue and turned off the DVD player.

"Ok, Rossi, let's start with this—did you recognize anyone in the movie?" Roth asked.

"No, sir, I did not!" Rossi replied.

"How about you, Sawicki?"

"No, sir, not really. One of those women looked familiar but I can't place her. I don't know her name, but I see her every once in awhile at the court house, I think," Sawicki replied sitting with his hands folded.

"Very good, Sawicki, you've just pointed out our Assistant District Attorney, Becky Colt, fornicating with none other than Joshua's boss, while one of the city's top judges was making out with the senator's wife. The tall blonde with the nice breasts is a Robin Willingham, presently a person suspected of murdering her husband, the Reverend Roy Willingham. She is only a secondary interest right now.

"The other disc shows another tall blonde with nice breasts by the name of Paula Tidwell," Roth said, looking over at Josh. "She is a Doctor of Toxicology and her husband a Doctor of Homeopathic medicine. I believe her husband is not involved with these murders and he's nothing but a prop in all of this. I personally think that it's his wife but can't prove anything, yet.

"So, Sawicki, Joshua is going to give you two phone numbers. Take note that these numbers have 212 area codes, which is New

York City. Joshua thinks they're Russian and if he's correct then it's a good bet the voice on the other end will be someone in or connected with the Russian Mafia.

"I'm certain these numbers will lead to the drug suppliers. These suppliers did business with a Mr. Leo Kaczynski who was killed by a Mr. Tim Hill of the Ohio Bureau of Criminal Investigators Office and that's how Joshua became involved. Subsequently, Hill was murdered by Deputy Sheriff Bean who, by the way, was consequently murdered in flight on his way to Columbia. Therefore, we are after the persons supplying the drugs to our city and the person who ordered the hits on Kaczynski, Hill and Bean and remember; please, silence is our protection. As of now, trust no one but the people in this room."

37

Rossi remained silent, wondering what her role would be in Roth's plan. She didn't have to wait long as Roth turned to her first.

"Rossi, your job is twofold—two important tasks—first infiltrate their inner circle and get to know who's who in the zoo, the other…help Sawicki set up a rival drug operation to force whoever is behind the drug distribution ring out in the open. We will use a safe house wired for sound and cameras. How you do it is your business, but makes it worth your while and ours, understand?"

She nodded her head in agreement. Roth wanted them all, not just the ho hums but anybody and everybody involved down to judges, lawyers, police officers, even the Attorney General herself. Joshua was correct—they would be all alone, no doubt. *Yeah…but Joshua and Roth forgot one thing—it's us versus them,* Rossi thought to herself.

The meeting lasted only forty-five minutes, Roth had seen to that. He had broken down every aspect of the plan like some great general on the eve of the battle. Roth carefully unfolded his plan of action, explaining every single detail, not leaving out a thing. Each person was told their tasks and how these essential elements affected each person and worked to make the whole a doable thing. A few questions were asked then answered, and then it was over. Roth's last words were simply, "People, there is simply too much to do and sitting around a desk isn't going to get anything accomplished."

"I take it, Roth, you don't approve of my tough-bitch costume?" Rossi asked him as she and Sawicki filed past him.

"I think, Sam, what we need is a gentler, kinder bitch," Roth replied smiling at her.

"Gotcha!" she replied, smiling and taking her leave.

Joshua waited as Rossi and Sawicki left the room. He had a concern—he had told Smitty about the meeting and what it probably would entail... Now he had learned the attorney general was a cocaine abuser and liked extra-marital sex. He had been on trial this morning with Smitty as the executioner. That's why she asked what was going to be done with the evidence and why she wanted to know who was the in-charge homicide detective. When he replied Roth, she just smiled. The whole case was becoming a game of cat and mouse.

"Yes, Josh, what is it?" Roth said, motioning Joshua to sit down.

"Roth, I think I have compromised you and the others," Josh said, hanging his head down and not looking at Roth.

"How?" Roth said quietly.

"It's the darndist thing… This morning Dakota Smith assistant to the attorney general tried to knock my head off with a round-house right. He was unhappy over my interim report about Hill. I told him that I had evidence Hill was dirty and asked if he wanted to see it. Well, he did, so we went back inside and I went to my office to get the files and then took the elevator to his floor. I walked into his office and he immediately excused himself, saying he wanted to clean up. Next thing I knew Smith walked back into the office and called the room to attention and in walked the attorney general. She asked only two questions, what my intentions were regarding the evidence and who was in charge of the case. When I told her that you were, she smiled and walked out. Now I see her in this amateur fuck flick snorting cocaine. As I see it, Roth, the circle is getting bigger and bigger each day and pretty soon it just may turn out that the cool cats get eaten by the big dogs."

Roth did not speak, he merely sat quietly in his chair with his arms folded neatly across his chest, head bowed, eyes closed as he waited for Joshua to continue.

"God damn it, Roth, we didn't just open up a can of worms we've uncovered corruption from here to the state capital," Joshua said, finished now.

"Do you want out, Joshua?" Roth asked.

"Hell, no!" Josh growled his anger clearly visible.

"Then do this, Josh, play this Smith fella and Maggie like a couple of violins, use them, and help lead them down the primrose path to self destruction. Feed them credible information mixed with lies and then when they least expect it, we'll nail their asses to the courthouse wall, along with all the rest," Roth's voice had become so vicious and so guttural sounding that Josh dared not speak. He simply nodded his head in assent to Roth's request and quietly stood up, slipping on his jacket.

"Turn the lights off when you leave, Josh," Roth said.

Joshua did as requested and left Roth alone in the dark with only his thoughts.

Roth pulled out the large desk drawer and placed his feet across the file folders that served no real purpose as everything was now stored on computers. He closed his eyes and began to rub his temples, feeling tired the tryst with Dixie had completely drained him of any vigor he might have had.

The thing that was bothering him most was the ever widening game of cat and mouse, a circle of corruption so large that it could eventually cost him and those close to him their lives if they weren't careful. The gentle vibrating buzz reverberating in his front pants pocket caused him to stir. Then another pleasurable buzz caused him to open his eyes. He had fallen asleep on the job. Something he hadn't done since Otis and he were driving patrol cars.

"Hello!" Roth said into his phone.

"Toby, why are you the only man I let treat me like this?"

"Excuse me!" Roth said stalling for time as he tried to move his legs and found them unresponsive as they too were asleep and unlike him hadn't woken up yet.

"This is Toby Roth, is it not?" the female voice asked.

"Hello, sweetheart, yes, it's me. I was taking a nap, believe it or not, at my desk. Something I haven't done in years," Roth said, pulling his legs one by one off the desk drawer and gingerly placing them on the floor, flexing his calf muscles, trying to get the circulation going.

"Oh, I get it—my tax dollars at work!" she said in a mock huff and then began to chuckle.

"Yes, April, your tax dollars at work," Roth replied.

"I called, Toby, because you wanted to get together with Aunt Dorota. Do you even remember that?" she asked sweetly.

"Funny thing, I was thinking the same thing this afternoon," Roth said, hoping April didn't see through his lie.

"Then why don't you come over, I'll make a nice supper and then we'll call her?" April said softly.

"Hmm…tell you what, let me go home first and change and I'll see you around 7:00 p.m. How does that sound?" he asked.

"See you then! Ciao for now—"

38

Paul didn't say anything, preferring instead to listen to Rossi talk about her army days as they walked into *Dante's Coffee Shop*. In truth, he was scared of her. She was a very street-wise cop, and he was betting by her build and muscle tone that she was a tough little cookie as well. He knew she had to be tough, otherwise, Roth would have sent her packing when she offered her little war of words.

The other thing that frightened him was failure. He didn't want to let Roth or his new partner down. The other guy, Joshua, seemed to have his act together, was polite and quiet and exuded what could best be described as an arrogant confidence, something he needed to cultivate.

"So, Paul, is this your first undercover assignment?" Rossi asked as she looked at the menu.

"Does it show?" Paul replied.

"Just a bit," Rossi teased.

"Hmm…ok, then, what must I do to blend in?" Paul said as he perused the menu that he already knew by heart.

"First we must get rid of that uniform, that's a given. Another thing, don't shave for two days maybe three I want you looking scruffy. I also want you to wear turtleneck sweaters, preferably black or gray with a matching sport jacket. That'll do for starters. Next, you must obtain a set of wheels, preferably a Cadillac or perhaps a big Town Car, but whatever car you pick it must be black or silver in color and fast. With me so far?" She put down her menu and looked at him, trying to decide if he really was worth the risk.

Rossi knew from personal experience that partners had to trust each other and be able to read each other's minds, including body language, and right now, he wasn't giving her the right signals.

"So, Paul, why do you think Roth picked you for this assignment?" Rossi asked, motioning to the waitress to get her attention.

"I suppose, ma'am, it's because I speak Polish and Russian," Paul replied.

"Oh, my god, I see it now!" she exclaimed.

"See what?" Sawicki said, puzzled by her sudden outburst. He looked at her and shrugged his massive shoulders wondering what the hell she was talking about.

"His Plan, Roth's plan, don't you get it?" she chided. "The plan is so simple it's actually brilliant. Those two telephone numbers that Joshua gave us? Do you still have them?"

"Yes, I do!" Sawicki said, reaching into his shirt pocket and handing her the slip of paper.

"Good, we will need to get a prepaid cell phone. Once we do, you will call one of these numbers. You will speak Russian or Polish and tell the person you killed the dumb Pollack and you're cutting yourself in. Then you'll negotiate a price for a couple of kilos. Tell the bastard you're testing the waters. Tell him you have no distributor yet and that you're looking for somebody in this area. If we're lucky, he may give up a name. If he asks about Hill, tell him you killed Hill as well. Both killings are easily verifiable anyway and since no arrests have been made why not take the credit? Besides it will give you some credibility with these people."

Sawicki looked at her across the table, not believing what he was seeing. Rossi was actually salivating—she wanted these guys that badly. *Judas Priest*, he thought, *this woman is a fucking animal! What will that make me?*

"Ma'am not to be impolite or anything, but while letting my beard grow and doing all this shopping and calling and getting the big black car, what is it exactly that you'll be doing?" Sawicki reasonably asked.

"Why shopping for clothes of course," she replied, taking a sip of water.

Joshua pressed hard on the old cruiser's accelerator, allowing the large Intruder engine to enter the freeway traffic with gusto. Still feeling the need for speed, he flipped on the emergency lights that allowed him uninterrupted passage on the Interstate. A quick scan of the western sky showed silver gray clouds rushing towards him, obviously pushed by a strong west wind. He wondered if a snowstorm was on its way.

He thought the meeting went especially well. He loved how Roth detailed his plan in just the right way, making each person feel important. The plan itself was part razzle-dazzle followed up by some good old-fashioned bullying and bullshit. Josh chuckled to himself when he thought about Roth making the remark about Tidwell. He slowed the cruiser, turning off the emergency lights and flipping on his blinker, telling fellow highway travelers that the big bad Smokey Bear was getting off the freeway.

Doctor Paula Tidwell was the key to this case—he just knew it, although he would be hard pressed to prove anything against her. However, she was a toxicologist and had access to all kind of drugs purposely so that was part of her job! Perhaps Roth was correct. Maybe it would be a good idea to talk with Smitty who in turn would talk to the attorney general who would tell Paula she was being investigated. He would ask Smitty in the morning for permission to review her bank records and credit card purchases.

As Josh neared his home, he realized he missed his wife Amanda, especially on dark gray, cold days like this as it always made him horny. He began feeling the familiar stirring deep in his loins as he began to imagine Rossi lying nude in his arms, her soft breath caressing the hair on his chest as she slept. As he turned the cruiser onto his street, he started to feel the urgent need for sex that he had been repressing for the past six months. He felt his throat tighten and the silent sting of tears burning his eyes as he walked into his empty house. Joshua knew it had been too long. He needed a woman, any woman would do, just one to be intimate with if only for an hour.

39

She lit the two candles that sat prominently in the center of her square dining room table then poured the water over the ice cubes, pausing a moment and to take in the intimate setting she had created. She tried to remember the last time she had cooked for a man but couldn't. Since she was a little girl, she had liked cooking, especially around the holidays. Tonight she was fixing her favorite cordon bleu with mashed potatoes, green beans and apple pie. *The wine,* she thought, *should be white.* She also had some beer stashed away, just in case Roth didn't like the wine.

Roth felt the cold wind as it whipped around his head, biting his ears and nose as he hurried up the walk towards April's condo. He thought he would have a bite, talk to her aunt Dorota, kiss April goodnight, and go home. Dixie had really taken a toll on him this afternoon.

Pushing the condo's buzzer, he proceeded to wait for her to let him in, hoping she wasn't busy doing woman stuff like bathing or washing her hair. A quick check of his watch told him he was on time. Growing impatient with the damn cold, he pushed the buzzer again. Despite his winter overcoat and fleece-lined gloves, he was cold. *To hell with this noise,* he thought, wiping his nose with his glove. He would give the damn buzzer one more push wait thirty seconds then leave.

"It's open," came the invisible voice from nowhere. *Just in time too,* Roth thought, grabbing the door handle quickly and pulling it open, allowing the warmth of the building to envelope him as he stepped inside.

Roth walked straight towards the brass-plated elevator and pressed the solitary button, once again forced to wait for April. As Roth waited on the elevator to collect him, he noticed how beautiful the lobby was. *Just like the owner,* he thought, stepping into the elevator and pressing the up arrow.

Dinner was subtle and romantic, just as she had planned it. She noticed Roth couldn't keep his eyes off her—something she found amusing, considering his tough guy demeanor towards her when they were in public.

In truth, Toby was a softy when it came to prostitutes. They were his major information source, and he borrowed their bodies when he was in need, but in reality he cared about them as people and the girls knew it and loved him for it, especially since he killed Shaquille's murderer and paid for her funeral.

Roth looked across the table and stared into April's eyes, noticing how they seemed to sparkle in the flickering fire of the soft candlelight. Her smile seemed more radiant, her mood jubilant. *Too much wine,* Roth thought, feeling his lust beginning to rise. He reached into his jacket pocket and retrieved a legal size piece of paper folded in thirds.

"What's that?" April asked, taking another sip of wine.

"It's the questions I want to ask your aunt."

"Here, let's have a look," April said holding out her hand.

Roth smiled and handed her the paper.

April held the paper close to the candles, her eyes moving quickly from right to left as she read each question carefully.

"No, you mustn't ask her these questions the way you have them written down. You'll scare her and she will not say a word. I'll ask her the questions in my own way," April said handing the paper back to him.

"Ok, you win!" Roth retorted.

"Good, now that we have that settled would you care for some dessert?" April asked.

"How about later on the dessert, sweetheart? We'll call Aunt Dorota now," Roth pushed his chair back from the dining table and proceeded to walk into her den. He took a chair next to the telephone. April smiled at him. *He's all business,* she thought dabbing her lips with the linen napkin that had been perched so daintily on her lap.

April sat down opposite him and picked up the telephone receiver. Roth noticed how her fingernails shined in the soft lamplight as she started to dial, and for a brief fleeting, instant he wondered if perhaps maybe he was falling in love with her. Otherwise, why would he notice such a trivial thing?

April smiled back at him as she dialed, watching Roth as he fidgeted in his chair, unloosened his tie, wiped his brow with his hand, then wiped his sweat on his trousers. She was getting to him, she could tell. He was just pretending to read those silly questions of his and all he really wanted to do was look down her blouse. *Men are all the same,* she thought, *they're either stud muffins, players, liars, or cheat. That's all they are and they would do just about anything to get in a girl's pants.* Roth was no exception, except for the fact that she liked him.

"Hello…Aunt Dorota? This is April—"

Roth noticed the change in April's voice, somewhat motherly and caring, a quality he had never seen her exhibit before. He chuckled to himself, thinking how odd it was to find a hooker with a heart. "Dorota, sweetheart, I'm calling about a package that Uncle Leo gave you when you worked at the bank. Do you remember what I'm talking about?" April said. She covered the mouthpiece and whispered, "She still has it. Dorota says the package is full of money."

Roth smiled and nodded, "Ask her if there are papers with names on them."

April did not relay the question but slowly nodded her head to Roth as Dorota told her that the box was hidden in her clothes closet, covered by other boxes.

"Aunt Dorota, listen, I'm going to drive down and visit with you and your new husband for two or three days, will that be okay?" April asked. She put the phone on speaker.

"Oh, thank you, April that would be so nice of you to help me with all of this sorrow."

"What sorrow, sweetheart?" April asked, her soft, soothing voice going up an octave.

"My husband died in his sleep yesterday morning and I'm afraid I have no money to bury him. I was going to ask if you could help with the funeral. He was a very good man, despite not being Polish."

"Tell you what, sweetheart, I will leave tomorrow morning and be there sometime the day after tomorrow. Will that be okay Auntie?" April asked. Dorota was appreciative. "Ok, then, see you soon. Bye for now, sweetheart," she said as she hung up the phone.

"She has the money?" Roth asked.

"Yes, Toby, she has the money."

"What about the papers, did Dorota say anything about the papers?" Roth asked his sweating more noticeable now.

"No, Toby, I didn't want to get into the papers bit, but I will look when I'm there, and if there are any papers I'll fax them to you immediately," April replied as she stood up and walked towards the kitchen. Toby wondered if he was making a serious error in judgment, trusting her and relying on her to do the right thing and want as much as he did to reel in the bad guys.

Rossi watched her protégé from the right seat of the big, black Lincoln Town car he had commandeered from the local Ford dealership. She had to admit he looked good dressed in his turtleneck sweater and sport jacket, accentuated by a two-day growth of facial hair. His shoulder holster was clearly visible under his jacket. His Bogart look could only be described as macho. His size and his looks would make him credible—a good first impression with the Russians, that much was sure.

"Ok, now what?" Sawicki asked, slowing for a traffic light.

"Partner, its show time!" Rossi replied.

Sawicki began to chuckle, "It's about time, let's go kick some Russian booty."

Rossi was beginning to feel comfortable with her new partner. Usually it took months before two detectives began to click as a team, but Paul was insightful and intelligent and his questions were always purposeful and respectful. Another nice thing was that he treated her with respect, an oddity in today's law enforcement circles.

"Is there a restaurant close by?" Rossi asked.

"Yeah, a Horton's up ahead," Sawicki, replied.

"Good, let's have a go," Rossi said, reaching down and grabbing her purse.

As soon as they entered the restaurant she said, "I'll have what you're having," and made a dash to the restroom.

Sawicki ordered two large black coffees with two bagels and cream cheese. He wasn't sure but he figured her for someone who liked bagels. He took the middle table close to the entrance so he could watch the Lincoln and pretend that it was his.

Rossi got to the table just as the server brought the order.

"Mmm...I love coffee and bagels with cream cheese," Rossi said, pulling out the chair next to him.

Sam wasted no time. She opened the small container of cream cheese and at the same time began talking. "Ok, Paul, our next move is critical. We must sell ourselves and our story. I don't know how the Russians will talk to you, but I don't expect anything right away until they check you out. So we must be convincing. I want you to tell them you killed the Pollock for shorting you on the count. Further, that Hill was working undercover and was going to arrest them and all the others, but you were suspicious of him and killed him after the Pollock told you that Hill was using his badge to cut himself in.

"That should make them curious at least. Now, two things can happen as a result of that game plan and my experience tells me that the Russians will probably, at first anyway, view you as a threat and if they do they'll probably have someone make an anonymous call to the local police giving them all the sorted details. However, another option is they will simply set up a meeting some place and kill you. Therefore you must be convincing from the get go. Do you understand what I'm saying here?"

Paul did not speak but sat quietly, taking a sip of his coffee to wash down the last of his bagel. Eventually, he said in a soft and reflective voice, "I understand, Sam, that we have to get it right the first time because there will be no second time."

Paul reached into his jacket pocket and pulled out his cell phone, already having programmed both numbers Joshua had given him.

"Shall I?" he said, a wry smile growing on his face.

"By all means, please do!" Sam replied demurely.

Paul flipped open his cell and began dialing. He felt his heart beat a little faster as his hand slowly tightened around the small phone. He took a sip of coffee, lubricating his dry mouth knowing that show time would begin in just a moment—

40

Mondays were shit for Joshua and he thought about pulling his cruiser into the state employee parking lot, especially since he was hung over. Instead, he decided to do what Roth had suggested and that was to play Smitty, who in turn would inform the attorney general. He had lost all respect for Maggie and Smitty and in the interest of justice and a nice promotion he, along with Roth and the others, was going to enjoy bringing them down.

Over the weekend, Joshua had written his make, believe report, informing Smitty that Roth had brought in two undercover officers. One was a man named Sam Rossi and the other guy was a DEA agent from Cleveland. Joshua went into great detail explaining Roth's plan of action. Of course, it was all bullshit, but Smitty wouldn't know that. He went on to inform Smitty that Roth was going after the Russians in hopes they would lead him to the killer of Deputy Sheriff Bean. Joshua deliberately ignored mentioning anything about Criminal Investigator Hill or Kaczynski, choosing instead to concentrate on the drug trafficking part of Roth's plan, lying in an attempt to provoke some kind of reaction from the attorney general. Slowly, he inserted the hard, little, green colored disc into his computer, pausing momentarily to say every investigator's prayer: *Oh, heavenly father don't let me screw this up!* He then pressed the SEND button and in the blink of an eye, the report was gone. He could only hope

Roth was right about feeding the attorney general lies; otherwise, his law enforcement career was over.

Smitty read Joshua's report twice and, when done, he forwarded Joshua's report to the A.G. Normally, he wouldn't have sent her the report but she seemed to take an active interest in Ledbetter's investigation and every time Roth was mentioned in a report, she paid particular attention to it. He didn't know why Roth's name lit Maggie up, it just did.

Margaret (Maggie) Hennessey was lost in thought as she stared out her large office window at the blue-gray sky of a February morning. Ever since they attended high school together, people had always under-estimated Roth. *Up to and including now,* she thought. *Toby Roth has always been my first love, but life had different plans for us both.*

Toby's fault, which was not of his own choosing, was that he was born poor in a time when it took money and references to get into a good college. Although bright and cheerful, he never seemed to fit in with his classmates, which over time created moodiness in him that as far as she knew he still harbored. She remembered one night during a very heavy petting session when he told her that his ambition was to be the first Roth to attend and graduate from college, sort of an ultimate dream. So being poor, Toby did what hundreds of other Appalachian boys did he joined the military. He joined the few, the proud, and the brave, because they were the best and because it didn't cost anything to get in. The Marines taught him discipline, self-reliance, and survival skills, the very skills needed to be a police officer.

She knew by his reputation as a homicide detective and that damn determined perseverance of his that he possessed what it took to find his killer. The fact that he had created a task force proved as much.

Now she was trying to decide if she should resign from her post or finish out her term of office hoping Roth wouldn't discover her indiscretions, that by some miracle that would be overlooked. If she let Joshua continue working with Roth, he could be her eyes and ears to Roth's investigation. Technically, Josh's involvement in Tim Hill's murder was over. Knowing this, she could at her discretion reassign him to another case. But if she kept Josh involved with Roth, she could keep an eye on him from a distance. And when he got too close she would pay him a personal visit and perhaps rekindle their romance or something else, something sinister but necessary.

In the meantime, she would call Paula and inform her about what Roth and his task force were doing and warn her to be on guard. She was also going to call Becky Colt, the young assistant district attorney in Zanesville and ask her to snoop around and find out more information and, above all, to keep her informed.

Paula flipped her mobile phone closed and slowly let it slide into the deep pocket of her lab coat. Maggie's warning about Roth and his team was also a growing threat against her. She walked over to her desk and took her chair, a quick peek at her watch told her that she had class in ten minutes, not enough time to call Heather and ask for an accounting of the merchandise. She would do that on her way home it would be simpler that way. Satisfied with her plan she turned her attention to the student's accountability sheets required by law when any narcotic was being used.

Personally, Paula thought the law of accountability for class one and two narcotic material dim-witted, and being enterprising, she used the law to her advantage. The federal inspectors who appeared like clockwork examined only the students' worksheets, not what was done with all the grams of narcotic material that she would so precisely weigh, record the results of, and supposedly destroy. Instead, she would place the narcotic material into a bio-hazard bag and when class ended simply place the neatly folded, bright orange bag into one of her deep lab coat pockets and take it to Heather to be used later for more profitable ventures.

Paula felt tired as she pulled the big SUV Navigator out of the university's employee parking lot and headed home. On impulse, she tried calling Heather once again but still there was no answer. She flipped her phone closed and decided to go to her apartment. It was close by and if the inventory wasn't done, she would do it.

Paula pulled the SUV into the apartment building parking lot. She noticed an older Buick parked in Heather's assigned parking spot. Curious, Paula looked in the Buick's driver side windows and said straightway, "Damn it, I don't need this!" and headed to Heather's apartment.

A fucking Jehovah Witness trying to recruit Heather was just too much for her to cope with right now. Paula stopped only long enough to insert her key into the door lock, calling out to Heather as she tossed her purse into the over-stuffed lounge chair.

Paula walked down the hall passing the bathroom on the left two more steps, she was at the bedroom door. Slowly she pushed the door open and found Heather asleep.

False alarm, she thought, tiptoeing into Heathers bedroom. Paula looked down at her and thought how sweet and innocent she looked. Paula began slipping off her shoes, followed by her blouse and jeans. She got into the small double bed and cuddled up to Heather pulling her close and slipping her hand over Heather's breasts. She would take a power nap for now and worry about her inventory and Roth later when her mind could deal with it all.

The young, sexy Assistant Prosecuting Attorney of Muskingum County hung up her phone. She had just talked to the state attorney general who told her about Roth and what he was doing. She reached for her desk phone and picked up the receiver to call Roth, then gently positioned it back in the cradle, deciding to wait and see.

Becky Colt was a direct descendent of Samuel Colt, inventor of the rubberized cable that was used by Sam Morse to establish communications between cities and states. Placing the cable under lakes and rivers both in Europe and the United States steered the development of the fledgling telegraph industry, and along the way Colt invented and patented the underwater mine. Old' Sam gave a demonstration of his underwater mines for the U. S. Navy one cold November morning along the banks of the Connecticut River, accidentally sinking two moving boats. The Navy bought all the mines he could produce. Not stopping there, he started toying with firearms, establishing the Colt Fire Arms Company, which invented the *Peacemaker* revolver, the gun that changed the west. Upon his untimely death in 1862, Sam Colt had amassed a personal fortune of fifteen million dollars and the companies he established to manufacture revolvers and coated cables were still in business, providing Becky with a nice monthly income. Still with all that money, her beauty and education Becky Colt didn't know what to do with a lowly county sheriff's deputy by the name of Toby Roth.

Becky was a true aristocratic blue blood in Connecticut, born to privilege and accustomed to having her own way. The old-silver-spoon-in-her-mouth kind of life, where only the very best would do for the great, great, very great granddaughter of the first real weapons merchant in the world, was a thing only privilege could appreciate. Young Becky knew only the best of schools, the best of clothes, and the very best of men, and drugs would do for the young prosecuting attorney who had never been on the short side of a losing argument. Graduate of Princeton, law degree from Yale and now the Assistant Prosecuting Attorney of Muskingum County, a job she truly enjoyed, putting all those bad people in jail. She had justifiably earned her very solid reputation in criminal law.

Joshua called Roth late Monday afternoon and told him what he had done to this point, even emailing him the same copy he had given Smitty.

"Good, now we'll wait and see what direction the attack will come from," Roth said, then he hung up, leaving one pissed off criminal investigator on the other end of the phone. Joshua closed his cell phone and tossed it back onto his desk.

"Adrik, you know the Pollock was a piece of shit, why you talking to me like that? I want to cut myself in on the action. Yes Adrik, I did kill the fat Pollock, and if you must know, I also killed that two-face Hill. He was no fucking good, Adrik, you hear me. I don't care if you do send Baran to kill me. I'll just kill him and you will no longer have a bodyguard!"

Sawicki could feel his stomach churning as his nausea kept rising and falling in the pit of his stomach, but still he sweet-talked and argued with the faceless voice named Adrik on the other end of his phone. Sawicki could hear car horns in the background, and knew that he was talking to the Russian Mafia someplace in New York. This caused him to sweat so profusely that Rossi started wiping his face with napkins.

"How much you looking' for?" Adrik asked, not in Russian but in Polish.

"Two kilos for now. Then if I can find the Pollock's buyer I'll buy lots more," Sawicki replied in Polish.

"Call me on Thursday, around 3 o'clock!" Adrick replied and then there was silence.

"He hung up!" Sawicki said, looking at Rossi.

"You were great. He hung up because he's going to check you out. Did he say to call him or did he say he would call you?" Rossi asked handing him another napkin.

"He said to call him Thursday afternoon around 3:00 p.m.—" Sawicki replied, wiping his hands.

"Good, he's going to check you out," Rossi stood up, signaling to Paul that she was ready to go.

"Where to now?" Sawicki asked.

"We make no further contact with what's his name—" Rossi said, looking at Sawicki and fishing for the man's name.

"You mean, Adrick?" he replied, his brow looking like a new-plowed furrow.

"Yes, Adrick. We will call Joshua and ask him to call someone in New York and check on Adrick and the other guy he mentioned.

"You mean Adrik's bodyguard, Baran?"

"Yes, him, then when we know what we're facing we'll proceed accordingly," Rossi said, wadding up all the napkins she had used on her partner.

The young intern detective nodded his head and stood up.

"Now it's my turn!" Paul said.

"Your turn? For what?" Rossi asked puzzled by her partner's words.

"Why to use the restroom, of course," he said, beginning to laugh as he walked away from her.

"You know, Sawicki, you're a real asshole, you know that?" she said as he laughed out loud, noticing the restaurant staff smiling at them.

41

"Hello, Roth!"

"Hello, sweetie, do you miss me?"

"Like a toothache!" Roth replied caustically.

"Hmm...you're so mean to me, Toby, I don't know if I should tell you what Aunt Dorota and I found," April said laughingly.

"Well, if you put it that way... Yes, sweetheart, I miss you, but you already know that," Roth replied in a voice warm and soft, lighting up April's heart.

"Toby, I found what you were looking for!" April said softly. "Along with disc recordings, videodiscs and CDs. My aunt isn't exactly into that type of equipment so I don't know what's on them but I did get them all packaged up and sent express mail to your house."

"Express mail? My house?" Roth replied.

"Toby, honey, I read some of the names on the list and frankly I was afraid for you, and me. If anybody got hold of that stuff I think you'd be a dead man," April said, her voice clearly registering concern for his safety. Her words were not an act.

"It's, ok, sweetie, and it was probably the wise move, now that I think about it. What did you do with the list of names?" Roth asked in a voice soft and warm to try to calm her fears.

"I put them in the shipping box as well," she said.

"Good enough, then, when are you coming home?" Roth asked.

"I must take care of my aunt first. She's in no shape to live alone so I'm going to find her an assisted living home and finish up some loose ends, then I'll come home," April said, sadness resonating clearly in her voice.

"Listen, be careful and call me when you get home," Roth said.

"Ah, Toby, you do miss me," April replied and began to tear up.

"Of course I do!" Roth said his voice in its matter-of-fact mode then he simply hung up the phone.

"Damn that man! He is so infuriating," April mumbled, flipping her cell closed.

"Did you say something, April?" Dorota said, looking up from the kitchen table.

"I said men are jerks!"

"Oh, tell me something I don't know! I've known that for years dear, but they do have a place in our lives," Dorota said, chuckling as she looked down through her bifocals searching for a piece to her puzzle.

"Yeah, like killing spiders and picking up dog poop!" April said, picking up a piece of puzzle that she identified as a sure fit.

* * *

"Adrik and his side kick, Baran? Yeah, we know them, sir as does the DEA and FBI. We've been trying to nail those two for years."

"Detective Brown, think positive— maybe I can nail them," Joshua said.

"You're welcome to try, inspector, but they do everything through a third party and never venture out of the New York area, which makes it damn near impossible to prove anything against them. Twice we've gotten close and twice the middleman ended up dead. They play for keeps, sir," Detective Rollin Brown said, knocking the ash off his cheap cigar and watching the hookers practicing their trade. He was looking for another drug bust.

"Well, sir, I'm committed to this and I'm going to get them," Joshua said, thanking Brown.

Joshua put the phone back into its cradle thinking it had taken more time to find Detective Brown than the time span they had talked. However, he now had confirmation from an outside source the bad guys were big time, smart, not trusting even among themselves and not afraid to kill. He would pass on the information to Samantha then reluctantly return Roth's call.

Paula folded the sheet of paper that had her inventory neatly penciled on it. According to her calculations at the going rate, she had just over five million dollars in pills. She would discount her inventory and sell everything for four million. Then she would discreetly quit her job, board a plane, and disappear into a country with no extradition to the United States. Maybe Brazil, Bolivia or Ecuador, she didn't know for sure but she'd find something suitable. Better yet, she'd call Maggie, and ask her to recommend a safe house country.

Joshua listened as Roth told him about his discovery and what it entailed. Joshua's enthusiasm began to return, forgetting Roth's earlier slight against him. "Ok, Roth, sounds good, call me when you're ready and I'll be right over," Joshua said snapping his phone closed.

He then smiled, thinking to himself, *How does it feel jerk?* But somehow, he didn't feel all that superior at the moment. Maybe he wasn't as smart as he would have to be—

42

Otis was wrapped up in an electric blanket and sat silently in his favorite chair watching *She Wore A Yellow Ribbon,* an old John Wayne movie of the late 1940s. The chemo treatments were taking their toll upon his body. His once robust looks and glib demeanor had fallen away, exposing a man who was now skeletal, having lost more than seventy pounds. His attitude could best be described as dour. He had heard the doorbell, despite the bugle call on TV but was too weak to answer the door. He would have to wait until his wife, Edith, or Edie as he had called her for the last forty years, answered the door.

"Look who's here to see you, Otis," Edith said, taking Toby's coat and the flowers he brought.

"God damn, fuckin' flowers? You brought me a bouquet of fucking flowers!" Otis said, his voice registering mock disgust.

Roth smiled and began to laugh as he reached into the inside pocket of his sport coat and pulled out a pint of Seagram's Seven®.

"Now that's more like it," Otis said, a smile returning to his gaunt face."

"I don't know if you're allowed any whiskey, Otis, but I figured what the fuck! He's dying' anyway and knows it! So we'll have a few drinks to old times and have an Irish wake a tad early," Roth said, breaking the state seal with his fingernail.

Otis leaned over, looking towards the kitchen to see if Edie was there.

"What is it Otis?" Roth asked.

"Nothing, nothing at all, I was looking for Edie. I think we still have that bottle of ginger ale left over from Christmas. If we do, it's on the back porch," Otis said setting back into his chair.

"I'll go check, Otis, where are your glasses?" Roth said, walking towards the kitchen.

"Second cupboard on the right," Otis replied.

The drinks were stiff and the conversation lively, despite Edie's constant pleading to stop drinking. Roth felt guilty and placed the cap back on the whiskey bottle despite it being almost empty then slid the bottle into his jacket pocket. By the looks of him, it was obvious Otis was not feeling much pain now. His complexion once jaundiced had changed to a rosy red. He made no complaint when the whiskey disappeared from view. Otis just sat there, his eyes glazed over with a big shit-face grinas if someone had drawn it on his face.

"Yah, ok there, Otis?" Roth said, shaking his friend's shoulder.

"Oh, yeah, Toby, I feel fine, what I need now is one of Paula's blow jobs.

Roth said nothing, choosing to play it straight and ask a question he did not want to ask.

"Paula who?" Roth asked his voice barely above a whisper. "Paula Tidwell? You mean the toxicologist?" His voice took on an urgency all its own.

"Yeah, the rich bitch."

"How the hell do you know her?" Roth asked, trying to keep his temper under control.

"She sends me money, Toby, to help me with my medical bills," Otis replied as small tears began to form in the corner of his eyes.

"Why does Paula Tidwell send you money, Otis?" Roth asked quietly, not wanting to create an ugly scene with Edie nearby. But still the question had to be asked.

"She sends me money to help pay our bills!" Otis stammered.

"And what, Otis, do you do for her in return?" Roth said, his body starting to quake with rage.

"I tell her what the city police are doing to catch her. I told her to watch out for you as she's no match for you, Toby," Otis said, looking up at Roth for some sort of absolution.

Roth sat down. He needed to think but was too drunk to do so. He began rocking back and forth, holding his hands down between his legs. He began to vent his wrath cursing one moment, yelling the next. "Who hasn't this bitch corrupted?" Roth finally managed to say. "The state attorney general, the county prosecutor, a state senator and his wife, a state criminal investigator, a sheriff's deputy, two local judges. Who else has this evil maniac-bitch corrupted that I don't know about?" He went silent—his blood shot eyes boring holes into Otis. He grabbed his overcoat and stood up saying nothing.

Roth pulled on his coat, made his way quickly through the house and to the front door, and silently turned the knob, choosing not to say goodnight. As he walked down the drive headed towards his car, he could feel the cold winter air clearing his mind and cooling his rage. He needed sex to get over this revelation and he needed it badly. Sliding his hand into his jacket pocket, he retrieved his phone and called Dixie. He needed her now more than ever.

It was 06: 09 a.m. when Paula begrudgingly answered her home phone. "Paula, it's me, Otis."

"Jesus Christ, you old fart! Why are you calling me so fucking early?" Paula said, slurring her words, trying to gain some semblance of conscious thought.

"Sorry about that, but I thought you would want to know that Roth knows about you, me, and everyone else connected to you as well," Otis said.

"What? Did I hear that right? How does he know, Otis?" Paula said, her voice no longer sounding sleepy.

"I don't know how he knows but he does, Paula. He knows about Deputy Bean. I must admit, Paula, I didn't know about him.

He also knows, and again I don't know how, that you killed him." Otis caught his breath and went on. "Did you kill him, Paula?" Otis asked out of curiosity, his voice taking on the authoritative tone of a sheriff.

"You're stalling, Otis, keep talking!" Paula said her voice just a couple of octaves below a scream.

"He also knows about Maggie and Colt, plus the senator and his wife and the judges," Otis said, stopping because he had no more to say.

"I guess there's only one thing to do and that's to kill Roth," Paula said her voice venomous and already thinking about how to do it.

"Not on my watch, Paula, you understand me? You try that and I'll kill you myself, you hear me, girl?" Otis yelled, the anger in his voice resonating so loudly that Edie heard him in the kitchen.

Paula shut up, never hearing Otis talk like that before, especially to her.

"Ok, how's this for an alternative—I'm in the process of liquidating all my merchandise. If I do that and disappear, will Roth come after me?" Paula asked.

"Probably, unless you disappear to some South American country like Brazil or Bolivia, hell, girl, maybe even Argentina," Otis replied his voice softer now.

"I was thinking the same thing only yesterday…" Paula said.

"Can you be done with everything say in a week or less?" Otis asked.

"Yes, I think so!" Paula replied.

"Don't *think*, Paula, just do it— and by the way, this call is not free. I want some big bucks girl," Otis said just before he hung up… and he meant it.

"Like hell I will, you old fart! You're no use to me now!" Paula said, pulling back her blanket and making a beeline to the bathroom. She had to get ready for work.

"Edie, honey, after we eat breakfast, I want you to bring that disc recorder you bought me for my birthday. You'll find it in the lower left hand drawer of my desk," Otis said being the betting sort when it came to human nature and figuring Paula would go back on her word and kill Toby like she did Beanie.

His plan was to record his dying declaration and upon his death have Edie hand carry it to the Governor. Otis and the governor were childhood friends and, in fact, the governor had been the best man at his wedding. There was nothing they didn't know about each other—until now.

43

Maggie sat in the back seat of her chauffeur-driven Crown Vic listening intently on her cell as Paula told her about the conversation with Otis. She knew Roth was getting close and somehow had managed to get to Otis. Call it intuition, but Paula didn't even have to mention his name, she just knew it.

"Paula, I'm almost at work now. I'll see what I have on my work calendar, and if I can get away, I'll drive down to Zanesville and talk with Otis and Becky, and if possible with Roth. Ok?" Maggie closed her cell and removed Paula from her mind. She needed to think things through and she couldn't do it with Paula screaming that she's too beautiful to go to jail.

Roth needed to be dealt with and soon as he already knew too much. *Hmm, come to think of it, Josh does too. Too bad though, both suffer from the same affliction—honesty. They have this incorruptible code of honor, so endearing, yet so dangerous.* Paula had suggested killing Roth, but Otis told her no, which at the time was good advice. Although corrupt, Otis was still loyal to his men, but that was ok, she reasoned as she walked into her office. Otis' days were numbered anyway and, once done; Roth and Joshua would be easier marks.

April felt anxious as she crossed the state line into South Carolina. She couldn't believe it but she missed Toby and needed to get to work investing Uncle Leo's ill-gotten gains so she could retire.

Aunt Dorota would have to adjust to a new assisted living condo without April's supervision and that was just the way it was—she paid a pretty penny for it but it had everything Dorota would need and more. She had placed Dorota mobile home with a real estate agent before leaving and the property sold two days later. That money she placed in Dorota's bank account. She also had Dorota add her to both her checking account and savings. This way she could add money and pay Dorota's bills without her aunt worrying about too much.

Lost in thought, April smiled as she pulled off the interstate for gas. She was thinking of her sainted mother and how pleased her mother would be for her daughter's generosity toward her beloved friend. As she was filling her BMW, she noticed the dash clock. Seven hours had passed by since her pit stop in South Carolina and she had to pee badly. Another obvious thing was happening—darkness was closing fast. Across the highway she spied a large hotel sign and decided to stay the night and rest. She would get an early start in the morning—although early to April was nine, maybe ten.

She needed to rest and think. After all, she had over three million dollars in the trunk of her car, all neatly stacked in large cardboard boxes labeled glassware. Placing her Aunt Dorota in the assisted living complex gave her an idea to build one someplace quiet, maybe close to a lake or a river. She would build it and pay cash for it. Then she'd hire a staff to run it, official people with approved state papers and would retire off the income. It sounded like a good plan and she'd hire Toby as chief of security.

Speaking of Toby, she missed him and his snide remarks, but he cared for her, that she knew. She would call Toby tomorrow to check in and also find out if the package had arrived. That would make him happy. She thought turning down the bed and climbing in.

Joshua picked up his office phone it was Smitty. The attorney general had requested his presence in ten minutes then nothing—

the arrogant son of a bitch had hung up. *Maybe you have to be rude and arrogant to get anyplace in this world,* Josh thought, deciding whether to take his coffee cup with him.

His meeting with the attorney general could best be described as awkward. Fortunately, Smitty was not in the room, which he appreciated greatly. He didn't like Smitty standing at his back for fear of being knifed. Maggie's questions were odd and inappropriate, and even if he had known the answers to her questions, he wouldn't have told her. She was obviously scared, that much he knew. Her face was paler than usual, her big blue eyes redas if she had been crying, and she was trembling not from cold, but from fear.

Joshua sat quietly sipping his coffee, watching her closely as she tapped her pen on the back of her left hand as she thought of more inane questions to ask. *She's fishing for something. Maybe she knows!* Josh thought. *Somehow, Maggie found out about what we know. What if someone told her that Roth was on to her—and the others as well? She'll probably take me off this case, or maybe she's going to set Roth and me up for a big fall or worse.*

"Joshua, tell me about this task force?" she asked.

"I don't understand the question, ma'am, what about the task force?" Josh replied, answering a question with a question.

"What's its focus and make up?" Maggie asked, smiling like the big fat cat that ate the fucking canary.

"Oh, I see!" Joshua replied, sitting up in his chair and taking a big deep breath. He was getting ready to tell big fat lies to a dirty lying bitch. "Like I said in my report, Roth is convinced the Russian Mafia is involved somehow. Not with the murders of Bean, Hill and Kaczynski, but with supplying cocaine and heroin into the Zanesville economy. He wants to find out who the big buyer is because whoever that individual is he murdered Officer Bean, according to Roth.

"He has borrowed two out-of-town agents, one from Cleveland the other from Cincinnati, plus the NYPD is helping him," Josh said, taking the last gulp of his cold coffee.

"Did Otis approve all this?" Maggie asked calmly.

"Yeah, I guess so, he's the sheriff," Joshua said, his voice flat and direct.

"I only ask because Otis never asked for your services in writing. Why do you suppose he did that, Josh?" Maggie said her voice cold and calculating, her eyes staring directly into his, looking for the slightest hint of a lie.

"I don't have the foggiest why Otis didn't notify you," Joshua replied. "...Unless Otis was afraid that by notifying you it would jeopardize Roth's task force."

"Hmm...could be!" Maggie replied. "Or maybe Otis doesn't have any idea what's going on because Roth didn't tell him."

"What would make you believe that about Roth, ma'am?" Joshua said, still playing naïve.

"Josh, maybe you're letting your misplaced loyalty to Roth cloud your judgment. It's a known fact that Roth sleeps with prostitutes and other women of, shall I say, questionable morality. Hell, Joshua, last year he dressed a young hooker up as some sort of psyche and took her to a crime scene along with the man he suspected of killing his wife and somehow she got him to confess. Now I ask you, what kind of police work is that?"

Josh began to laugh, causing the attorney general to smile. "I'd say, ma'am, there are no rules when it comes to killers and that was a masterful job of bluffing on Roth's part..."

"Surely, Josh, you see what I'm saying. Roth is nothing but a dinosaur, maybe disaster is a better word. He should be pensioned off, for Christ sakes."

"*I bet you'd like that bitch!* Joshua thought, saying nothing further. "Is that it, ma'am?" Joshua asked, picking up his coffee cup.

"One other question, Josh?" she asked looking up at him.

"Yes, ma'am!"

"When is your next visit to Zanesville?" she asked.

"Today!" Joshua replied, turning his back to her and starting to walk out.

"Good, I want to go with you," Maggie said, standing up as if getting prepared for a fight.

"Ok, ma'am, my car or yours?" Joshua asked without the slightest hint of giving anything away.

"We'll take my car," she said, smiling at Joshua.

"Will I be driving or is your chauffer driving?" Joshua asked, holding on to the doorknob.

"My chauffer will drive," Maggie said in a flat and authoritative voice.

"Very well, I'll leave my driving gloves in the office then," Joshua replied.

As he walked to his office, Joshua made a quick call to Roth. He did as instructed—left a message hoping Roth would hear it before they got there—

"Damn it!" Roth yelled to no one. "That sly, conniving, meddling bitch doesn't miss a trick. Or did Otis sell me out?"

A quick glance at his watch told him he had maybe ninety minutes before the attorney general and Joshua arrived. No time for a dog and pony show but enough to drive over and have a *come to Jesus* talk with Otis. Roth pulled his cruiser into Otis' driveway, yet to be shoveled free of ice and snow. As he turned off the ignition, a strange sense of foreboding came over him. He didn't know why, but he sensed danger.

He opened the car door and despite the icy steps took them two at a time. He ignored the doorbell and instead hammered on the door, calling for Edie. In frantic desperation, he tried the door handle putting all his body weight into it and pushed. The door was not locked.

Frantic he called out to Edie.

"In here, Toby! Hurry!"

Roth followed the voice. He wasn't expecting what he saw. Otis was stretched out flat on the sofa bleeding from his mouth, a strange smell permeating the room. Roth recognized the smell at once it was death.

He looked down at Edie who was kneeling by Otis' side and wiping the blood away with an old kitchen towel, crying, obviously scared.

Roth stepped back and pulled out his cell and called 911, telling the dispatcher to send an ambulance and to alert ER that a great officer was down and in peril.

Edie reached up and took Roth by his hand and kissed it.

"Toby, thank you for that call," she said as she broke down, continuing to attend her husband knowing that he would be dead soon.

"Edie, listen to me. I know this is a bad time to be asking but can you tell me if Otis called anybody after I left last night?" Roth asked.

"No, Toby, he didn't! He just turned out the light and went to sleep. I think he was drunk as he kept saying, excuse my language, 'Fuck'em all! Toby will get the bitches.' He said that over and over until he went to sleep."

Suddenly, the house was surrounded with an explosion of sirens followed by Sheriff Deputies followed closely by the EMTs who pounded on the door and simply burst into the house announcing their presence with a collapsible gurney.

Roth reached down and gently took Edith by the hand and helped to her feet. Stepping back out of the way, they watched helplessly as the young medics demonstrated their oft-practiced life saving routine, racing against time—trying to save an old and valiant civil servant.

"Edie, have you called Tabby and Milo?" Roth asked, his voice gentle and soft and yet at the same time reassuring.

"No, I just can't bring myself to do it," Edie said, trying to hold back her tears in front of the others.

"Get me their numbers, I'll call the kids and let them know what's happening here while you stay with Otis."

Edie turned away and walked back into the kitchen. She stopped and stared at the old corkboard that had hung next to phone for thirty years. She spotted the pink sticky note pinned with both her daughter's names and phone numbers. The paper was so old that over the years, it had become faded and brittle but the writing was still visible.

She returned to Toby and handed him the slip of paper, her attention focused on the EMTs working on Otis, preparing him for transport. Toby merely took the paper from her trembling hand and he neither spoke nor acknowledged her presence in any way. Toby was engaged with a young, black sheriff's deputy who was standing at attention facing Toby as Roth barked out orders to him.

"You will stay with Edith as long as she needs you. You will assist her in anything she needs or wants. You understand me, Brown?"

"Yes, sir! I'm to stay with Mrs. Swanson until we know for sure one way or the other. I will do my best, sir," Brown replied, his voice deep and boastful.

"You damn well better!" Roth barked as he turned, leaving the young deputy and Edith alone.

"He has a good heart, deputy, and he means well," Edith said, patting Deputy Brown on his upper arm comforting him.

"Yes, ma'am, I understand the sheriff and he are good friends and Detective Roth is very concerned," the young deputy said, turning away from Edie and looking around to see if there was anything he could do to help.

Roth walked out the kitchen door into the crisp cold air. He was perspiring and the cold wind quickly cooled his skin but the nausea remained. He felt the need to vomit as the smell of cancer once learned is never forgotten. He thought these things remembering his dad, wife, and now Otis.

He walked slowly towards the garage he and Otis had built so many years ago, remembering how they had laughed at the dumb mistakes and the silly fights they got into. Edie was pregnant with

Tabatha then and she would hear them fighting and bring out two beers, chips and ham sandwiches and tell them to behave.

He felt the tears as he blinked rapidly trying to make them go away as big boys don't cry. Roth heard the siren of the ambulance followed closely by sirens of the cruisers and found the sounds of the sirens to be distinctly different. Each siren had its own peculiar sound. The ambulance siren was weak compared to the cruisers, whose sirens were blaring and nerve jarring.

He walked back into the house and locked the kitchen door, then made his way down the hall towards the front door. Stopping at the foot of the stairs he yelled, "Hello, anyone there?"

There was no response. Satisfied, Roth opened the front door and was greeted by a blast of arctic air whipped around by a strong south wind. The cold momentarily caught him off guard and stole his breath. The sun was noon high and glared down upon the frozen snow, causing the millions of crystallized starbursts to reflect so brightly that he was forced to squint his eyes as he descended the icy front steps that led back to his cruiser.

Roth opened the car door searching his jacket pocket for his car keys. He spied his sunglasses lying on the dash. He was torn between meeting Joshua and Maggie and going to the hospital. As he put on his sunglasses and turned the ignition key, his cell rang. He flipped open his cell expecting bad news.

"Hello, Roth?"

"Hello, sweetie, you missing me?"

"Like a truck load of dead babies!" Roth replied his voice somber at best.

"Now that was cold and hateful. Nobody deserves to be talked to like that you pompous ass."

"I'm sorry, sweetheart, truly I' am," Roth said, his voice cracking.

"Honey, what is it? What's going on?" April's voice was soft and reassuring.

"I'm sitting in Otis' driveway. The ambulance just left and I have Joshua from the Ohio's Criminal Investigation Bureau coming here with his boss the attorney general who figures prominently in my murder investigation, and I have to assume she knows I'm on to her. Other than that, that's about it. Oh, along with a few crooked judges and other well-placed and heeled politicians with Otis being one of them. I'm not sure, honey, but I think Otis has compromised my on-going investigation which your uncle helped finance. Yeah, I think that's about it—"

"Ok, I'm beginning to understand, Toby. You're torn apart by loyalty to an old friend who may or may not have ratted you out to Maggie Henderson, and if Otis did then your investigation would be compromised, placing you in mortal danger. By the way, honey, I happen to know that Maggie is as crooked as a dog's hind leg," April said her voice betraying her emotions.

"Yeah, I know— I'm going to take her down as well as all the others," Roth said, his voice now gentle and warm towards her, making her realize that he really did care for her.

"Toby, honey, you don't understand, Maggie Henderson is a bitch and she's ruthless, plus she has connections. And if you're not careful you could buy the farm," April said, her voice sounding anxious.

"Where are you?"

"I'm about two hours from home!"

"Good…when you get there, call me. I have a couple of things to show you," Roth said.

Roth sat quietly listening to the cold wind as it swirled around the car causing it to rock from side to side. He found it odd that April would know so much about Maggie and her connections. However, he knew April made it her business to know her clients personally and obviously, Maggie was or had been a client of April. He needed to come up with a plan to keep Maggie away from him and his people.

Then it came to him in a sudden burst of genius—Dixie. He would call Dixie and have her meet him at the hospital then he would call Joshua in route and let him know what was going on with Otis. Once Maggie and Joshua showed up at the hospital, he'd have Dixie start questioning Maggie about drug trafficking and criminal activity among political figures in the state and local government, maybe even have Dixie drop a couple of names. That would keep Maggie temporarily at arm's length and buy him time to start pressing Paula Tidwell.

As he put his cruiser into reverse, another idea occurred to him. He would pull Rossi and Sawicki off the Russian mafia investigation and have them start pressing Paula. The plan was simple—he'd have them spook Paula into selling her drugs to Rossi and Sawicki.

44

Ok I'll tell her! That was Roth, ma'am— Otis has been rushed to Good Samaritan. He's not expected to make it," Josh said in a calculated, unhurried voice best described as cool and somber.

"That's a pity!" Maggie looked out the rear side window, her lying breath fogging up the window.

"Yes, ma'am, it is," Joshua said, looking out his window at the barren frozen fields that would be blessed with corn and wheat come summer.

"Will Roth be at the hospital?" Maggie asked guardedly.

"Yes, ma'am!" Joshua replied, turning his attention once again to his window view.

"Good, enough, we go and pay our respects to Otis and his family," she said, turning away with a sardonic smile on her lips.

Roth sat apart from the others as he watched the waiting room beginning to fill with family and friends. He could see the corridor lined with Sheriff Deputies who stood silently at parade rest waiting and wondering who would be appointed acting sheriff when Otis passed to greener pastures.

Roth sat with his arms across his chest, his head bowed as if he were praying. However, he wasn't praying, he was thinking. His thoughts were deep and dark as he tried to decipher what Otis meant when he said, "Roth will get the bitches." Up to then he had thought there was only one female suspect. Otis implied there were more.

Roth looked at his watch again. He figured fifteen maybe twenty minutes at most until Maggie and Joshua arrived. Agitated he began tapping his foot and rubbing his thumb and index finger together as if he were keeping time with some imaginary music playing in his head. He was hoping Dixie would arrive before the Attorney General as he needed five uninterrupted minutes with her to level the field.

His mind turned to April. He was missing her and at the same time wondering how she would react when he began asking her questions about the videodiscs, especially the one with her and Paula, and if she knew the person who did the taping.

Where in the hell was Dixie? He needed her now and he was running out of precious time.

"Hello Toby!"

"You're late, Dixie!"

"Sorry, but I couldn't find a place to park. What's going on? There are police cars everywhere," Dixie said.

"It's Otis, he's dying," Roth responded as he led her gently toward the alcove that hid the elevators from sight.

"Ah, you called to give me the story? Wow!" Dixie gushed, kissing him on the cheek.

"Not exactly, sweetie" Roth said, grabbing her wrists and pulling her towards him.

"Dixie, I don't have much time— I need you to take on the Attorney General… I want you to accuse her of using her office for personal gain in protecting drug traffickers. I want a catfight, Dixie. I want you to mention Becky Colt…and especially whiplash Criminal Investigator Tim Hill as being her enforcer…and whatever else you can think of—"

"Why? What's happening? Are you in danger?" she said quizzically.

"Dixie, I have a serious hunch the moment Otis dies, my life and Joshua's won't be worth much. I'm making some very important people very nervous and I need to buy myself time. I now think this drug ring that has infiltrated our city is controlled by a woman who has her hooks into our Attorney General and Assistant Prosecuting Attorney—"

"You mean…Becky Colt?" Dixie said.

"Yes, and let's not forget those judges we saw on the videodisc and of course the state senator and his wife who has had relations with your friend the preacher lady and god only knows who else. I also have a hunch the preacher's wife you've been looking for is also involved."

"Are you sure about all of this, Toby?" Dixie said, seeing not fear in his eyes but contempt.

"All except for the other woman," he replied without missing a beat.

Roth was about to say more but was cut short by the sound of the bell announcing the arrival of an elevator.

He didn't have to look, Roth knew intuitively who it was going to be and was hoping his plan of going on the offense would keep Maggie pinned down so tight she couldn't be much help to the other two…Paula and Lady X.

"She's here Dixie. Do your thing, sweetie!" Roth whispered and kissed her lightly on the lips.

45

Rossi rolled over and looked at the wall clock, 8:00 a.m. She smiled as she listened to Paul singing in the shower and felt abnormally womanly after last night's marathon love-making. Happy with herself, she began doing leg lifts and stomach crunches on the bed, something she had been doing since her Army days. When finished with those exercises, she would do pushups, maybe a hundred; maybe two hundred, depending on her mood then take a shower, eat breakfast, and go to work.

It had been four days since Paul had talked with the Russians and still no word. Obviously, the Russian's weren't interested in doing business. That didn't matter much as Roth had called and had another job for them, and this assignment would be a cakewalk. *Spook some fucking doctor bitch into selling the crew some drugs. Wow, Roth, how fucking exciting is that, huh?* She thought assuming the position for push-ups.

Traffic was exceptionally slow as Paula navigated her way through the morning rush hour mess. Each mile she traveled only increased her agitation towards Maggie's nonchalant attitude towards Roth. *Trouble is brewing; the kind that could not be bought off,* Paula thought as she passed some dumb ass on the right and flipped him off as she made her turn that would take her to the university. *Fuck Otis!* She thought, turning on her blinker and making the left turn into the staff-parking garage. She would kill Roth despite Otis' threats. *Maggie's "don't bother me bitch attitude" would end this bullshit once and for all,* she thought. Paula locked her SUV and proceeded to walk down the same ramp she drove up on, choosing to ignore the steps altogether as they smelled of urine and tobacco. She had a class at ten, a lab at noon. And would then be done for the day. As she walked towards her office a cold mist began falling, catching her without an umbrella.

Paula was thinking of various ways to kill Roth with each step she took towards her office. She ruled out a gun as too noisy. She even thought of hiring an assassin but ruled that out as to costly and dangerous as it set her up for blackmail. Clearly more thought was needed on the subject.

"Hello, Toby—longtime no see," Maggie said, extending her hand to Roth.

"Yeah, it's been a while," Roth said, taking her hand in his like he did many years ago when they were in love.

"How's Otis doing?" Maggie asked.

"Holding his own right now," Roth replied.

"I came to pay my respects to Otis and his family…and to discuss a couple of things with you and Joshua," Maggie said, taking Roth by his arm and leading him out into the corridor lined with sheriff's deputies and the local vultures that comprised the county and city officials.

Otis had little respect for most of them. Although he liked the County Safety Director, Bart Collins, old' Bart didn't always agree with Otis about some things. But when Otis was in budget trouble Bart would always come to his rescue, so it was sort of symbiotic. He liked Betty Monroe, one of the county commissioners. She was feisty and looked out for the county as if she owned it. Plus, she took no shit from anybody and Otis respected that. The two others he could do without.

As Maggie passed by each deputy as she headed towards Otis' room, they would come to attention in silence and then return to parade-rest. It was a sign of respect for the Attorney General and the great state of Ohio. Roth knew the drill from years past and wondered if sheriff deputies would show the same respect to Maggie if they knew what he knew about their Attorney General.

Joshua followed behind and watched closely, sensing something was about to happen. He wasn't exactly sure what it might be but knew enough about Roth after these several weeks of working with him that the old boy was nobody's fool. Another thing he just figured out—Roth and the attorney general had been lovers. He could see it in their eyes, the way they looked at each other and the way Roth took her hand. It was beginning to make sense why every time he mentioned Roth's name she would smile.

Dixie watched and waited, looking for her opportunity to strike out at the bitch. Alicia had told her one morning when they were in bed about the great Maggie Henderson, and what a two-faced evil bitch she really was. Nothing much had changed.

April pulled her BMW into her custom-built garage and turned off the ignition. She grabbed her cell phone and handbag, and opened the car door. She would come back later and get her clothes, and of course the money. As a general rule, she was both an opportunist and optimist. However, for the last hundred miles, a feeling of sadness had come over her, like a dream with wide-open eyes. The last time she had this strange feeling was when her mother died and immediately April's thoughts turned to Aunt Dorota. Before the elevator door slid open, she was calling Dorota. *Please, pretty please, pick up sweetie,* she mumbled as she stepped out of the elevator and walked down the hall towards the condo's front door.

"Hello..." came the sleepy voice of her mother's dearest friend.

"Hi, Aunt Dorota— It's April, sweetie. I called just to let you know that I'm home," April said.

"Oh, thank you for making this old lady happy. I enjoyed your visit and finding this home for me. I'm really enjoying myself," Dorota said. She coughed into the phone, causing April to jerk the handset away from her ear.

"Oh, sweetheart, it was a pleasure… I'll be talking to you soon. Love you!"

Good, it wasn't Dorota, she thought, setting her handbag and phone on the kitchen counter. As she scurried to the bathroom, she wondered who it could be.

Roth stood beside Edie, looking somber and protective. They watched as Maggie took Otis by the hand and nodded her head, supposedly in prayer.

Joshua stood at the foot of the bed watching his boss being a hypocrite, still wondering what Roth had up his sleeve. Whatever it was, it had better occur soon as time was running out for him. He figured Maggie would use the old divide and conquer method of stopping the investigation. She would simply downgrade him or exile the old warrior to some remote part of the state, perhaps even remove him from the state's employment. Disposing of Roth the old-fashioned way would be simple—she would simply discredit him, making him out as an incompetent nincompoop and forcing him to retire. Joshua chuckled over the thought.

Maggie was no match for Roth, plus he had the proof against her and the others, so what could she really do? Joshua never saw it coming but suspected Roth had a hand in the attack. He had noticed the blonde when he stepped off the elevator and the press-pass hanging around her neck, obviously the way Roth courted her presence gave her immediate credence. Joshua smiled as he watched the beautiful blonde start the verbal attack with accusations of infidelity, breach of faith, selling her office for political favors, and having drug-induced orgies. In truth, the attack was a masterstroke worthy of Roth's Hall of Fame. He would keep the attorney general so mired in political muckraking that everything she said and did would be scrutinized by the press. Joshua didn't know much when it came to reporters. He had always been very direct and honest with the press, but one thing he had learned over time was that reporters were like sharks at the hint of blood and did not hesitate to attack. The little blonde spitfire had just thrown raw bloody meat into the bay.

Roth watched the fireworks from the safety of Otis' bedside. Confused, Edie looked up at Toby, not understanding what had just happened. Toby knelt down beside her and took both her hands in his.

"Edie, I don't have much time to explain, but please trust me. I want you to call your friend the Governor, tell him about Otis, and ask him to come. When the Governor arrives, give him the disc that Otis made. Then give him my phone number and ask him to call me. He will call me, Edie, if you tell him to do that. I'm in danger, Edie, and Otis knows it and that's why he's protecting me."

Edie squeezed his hand and gently kissed his fingers, nodding her head as tears began to stream, knowing it was to be one last hurrah for her beloved Otis.

46

Paula decided to cancel her classes. The local news had pre-empted all programming, telling the citizens what they already knew—that the weather had turned to shit. Local schools and business were closing and freeways were jammed because of accidents, and since the mayor had laid off twenty-five police officers and firemen this past fall, no one in the protect and serve profession was rushing out to protect and serve distressed citizens who didn't have enough common sense to stay home.

With extra time on her hands, Paula called Heather to tell her she would be over later and spend the night. She really didn't want to drive home only to sit in an empty house. Mike had not taken her request for a divorce well and had moved out the next day. Except for Heather, she was all alone in the world.

Placing two apple-cinnamon tea bags in a 1500ml glass beaker, she added water and carefully placed the beaker over the Bunsen burner. She adjusted the flame, removing as much orange from it as possible. Looking out the window she saw that the mist she had walked through was now a freezing sleet. She took her desk chair, sat down, and tilted the chair back. Her thoughts turned to Roth and she wondered how best to dispose of him realistically, but really she would do whatever it took. She knew it would have to be some sort of poison, something difficult if not impossible for the coroner to detect. She also thought of the possibility of killing Maggie, and

219

wondered how she could do it. Of course, Roth would undoubtedly be her ultimate target, and maybe even Joshua. Maggie had warned her about Josh and advised her to stay clear of him.

Seeing the beaker beginning to boil, Paula stood up from her desk and carefully placed a small ruler in the book to mark the page she had been reading. She reached across the countertop and grabbed a set of lab pliers. She gently placed them around the long contoured neck of the beaker and poured the freshly brewed tea into her mug. She was ready now for some serious maniacal thinking.

She knew herself well enough to know that she could never kill someone face to face with a knife or gun. Like the Venetian Countess Lucricia Borgia, Paula knew that poisons were her weapons of choice. She reasoned that conventional poisons would not work on Rothas he was too well known and the coroner would easily detect any obvious poison. Another thing Paula was sure about was that she would need a scapegoat, someone the police would immediately suspect, and that left her with three people, Heather and Maggie were the first two choices and then the rich, prissy bitch that also happened to be Maggie's personal leg-lapper.

Heather would undoubtedly be the most logical choiceas she was already wanted by the police for murdering her husband. Maggie would also suffice as a prime scapegoat, but how could she get the police to suspect their attorney general of murdering one of their own? However, if she somehow managed to do that, the media would be in a feeding frenzy and she could easily make her escape to Argentina. As for the pretty little dark-haired bitch, her death wouldn't raise so much as an eyebrow on the scale of humanity. She took another sip of tea and returned to her book of exotic poisons.

"Toby, just who in the hell was that little bitch?" Maggie yelled as she looked at him through tear-stained eyes.

"Her name is Cathy Dixon, a local news reporter." Roth pulled his chair around his desk, offered it to Maggie and at the same time nodded to Joshua to close his office door.

"Tell me, Toby, if you can, what did I do to her to deserve that attack?" Maggie said, unbuttoning her coat before taking the offered chair.

"Ma'am, Dixie obviously viewed you as threat to her man, Roth here," Joshua interjected as he held the chair for Maggie so his boss had time to remove his jacket and take a chair.

Sensing something dramatic was about to unfold, Joshua stepped back into the shadows and leaned his massive frame against the wall. He waited for Roth to commence interrogating Maggie, putting her on the defensive until she broke down.

"Is Joshua correct, Toby? Do you and this little reporter have a thing going on?" Maggie asked, a jealous snicker appearing on her face.

"Now, Maggie, I'm not one to kiss and tell!" Roth replied, opening up his desk drawer and pulling out a large envelope.

"So, Joshua is correct—you're fucking that little bitch and intentionally sicked her on me! Jesus, Toby, I've heard of carrying a grudge, but never like this," Maggie yelled, picking a half filled coffee cup off the desk and throwing it at him. It missed him by inches.

Joshua watched and smiled, listening to Maggie and Roth and thinking of a king cobra and mongoose fight he had once witnessed years ago in Thailand: The king cobra stood up, flaring its iconic hood and hissing, giving fair warning to the lowly mongoose that he was about to die. The cobra struck and missed. It retreated, while the mongoose circled behind the mighty cobra. The mongoose waited and waited and when the opportunity presented itself the mongoose attacked the cobra from behind, biting and killing it. Joshua imagined Roth as the lowly mongoose and knew when betting on a cobra-mongoose fight the smart money was on the mongoose.

"Why am I in your office, Toby? And where is my driver?" Maggie asked.

"We ditched your driver. He has absolutely no idea where you are," Roth, poured out the contents of the envelope onto his desk.

"What's that stuff?" Maggie asked, pointing to the pile of videodiscs.

"Evidence, Maggie!" Roth replied, giving a contemptuous smile.

"Evidence—against whom?" she asked, crossing her legs and showing a lot of thigh.

"Against you— Who else?" Roth replied. Maggie swallowed hard. "Yes, Maggie, you. I've known of Doctor Paula Tidwell for some time, and I also know she killed Deputy Bean. That leaves only one woman, and I want that name," Roth said, opening the plastic case and removing the DVD disc that would end her career and send her to prison.

"You're bluffing!" Maggie hissed, staring into Roth's eyes but finding no compassion.

Roth did not respond. He simply held the disc up and allowed Joshua to take it from his hand.

"Maggie…while Joshua loads the disc, let me explain a few things that led us to you. It started with the murder of Mr. Leopold Kaczynski, the Criminal Investigator who was in your employ. The triggerman? Tim Hill. He killed poor Mr. Kaczynski. Now, I would like to take the credit for discovering that little detail, but Joshua discovered it. Three stars to Joshua!" Roth said, nodding to Joshua who stood at the ready, waiting for Roth to signal the start of the disc. "…So then came the logical question. Do you know what that question was, Maggie?" Roth asked, not waiting for a reply. "It is why. What caused the state drug czar to kill a supposedly peaceful Polish immigrant? Well, that one little question, Maggie, resulted in more and more questions. Each question answered led us to you, Maggie Hennessey.

"Look at the ink boards on the wall over there, Maggie." Roth pointed to the post ups. "See where Joshua and I started asking each other the big question?" Joshua stepped away from the video machine and pointed to the first question. It read simply, 'WHY?' Now, Maggie, here comes the coupe de gras…"

Roth turned to Joshua and nodded his head. Joshua aimed the remote and pressed PLAY, lighting the small screen. *Its show time,* Joshua thought as he walked towards the office door. He heard the sound of footsteps coming up the stairwell and guessed it was Maggie's driver. Odds were he was not happy and Joshua quickly turned off the overhead light and locked the door, hoping the driver didn't notice.

47

Sawicki pulled the Lincoln Town car into Paula Tidwell's driveway. The house was dark. He looked at his watch, 4:45. He got out and walked up to the front door, remembering with every step what Rossi had taught him. Remember to speak in broken English—chances are she won't know Polish from Russian anyway. Be sure the doctor bitch can see your gun as that will tell her you're serious, and tell her a friend from Russia told you that she was in the wholesale business and that you're here to buy goods.

Sawicki remembered looking at Rossi as he waited for her to explain the term, wholesale business. When she didn't say anything more, he had mumbled in broken English, "Wholesale business."

He remembered her looking at him and then she had burst into high-pitched laughter. He had never heard Rossi laugh before. The best way to describe it was "bawdy," which surprised him somewhat as when Sam was not on duty she always gave the appearance of refinement and gentleness, nothing that would indicate she was an undercover narcotics officer.

Sawicki pressed the doorbell and heard the chimes echoing throughout the house. He pressed the doorbell again and stuck his hand into his jacket pocket pulling out a neatly folded napkin with a poorly constructed hand written note, which Rossi had written. The note was simple, and direct, "You sell drugs. We buy drugs. All you have if price ok…" The note was direct and short, closing with a telephone number. When it was obvious to him that no one was home, he stuffed the napkin gently into the mailbox and walked quickly back to the warmth of his car. *Now what?* he thought, putting the big Lincoln in reverse and backing out of the driveway.

* * *

Edie gently let go of Otis' hand for fear of waking him. The doctors said he was stable now and sleep would do him good but they weren't optimistic about his chances. The cancer had spread since his last x-ray and now ever so slowly was destroying his lung cells, decreasing the odds with each passing hour. According to the local news, the sheriff had been rushed to the hospital and was in critical condition. They never said why—however, it must be very serious as the state attorney general stopped by to give her well wishes and a catfight broke out between a local news reporter and the attorney general, undoubtedly staged by Roth. She didn't know what to think about him leaving, especially when things were getting interesting.

Edie took Milo by her hand and whispered she was going to the restroom. Milo smiled and nodded, saying nothing and choking back her tears. Tabby slid into her momma's chair, taking quick advantage of the abdication. She held her daddy's hand—all the while taking comfort in the fact that she had a daddy for a little while longer.

Edie walked into the women's restroom and turned on the light. The room burst forth in an array of soft purples, blues and silvers with black floor tile. She thought the room was quite lovely considering it was only a restroom. She placed her purse on the solid green granite counter top and pulled out her lipstick and makeup, having left the house in such a hurry she hadn't time to apply it. As she looked into the mirror, the harsh fluorescent light revealed her deep facial wrinkles caused from years of tobacco addiction. Her eyes were red surrounded by deep, dark circles that hung like heavy bags under her eyes. *I look a fright and Otis must not see me like this*, she thought as she started to apply her foundation.

As Edie worked to make herself presentable, she remembered Toby asking her to call the Governor and tell Michael to come to Zanesville. Finished with her make up, she placed her mascara in her purse and retrieved her phone and glasses. She placed the small bifocals on her face and carefully scrolled down the menu looking for Marjorie, the Governor's wife. She didn't have Michael's office number, only his home phone. Gently, she pressed the little green button and waited, counting each ring. With each passing second, more precious time was wasted that otherwise could be spent with Otis.

48

Paula sat on the cold leather sofa listening intently to the breaking story on the local news channel. The Governor had relieved the State Attorney General from office pending a full-scale investigation for malfeasance and obstruction of justice. However, the TV reporter began describing Maggie's sexcapades in the most intimate details.

Fucking Roth! Paula thought. *He actually lured Maggie into a trap...* She didn't know what Roth had used as bait, but whatever it was it had to have been too irresistible for Maggie to resist. Panic began to envelop her and she wanted to run, but where?

Heather appeared from the kitchen holding two plates of spaghetti. She handed Paula one plate along with a paper towel. Paula smiled, thanking her as she took the dish and placed it on the coffee table. Heather returned Paula's soft smile and turned back to the kitchen to fetch the ice tea. *How beautiful she is,* Paula thought when an idea occurred to her. *Why not use Heather to kill Roth?* According to Maggie, Roth had a weakness for prostitutes, and Heather definitely qualified as bait.

Sawicki entered Rossi's apartment and immediately sensed something wasn't right. The television wasn't on a prearranged signal between them, giving warning that something was wrong. He pulled his weapon and took off the safety. Using the two-hand grip, he proceeded slowly into the front room confirming what he already knew and began breathing a little easier as he walked the hall to the bedroom. The bed was neatly made, something Rossi seldom did. He returned to the front room and glanced across the hall into the kitchen and saw a note leaning against the sugar bowl.

Resetting the safety, he holstered his weapon and flipped on the kitchen light. The note simply told him that she had been called back to Cincinnati to testify and would he notify Roth, and that she would be back soon. He smiled, tossing the note back onto the table. He turned off the light, walked out of the apartment, and locked the door.

He flipped open his phone and dialed Roth only to be greeted by an out of service message. *Shit, nothing's going right,* he muttered, deciding to try later. He sat in the car trying to decide what to do next. He figured as a deputy sheriff, his loyalty was to Otis and the other deputies. He had learned in his short tenure that loyalty was a very precious commodity among the sheriff's department as they were so few. He decided to visit Otis and pay his respects to the old man who had hired him, that is of course if the old boy was still alive.

April slammed the phone back into its cradle, cursing Roth for not taking her calls. He knew she would be home soon, and he told her to call him when she got in. But the son-of- a-bitch wouldn't return her calls. Still cursing, she walked into her bathroom, deciding to take a bath and cool down. Using a long stick match, she started lighting all her candles, flooding the bathroom with soft, flickering firelight. She turned on the faucet, adjusted the water temperature, and poured her favorite bath salts into the water. She turned on the twelve water jets that would soon massage her tensions away and gently lowered herself into the tub. She reached forward grabbing her oatmeal soap and bath sponge and began to bathe, oblivious to the drama that would soon envelop her, forcing her to make a life changing decision.

Becky Colt sat in her office disbelieving what was happening around her. She had overheard two law clerks discussing the arrests of two local judges that she knew intimately and a state senator along with his wife, whom she also knew in the biblical sense. When told the news of the attorney general's arrest, the young prosecuting attorney locked her office door, refusing to answer her phone. Panic had overwhelmed her. She needed to think, and just as she did when she was a little girl, Becky kicked off her shoes, climbed onto the large over stuffed sofa, neatly tucked her legs under her small body, and inserted her thumb into her mouth, her index finger slowly wrapping itself into her hair.

Despite her bluster, her money and beauty Becky was nothing but a female sex addict. Her shrink had called it a histrionic personality disorder and in layman's terms, it meant she used her body and beauty to enhance her sex appeal, gaining the attention of men or women in order to bolster her self-esteem and gain self-worth by surrounding herself with the rich and influential.

She wasn't a bad person, she reasoned. So what if she liked sex and people with money and power. That wasn't a crime, was it?

The afternoon sun was beginning to cast long shadows across her desk, throwing bizarre silhouettes on the wall. She sat motionless enjoying her thumb and wondering why nobody had come to arrest her. Then it dawned on her. The others, except for Nancy and the senator's wife, were all elected officials. She was just a county employee like Roth. What was the worst that could happen to her? Being fired? Big deal! *Unless they ask me to testify as a material witness,* she thought. Then her only recourse would be to take the fifth. *Big Fucking' Deal,* she thought, *and Roth probably knows that and that's why he hasn't arrested me...*

Somewhere in the distance, she became aware of someone knocking on her office door.

"Who is it?" Becky called out, figuring it was someone from the janitorial staff.

"It's Doctor Paula Tidwell; I need to speak with you!"

49

Paula sat at her kitchen table reading a textbook on poisons. The plan was to kill Roth and Joshua using Heather as bait. Otis was out of the way and Maggie under house arrest, but still she was reluctant to call April to ask for permission to kill Roth. April had been slowly seducing him into joining her organization. Poor Roth didn't even suspect the woman he was screwing was actually the head of the largest drug ring in the state.

She picked up her pencil and began to write on an envelope, ignoring the loud whistling of her favorite teakettle. She had narrowed the poisons down to three. However, her immediate concern was in what form the poison would be administered. Perhaps homemade fudge would work to mask the bitterness of the leaves of the foxglove plant. The body would probably begin to react in twenty minutes, maybe a bit longer and, being forceful and determined men, Roth and Joshua would try and tough it out, refusing medical intervention. That refusal to take any positive action would be their undoing. Another option was the deadly Lily of the Valley. Her idea was to soak a few plants in water for a couple of days strain the water, boil it, and brew it into an extremely toxic tea. She would add some sweetener and voila! But the plants were unavailable this time of year. Therefore, that only left her favorite poison Yew, or perhaps Monkshood would be the better choice. She could easily make a salsa containing the deadly poison and—a few corn chips covered with her special salsa—it would be all over in minutes. Paula smiled at the idea and suddenly smelled the scorched teakettle.

April sat on her king size bed, gently brushing her long black tresses. Bored, she picked up the remote and pressed the on button, igniting the sensors of her wall-mounted plasma TV. She turned to a Columbus station to listen to the Five O'clock news, a decision she would come to regret. As she listened to the reporters and news anchors, April felt her stomach begin to souras she turned red from anger. "Fuck you, Roth!" she screamed at the television and threw her hairbrush across the bedroom into the heavy drapes. "I'm going to kill youas surely as god made little green apples! Toby Roth, you're a dead son-of- a-bitch. Use me like some common whore then cast aside the residue like some piece of human garbage. I don't think so, Mr. Roth," she yelled, punching Toby's pillow and asking herself the simple question, "Why, Toby, why?"

Joshua leaned back, allowing the waitress to pour his second cup of coffee.

"You know, Roth," he said, "I should be feeling elated over what we did today, but I don't. The fact of the matter is I feel sad."

"It's always this way, Josh, we get so caught up in the details of the chase, we forget the fact that the individuals we are hunting are people just like us. Except they have weaknesses that were exploited, and once exploited, they lost their individual identities and allowed themselves to be owned by someone else, who will do with them as they please. That's what happened in this case."

"You know, Roth, I don't believe I ever asked where you came up with those DVDs, and how the hell did the governor get here so fast? More to the point, why did he call you? How did he even know who you were?" Joshua took another sip of coffee.

Roth smirked and shook his head. He took a sip of his lukewarm coffee and set his cup down on the stained napkin. Leaning back, he crossed his arms, looked up at Josh, and smiled.

"Would you believe simple, dumb luck?" Roth responded.

"Hmm, how so?" Josh asked.

"Well, the news reporter who made the big scene at the hospital this morning actually should get the credit. Her name is Cathy Dixon and she and some young, beautiful intern pastor decided to locate the wife of a local minister that was murdered. The police theorize the wife killed her no good husband and fled with her lover. Dixie and this intern theorize the wife killed in self-defense. So using a house key, they crossed over the police disc and opened the backdoor of the house. Using her womanly intuition, Dixie theorized the home was devoid of love. She looked into a hutch and discovered dozens of porno discs. Two that happened to catch her attention were unmarked DVDs, so she "borrowed them" and showed them to me. Once the significance of it dawned on me, I knew they had to be confiscated. They were the ones I showed to you, Rossi and Sawicki, in part to let you know what we were up against. I recognized almost everyone except Paula Tidwell. Dixie pointed her out to me. Then I began putting all the facts together. Paula needed protection, so why not the Attorney General of Ohio, a couple of Judges, a Sheriff, a Deputy Sheriff and a Criminal Investigator named Tim Hill?"

"OK, then how does the sheriff figure into all this?" Joshua asked.

"The night before last I bought a fifth of bourbon and went over to his house. I already knew Otis was dying from cancer, so I thought I'd have an Irish wake with him while he was still alive. I know it was wrong of me, but Otis and I have been friends for thirty years, maybe longer. Anyway, we were feeling good as you can probably imagine, and Otis let it slip he was on the take from Paula. It appears Otis needed money for medical bills.

"Now, Josh, before you judge Otis too harshly, the best I can figure is that he never sold any of us out. He would just tell Paula to be careful and watch out for this or that. He never gave her names, which must have pissed her off big time.

"Anyway, after I left, he asked Edith to get his disc machine. I guessed when he told his wife to give it to the Governor that it was a full confession. I never knew this, but Otis and the Governor were childhood buddies. He was Otis' best man when he married Edith and is Tabby's godfather. So I just asked Edie to call and ask the Governor to come to Zanesville as I was in danger and Otis was trying to protect me. The rest you know."

"Sweet Jesus! I knew you had a plan when you called and asked me to bring Maggie to the hospital. However, I had absolutely no idea that Maggie was your target. I thought you were after Paula and that Assistant Prosecuting Attorney." Joshua shook his head and chuckled.

"No, I still need Becky Colt to secure a search warrant for us," Roth said.

"We do!" Josh replied, surprised at Roth once again.

"Yes, we do. Tell me, Joshua, what actual proof do we have against this Doctor Tidwell that she's dealing drugs? In the DVDs, she's certainly not using any drugs. There's no volume on the DVDs, so we don't know what is being said. We have her lying to you. You can't arrest her for that. No, Josh, we need Becky for now and can always get Paula Tidwell later. So for now let's use Miss Colt in her professional capacity and secure the warrant."

Joshua leaned back and crossed his right arm over his chest and rested his chin in the palm of his left hand. He scratched under his jaw looking at Roth.

"What?" Roth asked.

"There's more you're not telling me," Joshua said stretching out his legs under the table.

"Oh, and what would make you say that?" Roth stared back at Joshua.

"Money!" Joshua said softly. "Who is paying for all this Roth? An organization like this would require lots of money and who in this town has that type of money? No, I can't accept it. We haven't caught the money man—"

"You're correct as usual, but what makes you think it's a man?" Roth said, smiling at his dinner companion. Why couldn't it be a woman?" Over the brim of his coffee cup, Roth waited for Josh's reaction.

"Something tells me you already know who it is."

"No, Josh I really don't have foggiest idea," Roth replied.

"If you are correct, and the organization is headed by a woman, then what we have, or should I say had was an unholy trinity. One with the technical skill, one with the legal brains who could influence and direct any of the state run investigations, and last but not least a woman with money, connections and the ability to control everything without being conspicuous. Do you know someone like that?"

Roth did not reply to Josh's inquiry. He simply sat back and mimicked Joshua, crossing both arms and sticking his tongue into his cheek creating a very obvious bulge.

"Well, do you know someone like that?" Josh said again, a bit perturbed at Roth's reluctance to respond.

"No, Josh I can't say I do. However, I would travel in different circles than the person you're describing," Roth answered. He lowered his head, a signal to Josh that he was thinking.

Roth enjoyed brainstorming with Joshua. He was direct, honest with his feelings and didn't intimidate easily. Joshua would go far in life. However, at this very moment he wasn't concerned about Joshua's future. He was concerned about the third woman. He chuckled to himself; Josh had a unique way of encapsulating things: Calling the three bitches the unholy trinity, which equated to money, greed, and power—which all translated to Paula, Maggie, and Lady X.

50

April rolled over, still clutching Toby's pillow a strange yet familiar sound echoed in her sleep-filled brain. Blinking her eyes she focused on the alarm clock, which read a few minutes after eight. Hearing the sound again she rolled off the bed to answer the doorbell. A quick glance at the security camera told her that danger was not far behind the dark figure whose blond hair was blowing wildly in the cold winter wind. Against her better judgment, April pressed the buzzer and allowed the woman to enter; knowing the day's events and murder would soon be the topic of discussion.

Roth turned on his side and looked at Dixie's alarm clock, 3:00 a.m. He was chilled and had to urinate. He looked over at Dixie and discovered the reason why he was cold—Dixie had hogged the blankets. He got up answering natures call shivering uncontrollably. He made a dash back to the warmth and safety of the bed and tried to wrestle the blankets away from Dixie only to be greeted by a string of profanity. He stopped and looked down. Had she been awake and the light on, Dixie would have seen the contempt and anger on his face, usually reserved for harden criminals. He sat on the edge of the bed and got dressed, not looking back at her. A quick check of the kitchen clock told him only fifteen minutes had elapsed, and it would be a lifetime before he ever helped her or talked civil to her again. Softly, he closed the kitchen door not wanting to wake the sleeping bitch. Stepping off the back porch, he was greeted by the wind. He guessed that it was below zero and with the howling wind cold enough to burn his skin.

As he sat in his squad car, he mulled over the next move. He called to dispatch to report in and get a fix on the temperature.

"Yes detective do you want the actual temperature or just the chill factor as well" the dispatcher asked.

"Ok, dispatch, give me the good news and the bad news," Roth said.

The invisible and nameless voice chuckled. "Minus 20 as we speak, wind chill minus 41. Now that's cold!"

"Yep, cold enough for polar bears," Roth replied, chuckling as he waited for the car windows to defrost.

As Roth drove home, his thoughts were divided between Joshua's question of knowing a woman who was rich enough to front a drug ring and at the same time being inconspicuous a damn good question. He knew Josh's guess was right on the mark. The immediate front-runner would have to be Becky Colt.

She was rich and being the county's prosecuting attorney, she would automatically be above suspicion and in a position to ward off directed suspicion.

He made the turn into his neighbor's driveway and pressed the garage opener, something Roth had bought Henry a few years back. He didn't remember the occasion, but the old man did appreciate it. Now he was living in Florida for the winter and would be back in the spring. Henry had given him a key to the house and had asked him to check on things once a week.

Roth pulled the cruiser into that garage, being sure to take the garage opener with him this time. As he walked out of the garage, pressing the button that closed the massive garage door, he debated about going inside Henry's house. Shrugging his shoulders, he decided to go inside and turn up the heat.

At the back porch, he heard the sound of a racing engine and turned around to look over his shoulder. He saw a car speeding up the street and cross over into the left lane. He noticed that the car was dark, maybe black, or perhaps blue, and by the style of the car definitely foreign.

A quick twist of his wrist and the back door was open. He stood and watched the car coming closer and for some unexplainable reason, his cop instincts kicked in. Drawing his Browning 9mm he waited for what he suspected was a hit on him. As the car passed under the street lamp, he noticed the car's back window was down as was the drivers. He saw the gun emerge from the back window of the sedan first, then a gloved hand followed by an arm. He tensed, raised his weapon, and pointed it directly at the driver's side window. In an instant, the cold, crisp air of the early morning erupted into the sound of gunfire. In a blink of an eye, Roth returned fire hitting the car several times. It was all over in seconds—the car sped away.

Roth flipped open his phone and walked into Henry's house, thankful for the back porch that probably saved his life. As he turned up the heat to 65, he called dispatch, and this time the discussion wouldn't be about the weather.

Sergeant Caleb McCoy pushed against Roth's back door, twisting the doorknob so tight he bent it trying to escape the cold. Roth watched as his friend passed by him, observing that Caleb's ears and cheeks were red. He had never seen that on a black man before, and for some reason, thought it was strange that he had never noticed it before. Caleb knew where the coffee mugs were as he had been in the house many times over the years. He poured himself some hot coffee and walked over to the kitchen table that he had given Roth as a wedding present some twenty years before. He took off his insignia laden jacket that displayed all the honors he had accumulated over the past twenty-five years, and draped it on the back of the chair. He tossed two small bags on the table before taking his seat. Each bag contained bullets that were extracted from Henry's house and the back porch.

Roth reached out and grabbed the bag with only two bullets. The other bag he recognized as standard .22 caliber bullets and showed little interest in them already knowing they came from a semi-automatic pistol. However, the two bullets he held in his hand were most interesting to him. They looked to be from a Colt .38. And since Caleb found only these, two then it would be logical to conclude the bullets were fired from a big bore derringer. A *woman's weapon,* he thought.

Caleb sat back and watched Roth examine the two bullets knowing full well Toby had already figured out the bullets had been fired from a big bored derringer, and that it was the weapon of choice among prostitutes, call girls or any other woman in a dangerous vocation.

"Caleb have you ever been made a fool of by a woman?"

"Can't really say, Toby, I've been married for so long," Caleb replied.

Roth smiled at his friend and noticed that Caleb's ears and cheeks had returned to their normal color.

"I will bet you a hundred dollars that if you find any shell casings, they will be rim fire. I will also bet you another hundred the gun that fired these bullets belongs to a Doctor Mike Tidwell, who is married to a Doctor Paula Tidwell. As for these two little beauties, they belong to "Lady-X" whom I have been after for over three months. And I learned this morning the woman I thought was a non- player is, in fact, my Lady X," Roth said, throwing the bullets back down on the table.

Caleb began to laugh as he got up to pour himself another cup of coffee. "By any chance is this woman a shady lady you perhaps double crossed at some time in the past?" he said, retaking his seat.

Roth stretched his legs out straight under the table and crossed his arms. He looked at Caleb and smiled. "Caleb what would make you ask if the woman I thought I was in love with was a dodgy lady." Roth replied.

"Because every decent woman in the county will have nothing to do with you, and that leaves only the dodgy ladies," Caleb said laughingly.

Roth shrugged his shoulders and smiled at his long-time friend, preferring to say nothing at all.

Roth was about to speak when someone knocked on the kitchen door. Caleb was closest to the door. He stood up and opened it for Deputy Sheriff Brown.

Roth looked into the eyes of the young deputy and straightened up, sensing bad news.

"Yes, Deputy Brown" Roth asked.

"Sir, Mrs. Swanson needs you."

"It's Otis, isn't it?" Roth stood up and searched for his jacket.

"I'm afraid so, sir—" Brown responded.

"Last report I got; old' Otis was up and walking around," Roth said.

"That's true sir. He was," the young deputy replied.

"Well, Brown, is Otis dead or not" Caleb asked.

"Not at this exact minute sir, but soon."

"What the fuck is it then?" Roth asked his patience's running thin.

"Sir, Sheriff Swanson has suffered a massive heart attack," Brown replied.

"If Otis dies of a heart attack, would it be fair to say he, beat the cancer?" Roth asked reloading his weapon.

"I'd have to say yes!" Caleb replied.

"Then Otis wins!" Roth said, a wry smile forming across his face.

"So he does!" Caleb replied with a big grin.

"Deputy Brown, is your car warm?" Roth asked his voice showing no emotion. Brown did not reply, merely nodded his head.

51

April pulled her badly damaged BMW into the garage and shook uncontrollably from the near-death experience. She pressed the little black remote attached to her key chain closing the garage door behind her and hiding her sin from prying eyes.

As the elevator carried April upwards, she began to cry, not knowing what to do with Paula's body that lay silently in the back seat of her car. Roth's aim was deadly, blowing away part of Paula's skull and scattering her brain matter and bone fragments all over the back seat. Her own wound was just a nick on the back of the neck, a dab of hydrogen peroxide and band-aid being all that was required.

April opened the front door and walked into the house, mindful of the past evening with Paula clearly visible on the kitchen counter where two goblets that had been filled with gin and vermouth rested. They had been drinking into the early-morning hours. On the far end of the counter top laid Paula's favorite cookie recipe along with the poison she had intended to use on Roth. Walking into her bathroom, April glanced at the shower stall and noticed that it was still wet from their wee hour interlude there in the vain attempt to sober themselves up. As she walked into her bedroom, she picked up the damp bath towels they had used and threw them into the bathroom. She crawled back into bed, pulling the covers up to her chin. Reaching across the bed she pulled Paula's pillow towards placing the pillow over her eyes breathing in Paula's scent, trying to find a plausible idea on how to kill Toby and the others for the pain they had caused.

Roth stepped out of Deputy Brown's patrol car, the cold biting at his flesh until he walked into the hospital lobby. He knew the way as he had been on Otis' floor many times over the years. He pressed the little green button that would take him to the third floor.

Stepping off the elevator Roth turned immediately to his right and walked towards the critical care unit. A quick glance at the wall clock told him that it was shaping up for another brutal day, and it wasn't even 7:00 a.m. yet.

Roth didn't need to be told what room Otis was inas the line of deputies lined both sides of the corridor.

As Roth approached Sergeant Dana Calvin called the deputies to attention rendering a salute. "Dana, why the salute" Roth whispered returning Dana's salute.

"Sir, by the Governor's decree you are hereby appointed acting Sheriff!" Dana replied extending his hand to his long-time friend. "Toby, Otis asked the governor to appoint you." He pulled his hand back from Roth's grip.

"Come on, Dana, I'm in the middle of a case here... Hell, not more than an hour ago somebody tried to kill me. Caleb is at my house right now gathering evidence," Roth said, almost pleading with the deputies to choose somebody else.

This just complicates things all the more," he muttered. He slipped into Otis' room quietly, not wanting to disturb the old parish priest who was reciting the last rights to his friend. He stood at the foot of the bed with his head bowed, and his hands foldedas if he was in prayer. However, his thoughts were not on Otis' after life, but on the monitor that stood beside the bed. The numbers on the screen told him Otis would be dead shortly. He felt his throat constrictingas the priest made the sign of the cross on Otis' forehead and Edith screamed followed by the continuous sound of the monitor and the ominous flat line. Otis was dead. He had witnessed his friend's passing from this life to the next.

Roth stood silent, slowly becoming a pillar of strength as Milo and Tabatha came to him and buried their heads into his chest. He held them close like he did when they were little girls and kissed the tops of their heads. He wanted to say that things would be all right, but that would be a lie, so he stood silent, feeling the girl's tears as they permeated his shirt, damping his chest. Suddenly, the momentary silence was broken as Edith screamed, yelling at Otis to wake up then in desperation, she started pounding Otis' chest in a hysterical attempt to revive her husband, but to no avail.

From somewhere, two nurses entered the room and with practiced perfunctory care one went to Edith, and with the help of the parish priest pulled Edith off of Otis' body. The other nurse turned the monitor off then took Otis by his hand and wrote TOD 06:50. It was now official—Otis was legally dead.

"Nurse, would you ask Sergeant Calvin to come in please" Roth asked as she passed by him.

"Yes, sheriff…" the nurse said, smiling up at him as he continued to hold Milo and Tabby in his arms.

"Yes, Toby, excuse me, sir, I mean sheriff!" the red-faced sergeant said.

"Otis has just passed and will be buried with all honors, please see to it," Roth said in a soft voice.

Dana did not respond, he merely nodded his head and backed out of the room.

Roth heard the sergeant inform the other deputies that Otis had passed over.

* * *

Becky Colt sat quietly in her favorite chair wrapped in an electric blanket, a Christmas present from her mother. Despite the gift, she awakened hours earlier, cold and hungry. She was watching the local news paying particular attention to the growing list of schools and businesses that were closing because of the cold, but that's not why she was interested. She was looking for municipal and city building's closing. The news was also reminding parents not to allow their children outside under any circumstances. The temperature was a minus 22 and with the wind-chill factor; the temperature plummeted to minus 44 degrees below zero.

Suddenly, Becky's attention was drawn to the little red banner at the bottom of the television screen announcing a news flash. She waited annoyed that it was taking so long for the message to appear. Finally, the message began going across the screen one letter at a time. When finished the message announced that Sheriff Otis Swanson had died of a heart attack and to stay tuned for more details.

Becky looked at the time 7:10 a.m. and she had twenty minutes to shower and wash her hair before the local news came back on. As she showered her thoughts returned to Paula's convoluted conversation about disposing of Detective Roth and his sidekick Joshua Ledbetter. When Paula had finished with her intricate plan, Becky looked at her and asked the simple question, "Why?"

"Because he's a threat to us," Paula replied.

Becky smiled and held up her hand stopping Paula mid-sentence. Then in a soft, reassuring voice, the young prosecuting attorney went into great detail explaining the law to Paula and informing her that Roth was just trying to bully her into making a mistake. She told her to shut down her operation, getting rid of any evidence related to drug operations and once that was done, just ignore him.

Paul rolled over and turned on the table lamp. He felt Rossi snuggled up against his back enjoying his body heat as the room was cold. Looking at his wristwatch it was 07:30. He was startled when his phone began vibrating across the nightstand bringing to mind those grotesque chattering teeth he used to play withas a young boy.

"Hello Paul" the strange female voice asked.

"Yeah" Paul replied.

"Sheriff Roth wants you and the others to meet him in his office at 09:00, got it" the strange female voice asked.

"Got it" he replied, flipping his phone shut.

"Who was that" Rossi asked.

"Don't know exactly," he replied, lying back down and allowing Rossi to lay her head on his chest.

"What did they want" she asked, pulling her body closer to his.

"We are to report to Sheriff Roth at 09:00" Paul said, kissing the top of her head.

"Did you just say Sheriff Roth" Rossi said, pushing her body away from her lover.

"Yeah…"

52

April hung up the phone, thankful that Paula had talked to Becky, who told her about Roth's task force. Supposedly, the information had come from Maggie herself.

She learned one thing from Roth: Keep the conversation direct and short. Sawicki never asked who it was. He just acknowledged the message, and hung up on her, same damn thing Roth did. *It must be a cop thing,* she reasoned and walked back to the kitchen to check on the cookies.

April didn't remember the name of the poison, but Paula called it her special blend. Supposedly, the poison was slow acting, taking up to three days for the symptoms to appear and by that time; it was too late. The killer would have plenty of time to leave the city or develop an alibi. The individual in question would simply stop breathing, a victim of an apparent heart attack, and if her idea worked later in the week a whole bunch of sheriff, deputies were going to have heart attacks.

Heather sat at Paula's kitchen table wearing only her panties. She noticed the kitchen windows were frosted over obstructing her view of Paula's backyard. She turned her back to avoid the onset of a anxiety attack.

She waited for the teapot to boil and wondered why Paula had not come home? She didn't know exactly how long Paula had been gone, but it had been a while. Repeated calls and messages were not returned. She wanted to call Mike to let him know about Paula and to inform him that she was available. She decided to call him later, but for now she would call the police and ask them to find her friend.

Roth stood in front of his bathroom mirror shaving while Caleb proceeded to ask questions about some blonde woman. To each question asked, Roth replied with a simple "No!"

Caleb turned around and headed back to Roth's kitchen, stopping in front of the refrigerator. He opened the refrigerator door and pulled out a carton of eggs and some butter. He'd already started another pot of coffee.

Caleb was whipping eggs when Roth crept out of the hallway dressed in full uniform.

"How do I look, Caleb" Roth asked standing at attention and allowing Caleb to inspect him.

Caleb removed the eggs from the stove and stepped over to his new boss running his eyes up and down Roth's uniform.

"You're wearing the wrong belt and shoes," Caleb said. He turned his attention back to the toaster and butter.

Roth laughed and turned around. He knew where his dress shoes were, but the service belt might be a problem.

Roth sat at thes kitchen table looking down into his butter-stained coffee. His thoughts were interrupted by Caleb pushing a zip-lock bag across the table at him. The bag contained fragments of a human skull some with blond hair firmly attached.

"Is this all you've found" Roth asked taking a sip of his coffee looking at Caleb over the brim of his cup mug. He noticed that Caleb had one green eye and one blue one. Putting down his coffee cup down on the table a smile began to appear on his face.

"What" Caleb asked waiting for Roth to explain the grin.

"I know who the dead woman is, and I also know who the driver was!" Roth said, taking another sip of his coffee.

"You do" Caleb asked.

"Yeah I think so!" Roth said, looking up at the kitchen clock to check the time. He had been sheriff for more than an hour now, and he didn't feel any different.

"Care to let me in on it" Caleb asked.

"For weeks we have been concentrating on a woman named Paula Tidwell, who is or was a doctor of toxicology who liked to sponsor sex parties with the city's rich and political elite. She also videoed her parties using the videodiscs to blackmail her clients.

"Joshua Ledbetter, the criminal investigator from the attorney general's office, and I deduced that an operation of this size had to have protection to remain so deeply embedded in our community. Little did we realize the scope of Paula's operation, nor did we know how many influential people were involved," Roth said as he began tying his shoes.

"So who drove the car?" Caleb asked, his voice sounding commanding, as if he were talking to someone on the street.

"Becky Colt," Roth responded.

"No way" Roth Caleb responded disbelief clearly resonating in his voice.

"Let me explain it this way. Joshua and I saw it. We knew that an organization that catered only to the rich and influential had to have legal protection, muscle, a viable distribution system and money, clean or dirty.

"So that said we must digress back to last September when a Polish man was executed by a criminal investigator who himself was murdered by none other than our own Deputy Sheriff Bean. Then on a flight to Columbia, Bogotá to be exact, Deputy Bean was murdered. I suspected that some slow-acting poison was used.

"I then receive a call from Otis asking me to investigate Bean's death. However, I couldn't investigate Bean's death without investigating the other deaths, because somehow I just knew all the deaths were related. That's how Joshua and I brought down the attorney general, which led to the state senator and his wife, and our three local judges. The only one left is Becky Colt, the self-esteemed county prosecutor who I'm not finished with yet..."

"Why not" Caleb said surprised that all this investigation work had been kept so quiet for so long.

"Because I need her to get me a no-knock warrant on Paula Tidwell's residence," Roth said, standing up and putting on his Smokey the Bear hat. "Until then the rich bitch will be left alone."

April looked at the wall clock...she had thirty minutes to deliver her cookies to Roth and his merry band of men. Driving her BMW was out of the question and as far as the Corvette was concerned, she wouldn't even try to start it. She thought about calling a cab then decided to use Paula's Navigator.

Sawicki hated to be late for anything. Rossi could care less as her days on the team were numbered anyway and she knew it. A week maybe less she'd be back in Cincinnati doing her own thing busting pimps and drug pushers and any other low life creatures that roamed Cincinnati's streets.

As he approached the top step, Paul noticed that Roth's office was still dark. Maybe the lady who called meant Otis' office. Stopping in front of the office door, he removed his arctic gloves and pulled back the parka's ermine lined hood. To the left of the door, he saw the plate of homemade cookies wrapped tightly in cellophane. He noticed a white envelop, probably a best wishes card.

Flipping the light switch, Sawicki removed his parka throwing it over the back of the desk chair. A cardboard box sat on Roth's desk. *Interesting,* he thought. However, the most immediate concern was finding the thermostat. His eye's scanned each wall. He spotted the thermostat next to the grease boards and peeked at the dial, which told him that someone had set the control unit to its lowest setting. Paul set the temperature to 75 degrees and then rubbed his hands together, wishing Rossi would get here soon with the coffee.

Paul turned his attention to the box sitting squarely in the middle of Roth's desk. His curiosity aroused, he pulled the flaps open, not really knowing what to expect he looked inside the box. The box contained some video tapes and discs. Plus two pages of names with dollar amounts next to each name. Things were starting to make sense. He heard Rossi calling his name.

"YO," Paul bellowed back like some lovesick bull.

"I saw Roth downstairs—" Rossi said, handing over his coffee.

"I was wondering if we were in the wrong office," Sawicki remarked, taking a sip of his coffee.

"Maybe, but what with all that has happened this morning Roth is probably running late," Rossi said taking off her long winter coat, and pointing to the box.

"Don't know for sure, but I think its evidence," Paul said, suddenly realizing she wasn't pointing to the box.

"Oh, the cookies" Sawicki said, smiling as he handed her the plate.

"You said all that has happened this morning. Other than Otis dying, what else has transpired?" Sawicki said, taking two cookies off the plate and dunking one into his coffee.

"Someone tried to kill Roth early this morning," Rossi said as she took a bite of cookie.

"And you know this how?" Paul asked biting into his own cookie, chasing it down with coffee.

"I overheard a Sergeant Caleb talking to some of the guys explaining that Toby had returned fire and one of the assailants was probably hit."

"What was Roth doing outside in minus 41 degree weather so early in the morning?" Paul asked finishing off his cookie.

Roth stood in his new office. Marsha stood silently at her new boss's side trying hard to fight back her tears as she looked at Otis' desk.

"Marsha, I have a favor to ask. I want you to gather Otis' personal affects and you and I will take them to Edie when all this is over."

Marsha nodded, afraid to speak for fear of bursting into tears.

"Toby, the guys are assembled!"

Roth turned to see who was addressing him.

"It's Sheriff Roth! Lieutenant Luke, and never forget it. Do we understand each other?"

"Yes, sheriff!" Luke said, responding in a conciliatory way.

Roth patted Marsha's hand and whispered; "Now maybe I'll find out how you always knew it was me on the phone."

Marsha smiled and held his hand, whispering, "Never—"

Roth turned and placed his hat on his head, nodding to Luke that he was ready to inspect his deputies.

"Dixie you're late!" came the roar of Ogden's voice. Ogden was the newspaper editor and in possession of a voice reminiscent of a shrill, train whistle— He was also a pain in the ass and some reporters called him the hemorrhoid, though not to his face as this job was better than no job at all.

"Yes, Ogden I'm late, I couldn't get my car started. I had to call for a cab."

"Ok Dixie thanks for showing up. I know it's cold out, but the weather is not our lead story today," Ogden said handing Dixie her coffee cup.

"It's not?" Dixie replied, walking over to the coffee pot.

"No." Ogden filled Dixie's coffee cup then his own.

"Earlier this morning, a friend of yours, Toby Roth, was climbing up some back steps when somebody tried to kill him. Then much to everyone's amazement, the governor appoints Roth Sheriff to replace Otis Swanson who passed away this morning.

"Dixie, I want you to write Roth's bio. Have it done before we go to press," Ogden said as he walked away, leaving her alone with her anger.

Fuck Roth's bio. I'll write his obituary then a front-page story on why I killed the son-of- a-bitch, she thought. She said these words aloud as she walked back to her desk and wondered why Roth hadn't called her to give an exclusive story.

Sawicki excused himself as he knocked on Roth's office door. Rossi stood beside him holding a plate of cookies.

Roth looked up and smiled, motioning them to enter.

"Congratulations, sir!" Sawicki said as Rossi placed the cookies on the desk.

"Paul, shut the door will you?" Roth motioned to Rossi to take the chair on his left. Roth waited for his young deputy to take the other chair before he spoke.

"Your jobs are both coming to a close. Paula Tidwell is probably dead. Most likely I killed her this morning in the gun fire exchange and it appears she and Lady-X got spooked when we took down the attorney general and the state senator along with the judges. I also know who Lady-X is, and after we bury Otis we will arrest her as well," Roth said.

"Lady-X, sir" Rossi asked.

"Yes, Rossi, Lady–X. She is the money person who bought and paid for the drugs. With the exception of Tim Hill, she paid Deputy Bean to front as her enforcer then had Deputy Bean murdered. As for her rich and influential clientele, she began to blackmail using videodiscs of them having sex and abusing illicit drugs. She did this for two reasons as I see it; one to keep them in line, and the other for self-preservation.

"Sawicki this may interest you. Your little speech to that Russian fellow, Adrik, was very convincing. According to a Detective Rollin Brown of the NYPD narcotics unit you scared the shit out of him. In fact you pissed him off so much that he tried to come here and personally kill you. However, the FBI had been tailing him, and when he crossed the border into Pennsylvania he was pulled over. Supposedly a gun battle ensued and both Adrik and his bodyguard were killed. So kudos to you both and Rossi that was good police work."

"Thank you, sir," Rossi said.

"Now please take your cookies, and pass them out to the others. I have a lot of catching up to do," Roth said, picking out another folder from his in basket.

April sat in her favorite chair, wrapped in her mother's afghan, drinking her green tea and eating Melba toast. The television was tuned to the weather station, but she had quit listening. Her thoughts of the moment were on how to dispose of Paula and when was Toby going to come and arrest her for trying to kill him. She had to have a backup plan.

The weather guy said that this deep arctic freeze would last a few more days. This was good for Paula's body as the cold would keep her a while longer. She was about to help herself to another cup of tea when her phone rang.

"Hello is this April?" the female voice asked.

"Yes—" she replied, knowing the voice and trying to place it.

"Hello, April. This is Heather. I was wondering if you have seen Paula or perhaps know where she is."

"Hello, Heather, it's good to hear from you, sweetheart. How are you?" April cooed into her phone, trying to decide how to handle the situation.

"OK, I guess," Heather replied.

"Oh, you guess," April chided. "You're not sure that you're okay, sweetheart?"

"April, it's hard for me to explain. You see, I've been waking up at night with these terrible dreams. In one dream I'm happily married to some man. In another dream I have killed a man who proclaimed to be my husband. I've also dreamt that I'm a prostitute. April, I'm coming apart at the seams and Paula has my medicine in her purse."

"Where are you?" April asked softly.

"I'm at Paula's house. Why did you ask me that?" Heather asked in a defensive way, her voice sounding scared.

"Because it's very cold outside, and I'm alone, and I thought maybe you would like to come over and we could spend some time together," April replied, her voice soft and warm, trying to coax Heather as she was becoming a liability.

"OK, how do I get to your place?" Heather asked.

"Better yet, I'll drive over and get you," April said, still unsure of Heather's mental state.

"Could we please stop and eat? I have not eaten since Paula left me—"

"Sure, why not!" April said.

"The food in Paula's refrigerator is all poisoned, and she told me if I got hungry to eat the cereal and drink coffee until she got back."

"Sweetheart, I have a lot of food and I love to cook, so don't worry about the food situation. April replied, getting a little anxious. She did not know how she was going to tell Heather that Paula was dead.

* * *

Becky sat in her favorite easy chair as she watched television and tried to decide if she should get dressed for work or not. Her repeated calls to her office went unanswered and since it was after 8:00 a.m. she could only assume her office was closed. Her thoughts on what to do on this coldest day in local history were interrupted by the phone ringing.

"Hello, Becky? This is Sheriff Roth— I need a no-knock warrant," Roth said, telling her in lieu of asking.

"Oh, you do, do you?" Becky chided.

"Yes—" Roth replied.

"OK, what judge do I use? You've managed to remove some of them from office, and by the way, what judge is it that's going to swear you in, sheriff?" Becky said in a voice that bordered on disrespect, real close to venomous.

"Colt, what judge you get is your business. As far as my oath of office, the governor will swear me in at Otis' wake. Any other questions" Roth asked, his voice suddenly becoming cold and threatening.

"Who do you want the warrant for, and for what will you be searching?" Becky asked.

53

Despite the Lincoln's defrost on full, April was having a difficult time trying to see through the frosted front windshield of Paula's SUV. She was only a couple of miles from Paula's when she saw the flashing lights of a police car. Angry with herself, she pulled over and waited for the police officer to approach. She reached across the passenger seat and grabbed her handbag noticing another plate of cookies that hadn't been delivered. She removed her wallet and proceeded to extract her driver's license. The proof of insurance card was neatly inserted into the visor pouch just above her head.

Against her better judgment, she hit the auto-down button on the driver-side window and looked back over her shoulder wondering why the police officer was taking so much time.

Pissed off at the officer for taking his sweet time, April hit auto-up and began to curse under her breath. Finally, through the rear-view mirror, she saw the door of the cruiser open. The first thing she noticed was the officer's right hand did not have a glove on it. His hand was resting on his pistol, and as he walked towards her; he made a wide swing out into the street.

April hit auto-down again and the window quickly lowered, letting the young officer see her hands.

"Who does the vehicle belong to" the patrolman asked.

"It belongs to my girl friend, Doctor Paula Tidwell," April said, watching the patrolman approach her ever so cautiously, his hand still resting on his pistol.

"Where is Doctor Tidwell?"

"She's at my house, officer. We're baking and cooking for Sheriff Swanson's wake. In fact, sir, I'm on my way to Paula's house at present to get the rest of the food." April said, smiling at the freezing patrolman.

"Come here" April said, motioning to the officer and looking at his name tag as he approached her.

The officer moved to the side of the Lincoln, his eyes locking onto hers. Despite the bitter cold, he began to sweat as he felt a deep stirring in his loins, but he missed the cue.

"Please have some cookies. They're very good," April said. She handed Officer Bennington the plate and watched him take four of the poisoned cookies, all the while smiling up at him.

"OK, ma'am, you can go now and thank you for the cookies. I'll have them with my coffee at next break," Bennington said, turning his back on her and walking back to the warmth of his cruiser.

April smiled and waved good-bye. Dropping the shift lever into drive and pulling out into traffic she thought of the young police officer she had just murdered and wondered if he had a wife and kids. Then she merely shrugged her shoulders and muttered as if trying to justify the patrolman's eventual murder. "It was him or me, and he lost!"

As she exited Maple Avenue onto Dresden Road, April remembered what Heather had told her about the food in Paula's refrigerator being poison. Then in an instant of clarity April remembered Paula talking about her backup plan the night before she was killed. That was it, to serve the poisoned food at Otis' wake! Paula's idea of serving the sheriff's deputies and all the other dignitaries of the state, including the governor himself a slow-acting poison was a stroke of evil genius.

Dixie finished Roth's bio as Ogden had requested her to do with hours to spare. What she had learned about Toby helped clarify why he was the type of man that he was. Four years as a U. S. Marine, graduate of North Carolina, Masters Degree from Purdue in Forensic Psychology. Then it got even better: A Medal of Honor, two Medals for Valor, two Purple Hearts, and two Meritorious Service Awards. After the people read her work, they would understand why the governor appointed Roth as sheriff. What was peculiar about all of this was that Toby had never mentioned any of it to her. She once overheard some policeman refer to Toby as a cop's cop. She didn't understand the reference, until now, and yet that is exactly what he was—a cop's cop that obviously had better things to do than return her calls.

Roth sat back in the desk chair and yawned, stretching his arms and legs that had turned numb from lack of movement. He looked at his watch and saw that it had been close to five hours since he had left his office. He tried to get up but found it difficult as his legs would not respond to his wishes. Using the corner of his desk he managed to pull himself up and holding on managed to secure himself to the desk until his blood made a couple of trips through his veins.

"Excuse me, sir!"

"Yes, Marsha, what is it?" Roth asked lifting his legs to get the blood flowing.

"Edie is on line three, sir, and wants to talk to you."

Roth smiled at Marsha, nodding in acknowledgment. He pushed the little red button that would connect him to line three and Edie.

"Yes, Edie, what's up?"

"My priest, or should I say my ex-priest, is being a butt head. He has refused to say a service over Otis because I want him cremated, and he won't let me use the church basement for the wake. Toby, I don't know what to do. Can you help me?" Edie asked her voice sounding fatigued.

"Let's hold the service and the wake at the city's auditorium. After the service, we will slip Otis off the stage, so he can be sent to the crematorium. We can get a good Methodist minister to read over Otis. If you agree I'll have Marsha put everything in motion for you," Roth said his voice warm and loving towards his friend's wife.

"Oh, thank you, Toby, a wonderful idea and to hell with that old miserable asshole of a priest," Edie said, causing the new sheriff to chuckle.

"Marsha will call you with all the details. OK" Roth hung up the phone before Edie could say a word.

April sat alone in her living room. Heather was lying in her bed. Both women had been crying. It was an accident, really. It had occurred when she pulled Paula's Navigator around to the back of her condo to unload all of Paula's food.

Her idea was to place all the food in the elevator and then send the elevator up to the second floor where she, and Heather would take the food into her condo for safe keeping until she knew where the wake was to be held. However, as they walked back and forth from the Navigator to the elevator carrying food; Heather happened to notice bullet holes in the BMW. Curious, she walked over to the car for a closer look.

It was a scream that April would never forget. It started out as a low mournful howl and with each passing second, the howling became louder and finally, an ear-splitting shrill that curled her toes and made her blood run cold. She didn't have to worry anymore about how to tell Heather that Paula was dead. Heather found the body.

The shadows grew long as April continued to sit in the living room lost in thought. She was discovering that planning wholesale murder was not an easy thing to do. Especially the part about not being caught; that was the hardest part! Paula had told her the poison would start taking effect within seventy-two hours. The poison would not reveal itself using the standard forensic tests. That would give her an extra two or three weeks before the results could be determined and made known. However, April doubted that the powers to be would make the results public knowledge.

It was after 4:00 p.m. when April picked up her phone and dialed the sheriff's office, praying Toby didn't answer. All she needed was the time and place of Otis' wake. She would take care of the details herself.

The call took only a minute, and April had what she needed—when and where. The lady was also kind to tell her the time, 10:00 a.m. Figuring an hour give or take fifteen minutes the service would be over around 11:00 a.m. Lunch would probably be served around 11:30, giving her and Heather more than enough time to unload all the food that Paula had so graciously prepared beforehand.

Looking out her large picture window, April could see that the long afternoon shadows had given away to darkness. She turned on the table lamp. The hands on the mantle clock were just turning 5:00 p.m., and her stomach was beginning to growl. She paused for a moment to think when she had eaten last and determined it had been yesterday mid morning, just before Paula arrived.

Opening her kitchen cupboard, April extracted a can of tomato soup, her mind still on the details of killing Toby Roth and his minions. She stared into her refrigerator forgetting the reason she opened the door. She was focused on Paula's initial plan and realized that it was seriously flawed. What if Toby didn't eat anything, then what?

Her thoughts were interrupted when she felt two arms encircle her and felt the soft kiss to her neck.

"Hmm, that feels nice," April cooed as Heather pulled her close and squeezed her tight.

"What's for supper?" Heather asked softly kissing April on her cheek.

"Tomato soup, and grilled cheese sandwiches," April replied. She felt Heather's hands slowly inching up her body while she nuzzled April's neck. Goose bumps began to appear on her skin.

"Sounds yummy," Heather said, breaking her embrace and grabbing the cheese and the jar of dill pickles.

"Sweetheart, after we eat we must talk on how best to kill the man who murdered Paula." April cooed, kissing Heather on the lips and caressing her face with both hands.

54

Roth turned out the light and shut his office door. It had been a marathon day and tomorrow would be another. As he waited for his car to be brought around from the department's heated parking garage, a strange feeling began to take hold, like a one-way ride off a cliff. Was this the feeling of loneliness all men in charge must feel when there is absolutely no one to turn to or who even cared? At least Otis had Edie. All Roth had was a call girl and a newspaper reporter, both very dangerous women. He heard the car horn before he saw the car pull up. He had requested a driver to take him home. He did not want to wake up tomorrow morning and find that his car wouldn't start.

Roth sat calmly in front of his television watching a NBA game with the mute button enabled, preferring to watch instead of watching and listening. He could hear the cold, southeast wind battering his house and watched his curtains blow out away from the wall as he drank his beer.

Earlier in the day Roth had called Joshua to invite him to his swearing in ceremony and to discuss a few more details about the case. Joshua laughed, telling him that he would be bringing the governor. Thanks to Roth he had been promoted, replacing the legendary Dakota Smith as advisor to the yet to be appointed Attorney General of the State of Ohio. Dakota had been suspended with pay pending the outcome of his investigation into dealings with the former attorney general.

Roth did not mention to Joshua his concern about Becky Colt not being Lady-X. He based his decision on his phone call with her earlier this morning when she became belligerent with him. Had Becky said, "Why do you need a warrant for a dead person?" Then he had her, but she didn't. Instead she became flippant, daring him to accuse her of any crime, not knowing he had a video disc of her in the nude using cocaine.

Another little insignificant fact came to light when Caleb told him this afternoon that although permitted to carry a firearm she had never attended any firearm training nor did she ever apply for a permit anywhere in the country. Her bank records showed she was living on her salary and the biggest debt was her Honda Accord, and it was silver not black or dark blue.

Something else was beginning to cause Roth concern and that was this constant feeling of dread that was slowly enveloping him causing him to shiver. He couldn't shake the feeling that something ghastly was about to happen. Exactly what he didn't know, but when it happened a lot of people would be dead and he would be the reason for their deaths.

The steam from her bathroom's hot water faucet froze on the single pane glass window making beautiful intricate ice designs and also making it difficult for Dixie to look out the window. What she was hearing and seeing disturbed and scared her. She was listening to a howling wind that vibrated her apartment building and caused the window panes to rattle throughout her apartment. She watched helplessly as the wind pushed the snow up against her car, creating a giant snow drift and making it nearly impossible for her to get to her car and to work.

Lost in her thoughts, Dixie became vaguely aware that someone was calling her name, and although detached the voice sounded familiar to her. She jumped, startled when she felt Alicia's hand touching her shoulder.

"Wow, you were really out there," Alicia said laughingly.

"What were you thinking about?" Alicia turned and walked back out to the kitchen.

"I was wondering how I was going to get to work in the morning," Dixie replied, laying her hair brush down and following Alicia into the kitchen.

"How much food do we have?" Alicia asked.

"Enough until Saturday or maybe Sunday if we're careful," Dixie said. She sat down at the kitchen table across from Alicia, folded her toast in half, and dunked it into her hot chocolate.

"Then we will be OK until Saturday," Alicia said, taking a bite of toast.

"I suppose so!" Dixie said with anguish in her voice.

"OK, Dixie, what do you want to tell me?" Alicia asked.

"I'm troubled Alicia. Perhaps it's nothing, but early yesterday morning my phone rang. I answered it and a woman asked me if Toby was there. At first I thought it was someone from the sheriff's department. Then when I asked who it was the woman became belligerent and was slurring her words. I even asked her why she didn't call Toby on his cell phone and then it dawned on me—how did she get my landline number? Not even Toby has that number! When I asked the woman, she got ugly with me. I turned to give the phone to Toby, but he wasn't in bed so I told the insolent bitch that he had gone home.

"I didn't know it at the time, but he was in the bathroom. When he came back to bed I started cussing and he got angry at me and left for home, only to get shot at when he got there. Now he won't call me or return my calls. So despite this cold, you and I are going to Otis' service tomorrow so I can say I'm sorry and cover his swearing in ceremony.

"So you think this mysterious woman was the one who tried to kill Toby?" Alicia asked.

"Yes, I do!" Dixie replied.

"Do you have caller ID?" Alicia asked.

"Why yes, I think so—" Dixie responded, a big smile beginning to form on her face.

55

That's it, sweetheart, there're only two things to remember. First, pull back the hammer, and second, place the muzzle right on Roth's heart before you pull the trigger and if you do it correctly the murderer of Paula will be dead," April said with a certain satisfaction resonating in her soft voice.

"April, what are we going to do with Paula's body?"

"I don't know for sure, what do you recommend?"

"I want to bury Paula's body in the woods. I know the ground is frozen, but we could buy a sleeping bag and lay her body close to the river's edge and cover her with rocks, like they did in olden times—"

"Heather, how about we do this? Early tomorrow morning we load the Navigator with Paula's food then we go to Wal-Mart, where we will buy a sleeping bag and some large trash bags. We will simply return to my place, wrap Paula's body in the trash bags, place her inside the sleeping bag, and take her home. I will take my BMW since it already has Paula's body inside. You will follow me in Paula's Lincoln. The garage door opener is on the visor. You just pull to the curb in front of Paula's house and hit the button so the garage door will go up. I will pull the BMW into the garage and shut the door and you, sweetheart, will drive away, leaving me to clean Paula's house one last time. When I'm done, I will take a cab and meet you at the auditorium."

"What an ingenious idea!" Heather replied following April into the kitchen. "It's such a simple concept, and Paula would love you cleaning her house," Heather said, gushing like a school girl.

Sawicki sat at the edge of Rossi's bed and looked at her alarm clock. It was 3:00 a.m. Thursday morning and he and Rossi had been sick for the past 16 hours. Between the vomiting and gastric distress they could hardly breathe. They were weak and getting weaker with each passing hour. Samantha thought it was food poisoning and he silently concurred. He tried to recall all the meals they had shared in the last day and couldn't come up with anything, however, he hoped that whoever had made whatever, rotted in hell.

Debbie Bennington stood at her kitchen sink snapping green beans. She was surprised that Bruce was home so early. When asked why he had come home early that afternoon, he complained of an aching chest. She became concerned and told him to go take a hot shower. Although he looked pale he told her that he felt better. Then later that evening he began vomiting. She asked him to lie down on their bed. When she checked on him a little later he was cold and unresponsive. She called for an ambulance, but was told they were experiencing an inordinate amount of calls and couldn't guarantee they would get to her. The dispatcher told her she should take her husband to the ER herself.

Even though she was seven months pregnant she had found the will and strength to go out in the arctic cold and start the family van. She rushed back into the house and placed a satin sheet on the floor and rolled him off the bed onto the sheet and dragged him through the cold and snow to the van where she managed to place him in the back and drove him to the emergency room of Good Samaritan Hospital.

Debbie entered the ER and did not hesitate to scream "Police Officer Down— Needs Help," and within seconds she was surrounded by nurses and doctors running out into the freezing cold with a gurney and pushing her husband into the ER.

The nursing staff went to work immediately, slapping an oxygen mask on Bruce's pale face and sticking his arms full of needles. All the while a young doctor stood by her husband's side and barked orders to the nurses who each acknowledged his commands. Debbie heard what was being said, but her brain refused to comprehend.

"Doctor, I have no pulse!" the nurse said, her voice raised and emphatic.

The loud beeping noise of the monitor was followed by the doctor yelling, "Get me the paddles!"

At the tender age of twenty three, and seven months pregnant, Debbie Bennington watched helplessly as the doctor applied the paddles to her husband's chest and started to count, "One, two, three, clear!" And after repeating this action a few more times the doctor stopped. Sweat was pouring off his nose and chin. He looked across the gurney and asked the nurse for Officer Bennington's time of death.

* * *

Roth had just stepped out the shower when he heard his phone. He ignored it, choosing instead to shave and dress before he started taking calls. He was in the middle of making coffee when his phone rang again, and this time he picked up.

"Hello…is this Sheriff Roth?" the man's voice asked.

"Yes, it is," Roth said, curious as to who would call him so early in the morning.

"Sheriff, this is Doctor Clark Adams, and I'm the ER doctor on call at Good Samaritan. It's with deep regret that I must tell you that two of your deputies are dead."

"What! Who?" Roth asked.

"According to the paramedics there names are Rossi and Sawicki," the doctor said with as much emotion as one would ask for when ordering a cup of coffee.

"Were they shot?" Roth asked trying to keep his emotions in check.

"No, sir, they were not shot. I suspect like Officer Bennington they each died from a heart attack, but I'll wait for the medical examiner to make that call," the doctor said, hanging up and leaving Roth with a whole lot of questions and heartache.

"Sir, it's about that time!" Joshua said standing at the governor's office door.

"OK Josh, I'm just putting the finishing touches on my eulogy for Otis."

"How about Sheriff Roth" Joshua asked respectfully.

The governor began to chuckle then his chuckling became a laugh.

"Joshua, did you know this man Toby Roth who my best friend on his death bed asked me to appoint sheriff used a prostitute to help him solve a murder?"

"Yes, sir, I knew that!" Joshua replied.

"Did you know that he also cavorts with them as well?"

"Yes, sir, I know that too!" Joshua said, walking into the governor's office and pulling a piece of paper from his hip pocket.

"What's this?" the governor asked, sticking out his hand and taking the paper from Josh.

"Sir, that is Toby Roth's bio that I downloaded this morning. Please note, Governor, that Roth is a highly decorated law officer and he is the best homicide detective I have ever worked with. That's the man, Governor, you will be appointing sheriff this morning. As far as the prostitutes go, they give him a lot of valuable information that he uses to catch bad guys. So it's a trade off, sir, his respectability for the criminals he catches."

"I take it that Roth is a friend of yours and you agree with the choice that Otis made?"

"Yes, governor, he is and I do!" Joshua said, turning around and walking out of the office.

Heather sat at April's vanity table applying lip liner. She was wearing a beautiful strawberry blonde wig that belonged to April, appropriated from the bathroom walk-in closet. She wanted to look good for Roth so she could approach him easily and then execute the murder.

As they loaded Paula's Navigator with food April began to explain her plan. She called it the razzle-dazzle. The plan was based on two things: Surprise, and trickery. Heather was to wear a red winter coat that when reversed changed the color to dark blue. She also was to wear a simple dress with leggings. The dress was rather nondescript, neither fancy nor beautiful, but it did have an empire waist which made her look pregnant and it had a pocket. She was also to wear a frilly yellow apron. The apron was to conceal her hand from Roth as she pulled out the Derringer from her dress pocket and to wipe off her fingerprints just before she dropped the gun onto the floor. April deduced that a policeman would automatically react to a snub nosed .38, but not a large bore Derringer that was lying on the floor amidst people trying to render aid to a dead man.

Once situated inside the auditorium, she would remove her shoes and replace them with thick, woolen socks, which would not look at all suspicious for a pregnant woman. April cautioned her to take the containers and wash them if she could, thus removing all traces of the poison. She was to wait until everyone was eating, talking and not paying particular attention to anything.

Then all she had to do was smile pretty, walk up to him, extend her hand, and blast him to hell. After the shots had been fired, she was to drop the gun, and yell, "The sheriff's been shot!" and point towards any nearby exit door. Then while all the attention was divided between Roth and the exit door, she would simply walk to the back of the auditorium, pull off her wig, throw it onto the floor, and slip into a pair of mukluks that April had conveniently provided. Then she would simply walk through the same door she had come through earlier, get into the Navigator, and drive off.

Dixie anxiously sat at the kitchen table drinking her coffee and praying that Alicia's car would start. She knew that if it didn't she would be shit out of luckas no car meant no story, which equaled no job. As simple as that! Dixie wondered if the deaths of Sawicki, Rossi, and Bennington were related somehow. Perhaps it was a warning to Toby to back off, which was something Toby wouldn't do.

"Dixie, I've been beeping my horn for sometime now. Are you ready to go? It's almost 9:30—" Alicia said, her face red from the cold.

Dixie had Alicia stop at the coroner's office on the way to the auditorium. She knew that Doc Morgan was an early riser and was often hard at work before his staff showed up. She stood in the hallway outside of Doc Morgan's office peering into it and the lab. Both were dark. *Oh, well,* she thought, *no Doc Morgan means no story today. Maybe tomorrow, that is if I still have a job.*

Driving down Main Street Alicia noticed the time and temperature on the bank's electric billboard and pointed it out to Dixie. It showed -12 degrees. Compared to yesterday -12 was a heat wave, but it was the wind that hurt, that biting cold that would not let go, grabbing your flesh and causing your skin to burn.

Alicia managed to find a parking spot in back of the auditorium that shielded them from the arctic wind. Alicia was the first to notice the Navigator. It was the pearl white color that drew her attention to it. It was the same color as Paula's Navigator and the license plate read, TOXICDR. She was sure that was Paula's Lincoln.

"Dixie, look to your left. Do you see that Lincoln Navigator sitting over there?"

"Yes, what about it?" Dixie asked.

"Nothing except it belongs to Doctor Paula Tidwell, the woman who supplied the cocaine at our sex parties."

"She's here? Why that bold-faced hussy. I can't believe that bitch would have the nerve to show her face, especially knowing there would be so many police officers and sheriff deputies here," Dixie said, opening the car door and screaming obscenities at the cold.

Roth stood in front of his bathroom mirror at attention looking at the collection of honors that adorned his uniform. He thought them garish, but protocol demanded he wear them. He could feel his stomach begin to churn as that distinctive, coppery taste began to form in his mouth. Then it was from attention to humbleness as he vomited again. Next came the bone-chilling cold that caused him to shiver so violently the medals that hung around his neck began to sway.

He wasn't sick, or even scared. It was more an insidious feeling of dread that was shaking his very being and causing him to fear this day.

56

April heard the cab driver honk his horn. She had washed, mopped and dusted the entire house for Paula. However, truth be told it wasn't for Paula or Heather that she did what she did. April did it for herself as she didn't want to leave anything that could be traced back to her. So what if the police found her car in Paula's garage? All she had to say was that Paula had asked her to swap cars. For what reason Paula did not say and she did not ask. Then perhaps in a week or two she would report her friend missing along with the car. Hell, she may just drive over there, being sure to let the neighbors see her.

It was actually that simple and Toby knew that she and Paula were on intimate terms, so he wouldn't be suspicious. Providing of course he was still alive in two weeks. It was also nice to find two bags filled with thousands if not hundreds of thousands of dollars hanging on a hook in the garage.

Joshua turned on the limousines blinker taking the fifth street exit off the freeway which would put him only a couple of blocks away from the auditorium. The governor had hardly spoken to him since their little tiff. However, in fairness to the governor, he had been on the phone and going over Otis' eulogy. At certain spots in the speech he heard his boss fighting back tears.

"Sir, we're here!" Joshua said pulling the limousine to the curb.

"Thank you, Josh," the governor replied.

Heather looked around the auditorium and noticed a couple of ladies offering coffee to the police officers and sheriff deputies. She looked at her watch; it was only 9:30 a.m. That would give her about 30 minutes to pass out four dozen cookies. Giving each officer two cookies would account for two dozen soon to be dead police officers and sheriff deputies. Then after the ceremony the macaroni salad, broccoli salad and baked beans would certainly account for a lot more.

Roth put on his parka and gloves, walked outside, and stood on his back porch to wait for some young pimply faced deputy to take him to his coronation. He inhaled the frigid air hoping somehow that it would shake this unknown fear that had been stalking him since he had been informed that he was to be acting sheriff.

Seeing the emergency lights flash, he descended the three steps and walked out to his snow filled driveway to wait for the deputy. He was curious about the flashing lights and wondered if they were really needed to take him to his ceremony.

Opening the back door Roth slipped into the rear right seat.

"Hello, Deputy Brown. I haven't told you thank you for taking care of Edie," Roth said, smiling at the deputy.

"No problem, sir, I was very honored to do it," Brown replied as he slowly backed out of the drive into traffic.

"Why the lights?" Roth asked.

"Sheriff, every time I see you I have to report bad news," Brown said.

"That has always seemed to be the case, Deputy Brown," Roth replied as he removed his gloves and unzipped his parka.

"I guess, sir, this time is no different," Brown said, trying to control his emotions and drive at the same time.

"What is it, Brown?" Roth asked his voice deep and commanding.

Sir, Marsha is dead as is Sergeant Caleb and Lieutenant Luke. Only yesterday we lost Sawicki and that female partner of his, plus the police department lost Officer Bennington. Sir, what the hell is going on?" Brown asked.

"I'm not exactly sure, deputy, but logic tells me we are under attack and these attacks are directed at me."

"So what do we do, sir?" Brown asked.

"We fight back and kick ass. That is if you don't kill us both before I'm sworn in," Roth said pointing to a very large bus.

"Oh, shit!" Brown yelled causing Roth to laugh it was his first laugh in a long time.

57

Dixie stood at the top of the aisle and looked over the rows of seats, her eyes scanning the auditorium searching for Toby. She watched as the honor guard paraded the colors across the stage, followed by two more deputies pushing and pulling the flag draped coffee toward center stage. Next came the honor guard, she counted ten in all, each carrying a black rifle. She was quick to notice that each man was also a sheriff from various parts around the state. Following them was a minister carrying his bible.

She was about to take a seat when her cell phone rang. Quickly she rushed back out into the lobby and picked up the call—a decision that she would regret.

"Sorry I didn't come into work. I was trying to get a story about the three cops that died yesterday."

"Very commendable, but that's not why I called you!" Ogden said.

"Oh?" Dixie replied.

"Frank's wife, Marsha, died sometime last night. Rumor has it that two of Roth's deputies are also dead," Ogden said.

"Ogden, I know about them. That's why I went to see Doc Morgan this morning, but he wasn't there. So I came to the auditorium to cover both the funeral service and Sheriff' Roth's swearing in ceremony," Dixie said, getting a bit confused.

"No, Dixie. I'm talking about Sergeant Caleb and Lieutenant Luke," Ogden replied.

"Sweet Jesus!" Dixie screamed. "Ogden, do you know what this means?"

"Yeah, Dixie, it means banner headlines and revenue," Ogden replied sarcastically.

"Fuck you!" Dixie yelled. "Strong message to follow, you asshole—"

"Dixie, calm down please. You're shaming yourself!" Alicia said, taking her in her arms and hugging her.

"Frank's wife is dead, Alicia, and so are two more of Toby's deputies. And when I asked Ogden if he knew what this meant he replied, 'Yeah, headlines and money.' He's a heartless prick, and I told the son of a bitch off," Dixie said.

"Yes, I know. And so does the entire lobby," Alicia said, spreading her arms. "By the way, Dixie, what does it all mean?"

"It means that our police and sheriff departments are being systematically murdered in order to create fear and panic, and my intuition is telling me that Toby is the target," Dixie said softly.

"So what you're saying is that someone is deliberately killing Toby's deputies to create panic and erode his authority to punish him?" Alicia asked.

"Maybe, Alicia, I don't know for sure. What I'm sure of is that Toby is protecting me. That's why he hasn't returned my calls. It's because of the assassination attempt. What one thing did all of them have in common, Alicia? If we just knew that, I could help Toby catch the killer."

"How about some exotic poison? After all, isn't Paula a toxicologist?" Alicia said.

"And we saw her car in the parking lot. That means she's here to kill Toby. She must have been the one who tried to assassinate Toby," Dixie said, her voice trailing off as she began looking around the lobby for a tall, statuesque blond who was probably in disguise.

* * *

April tossed the two bags onto her bed and began to giggle like a little overjoyed school girl who had just gotten her first kiss. Kicking off her shoes she climbed onto her bed and emptied both bags, instantly discovering that it would take days to count all the money that surrounded her.

Remembering a money counter that she had purchased years ago for her dad's business, April got off the bed and walked into her bathroom and opened the closet door. She happened to notice that the wig stand was empty. She gave it no mind remembering that Heather had taken it to conceal her identity.

Poor Heather, so sweet, but so gullible! Imagine her thinking that she could kill Toby and get away with it. However, in the end when everything was sorted out months later Heather would be blamed for everything. Law enforcement officials would call her criminally insane. April knew that Heather would die because she was dumb. She was a sweet loving person who happened to be trusting, but very dumb.

Alicia took off the winter coat that Dixie had bought her and placed it over a straight back chair next to what appeared to be a table with a sign-in book for Otis. Alicia signed it and looked for Paula Tidwell's name, but as she expected it wasn't there.

She was wearing her minister's garb, black pants and shirt, white collar with a gold cross. Like the others wearing their uniforms, hers would allow her access to Toby. She had to warn him about Paula.

Dixie smiled at the very beautiful pregnant woman who asked her if she wanted anything to eat. She declined the woman's offer telling her that it was almost time for the service to begin.

"Oh, it is? Then I must get everything ready," the woman replied, smiling and leaving Dixie standing alone although she was surrounded by strangers all with one thing in common: To say goodbye to Otis and to watch Toby being sworn in by the governor.

Alicia had given up. Paula wasn't here despite her SUV being in the parking lot. She saw Dixie standing in the doorway talking to someone who actually looked familiar to her, but due to the distance between the front of the stage to the entrance doorway she would be hard pressed to say who it was. Of course it could be no one she knew.

As she walked up the aisle Alicia heard a deep, male voice come over the loud speakers asking everyone to take their seats. Looking back over her shoulder Alicia saw a bunch of somber looking men with rifles standing on the stage and looking out over the hundreds of well wishers and mourners. They stood in a semi-circle around the flag draped copper-colored coffin.

As she walked up the aisle she looked for Toby, but couldn't see him or the governor. Perhaps they were off stage waiting to be announced. That way Otis would be the center of attention and not Toby or the governor.

Alicia sat down watching as Dixie penned her notes. She wasn't sure, but Dixie's notes looked a lot like a bunch of nonsense, a scribbled line here followed by a straight line then a bunch of symbols. She waited until Dixie had finished with her note taking before asking her who that woman was that she had been talking to before she took her seat. Dixie simply replied that the woman wanted to know if she was hungry and when she told her no the woman smiled and walked away.

Alicia grabbed her gold cross and bowed her head as the minister began to prayasking the good lord to bless Otis.

When the minister finished with his short and well received prayer Alicia turned to Dixie, who was back to her note-taking, and told her for some reason the woman Dixie had been talking with looked familiar; in fact she even stretched it some and told Dixie the woman looked like Robin Willingham.

Dixie stopped writing in mid-note her brain trying to remember what Robin looked like. She decided to defer Robin's identification to Alicia as she couldn't recall what Robin looked like, just that she was beautiful. Well, the woman who had asked her if she was hungry certainly was beautiful.

Dixie leaned over to Alicia and whispered, "Let's go find Robin. She must be the one driving Paula's SUV and if so she's not here to say goodbye to Otis," Dixie said. They stood up as the organist began playing the National Hymn.

The lobby was empty. Prisms of light danced on the marble floor.

"I guess we should go to the basement?" Dixie took Alicia by the arm and pointed her towards the steps that would take them to find Robin.

"Governor, you're up next, sir," the soft gentle voice of the minister said, prompting Joshua, Toby, and the Governor to say thank you in unison.

The Governor wanted to postpone Roth's swearing in ceremony, but Roth simply smiled and grabbed the arm of the governor reminding him that these attacks were the work of drug traffickers much like the drug cartels use in South America designed to create panic and undermine law enforcement.

"You're up, governor," the minister said as he prepared to walk back out on stage as the choir finished singing Amazing Grace.

Roth turned his head and looked at Joshua, who had been standing next to him and listening as Roth and the Governor tried to decide who was right.

"Well, what's your take on all this?" Roth asked.

"My take is that I think you know who Lady-X is?" Josh said, a soft smile forming on his face. He looked into Roth's eyes and saw something that he had never seen before: *Fear.*

Roth smiled at his big friend and shook his head.

"Yes, Josh, I do know. Because I was in love with her I denied my own logic. Now I see it can be no one else but April! She's lady-x and when you start to unravel all that has transpired over the last six months, Joshua, it all becomes perfectly clear. So when this ceremony is over we will go after her and that should close that can of worms we opened last September."

"Toby, the governor is about finished. If you would, how about standing in the wing nearest him?"

"Will do, Mike," Toby responded.

"You actually know a minister?" Joshua asked.

"Yes, I do. He's my little brother," Toby replied, walking to the spot where Mike had pointed.

Alicia began walking around the basement trying to dodge the tables and chairs that had been set out. She would pass on the food, deciding that a hamburger and fries sounded better to her. She saw a few church women, obviously friends of Mrs. Swanson, way in the back preparing the food for the onslaught of dignitaries and plain folk that would soon descend as though out of the woodwork.

Dixie had returned to her seat to take her notes and watch for Robin. Alicia had been the one to come up with the idea of using mobile to mobile as a way to keep in contact with each other while they hunted for Robin.

Joshua couldn't see the stage from where he was standing, so he began to walk down a long hall that hopefully would give him access to the auditorium. He had taken only a few strides when he saw a woman coming up the stairs and walking towards him in her stocking feet. He noticed that she was pregnant and looked for a wedding band on her left hand. He didn't see a ring, however, that didn't mean a thing. She could be wearing it around her neck, or she could be unmarried. He noticed how absolutely beautiful she was, which caused a deep stir in his unemployed libido.

"Hello!" he said, watching her as she approached him.

"Hello!" Heather replied, looking up at this giant of a man who was blocking her way.

"I'm trying to get to the auditorium?" Joshua asked.

"That's easy! Just go down the steps, make a right, and walk straight until you see a flight of stairs. Then just climb the stairs, make another right, and you're there," she said, smiling up at him.

Joshua arrived in time to hear Roth repeat, "So help me, God," followed by the congratulatory handshake.

It was over—Sheriff Roth would now arrest April and that would be that. Joshua could go back to being an advisor to the next attorney general.

Joshua felt the gentle tug on his shirt causing him to look around. It was her, the same woman he had seen in the hallway.

"Hello again!" Joshua said, looking down at her wondering why he hadn't noticed the yellow apron that she was wearing the first time.

"Here, sir, I brought these cookies and coffee to you. I didn't know if you took milk so I just left it black. I baked the cookies myself. Hope you enjoy them, sir. Oh my, look at all these people coming up the aisle. I must get back downstairs and man my table."

She was gone before he could say a word.

Alicia stood near the back door of the auditorium. She had walked outside to check for Paula's Lincoln and saw that it was still there. That meant Robin was still lurking about. Dixie had just called to inform her that everything was over upstairs and still no sign of Robin.

Alicia smiled, knowing that whatever was about to take place would occur very soon. She noticed a pair of mukluks and thought the person smart for bringing them on a cold day like this. She was growing impatient with Robin, knowing she was here someplace, hiding in plain sight amongst the hundreds of people who braved the cold to say goodbye to Otis.

Tired of playing this cat and mouse game, Alicia approached the ladies who had been eyeing her, wondering who she was.

"Hello, ladies, it's so nice of you to help the Swanson family. I know Edie appreciates it very much," Alicia said smiling at them.

"It's our pleasure, reverend," the silver haired, pleasantly plump woman replied.

"Edie has helped all of us at one time or another and this is our way of saying thank you," the tall, attractive woman said as she filled the line of white Styrofoam cups with hot black coffee.

"I was wondering if you could help me. Earlier I saw a woman upstairs who appeared to be pregnant, talking to my friend. Have you seen her?"

"Why, yes we have. Phyllis is convinced that the woman is not pregnant at all and I'm just too old to care," the plump woman said laughingly.

"I saw her taking her containers to the wash tubs and cleaning them then she put them in a plastic bag and threw them in the trash. Which, I thought very odd. Why wash something if you're going to pitch it anyway?" Phyllis said.

"Very odd, indeed," Alicia mumbled.

"Anyway, to answer your question, she grabbed some cookies and without asking grabbed a cup of coffee and headed upstairs. You can't miss her reverend, she's wearing a bright yellow apron and gray socks," Phyllis chimed in.

"Thank you," Alicia said slowly extracting herself from the clutches of the gossip mongers.

The basement was beginning to fill rapidly as she climbed the stairs upwards towards the lobby, scanning the crowd for a blonde woman wearing gray socks and a yellow apron. It seemed impossible to her, but somehow Robin had become invisible.

Dixie stood off stage watching the people pay their respects to Otis and the governor. Toby stood silently by, blending into the background of the stage and not caring if people shook his hand or not.

Alicia, exasperated over not finding Robin, sat down and called Dixie. They had been on the prowl for Robin for over an hour and she had simply disappeared.

Dixie answered her phone talking softly so as not to draw attention to herself.

"Where are you?" Alicia asked.

"I'm here on the stage watching for Robin," Dixie replied, her eyes not leaving Toby's form for a second.

"Dixie, I can't find that little bitch anywhere. It's as if Robin has completely disappeared. I'm thinking we spooked her and she's left the auditorium minus the SUV," Alicia said.

"Is there a quick way you can look out the window to see if the SUV is still parked where she left it?" Dixie asked.

"See that exit door behind you? You can see the parking lot faster than I can. I'd have to walk back down to the basement," Alicia said.

"I'll check," Dixie replied, walking back to the exit door and sticking her head out despite the cold.

"Alicia, the SUV's still there," Dixie said, concern registering in her voice.

"OK, I'll go back downstairs and look around again. Over and out," Alicia said, trying to inject some humor into a tense situation.

Toby heard the slam of the exit door coming from his right. He politely excused himself and walked over to where the sound had originated.

"Hello, Toby," Dixie said, walking over to him and throwing her arms around him kissing him on his cheek before he could protest.

Toby pulled her close, kissing her neck while he hugged her tightly.

"Dixie, you shouldn't be here. I'm in danger and everyone around me is in danger," Toby whispered in her ear.

"I know her name— It's Doctor Paula Tidwell, and she's the one who is killing your deputies," Dixie said slowly, extracting herself from Toby's grasp.

"Paula—" Toby said, surprised then realized Dixie had no idea about Paula.

"Honey, I shot and killed Paula the morning I left your house. We haven't recovered her body or the car she was driving, but we will eventually," Roth said, taking her hand and leading her onto the stage.

The reception line had just finished when the governor walked over to Roth.

"Let me guess, sheriff, you caught her trying to break in to meet me," the governor said, chuckling.

"This is Miss Cathy Dixon of the Tribune. She's a newspaper reporter and my friend."

"A very good friend, I'd say, sheriff," the governor said, handing his handkerchief to Roth to wipe off the lipstick.

"I'm hungry and thirsty. Let's go downstairs and grab something," the governor said, leading the way.

As the three of them walked out of the auditorium and into the lobby, the governor stopped in his tracks. He looked right and then left as if he was uncertain where he should go. "Sir, the refreshments are being served in the basement, to your right."

"Yes, Cathy, I know. I'm looking for Joshua?"

"Knowing Joshua, he's already downstairs," Roth said, taking Dixie by her hand and leading the way.

Alicia waved to Dixie as she and Toby entered the room. Dixie watched Alicia shrugged her shoulders and threw out her hands indicating Robin was still nowhere to be found.

"Who's that?" Roth asked.

"That's Alicia!" Dixie replied.

"Oh, yeah, your partner in crime—" Roth said.

"Toby, can I get you something to eat or drink?" Dixie said, letting go of his hand.

"I can use a hot cup of black coffee that's for sure," he replied, watching her walk away from him and heading straight for Alicia.

Roth stood alone. Most of the sheriff's had departed as soon after his swearing in ceremony was over, each one asking his forgiveness for leaving early. The funny thing was Roth actually understood how they felt. Their respective counties were vulnerable without them being there to protect the citizens.

He watched Dixie and Alicia discussed something obviously very important and watched as they both screamed no to someone named Robin.

Roth turned around to see who Dixie and Alicia were pointing at.

"Hello, Toby, I have something for you!"

Toby heard the two shots then felt intense searing pain as the bullets entered his chest, lodging deep within his heart. As he fell to the floor he heard another two shots followed by screams. He could feel Dixie holding him—then came the infinite silence of death.

Joshua holstered his revolver and walked over to the body he felt for a pulse. She woman was dead— His aim had been deadly, one bullet through the back of her head, the other through her heart.

"Where in hell did this creature come from Joshua?" the governor said, trying to maintain his public image posture.

"You will find when you remove her wig and make up that she is wanted by the police for killing her husband. Her name was Robin Willingham, sir, and she was a victim of long term spousal abuse," Dixie said, gently placing Toby's head onto the floor allowing the EMT's to remove his body.

This is Jim Cantu reporting live from Zanesville, Ohio...

I'm standing in the midst of a city whose citizens are reeling from a series of bizarre and unexplained murders. The death count is now over a hundred and of those eighty are sheriffs, from every county in Ohio, and high ranking police officials. To make a bad situation worse, Sheriff Toby Roth, who had just been sworn in by the Governor of Ohio not twenty minutes earlier, was shot and killed by a woman who had been wanted by the police these past seven months for murdering her husband. She in turn was shot by Joshua Ledbetter, the governor's body guard, who had at one time been a criminal investigator working with Toby Roth when he was Chief of Homicide for the sheriff's department.

Together Roth and Ledbetter single-handedly brought down one of the largest drug rings in the state. In fact it has been reported that the former Attorney General was a key figure in the drug ring selling FBI and DEA information to drug traffickers.

Jim Cantu reporting for CNN—

www.ingramcontent.com/pod-product-compliance
Lightning Source LLC
Chambersburg PA
CBHW030031180626
46810CB00001B/311